TABITHA ORMISTON-SMITH

http://paradoxbooktrailerproductions.blogspot.com.au

Copyright © 2013 **Tabitha Ormiston-Smith**

All rights reserved.

ISBN: 978-0-6485519-2-8

❧DEDICATION☙

For Robert. Thank you for the rainbow days.

ACKNOWLEDGMENTS

Sadly, several of the people whose help I must acknowledge in writing Dance of Chaos are now deceased. Bettina Gallen, nee Peemoller, who was my best friend at the time of writing, gave me endless encouragement, and contributed vastly to the book by demanding to be in it. The character of Miss Peemoller, therefore, unlike all of the other characters who of course bear any resemblance to real people living or dead purely by coincidence, is taken from life.

I must also thank the late Jack Deane for invaluable help and advice on technical matters. His criticism of my first draft was most useful, although I did not take all of his advice.

Among the living, Senior Sergeant (now Inspector) Steve Dennis of the Victoria Police gave me the most generous and unstinting help, taking almost a whole day from his busy life to show me everything there is to know about getting arrested. Steve at the time was OC of Malvern Police Station, and it is completely due to his invaluable input that Chapter 11 has the gritty authenticity that it has. I cannot thank him enough. Steve also saved me from acquiring a criminal record, because, desperately conscious of my ignorance of the arrest process, my first idea was to kick a policeman on point duty in the shins just to find out first hand what it was like. I am so grateful not to have been reduced to such a shameful expedient, particularly as my conscience would have been very much troubled to have hurt an innocent person in my quest for experience.

John Henschke, when I enquired at his shop about renting a laser printer to print out my first draft, was kind enough to deliver a printer to my house, lend it to me free of charge for a week and come and pick it up when I had finished with it. I was, and am, in awe at his generosity, and will never forget his kindness.

To Alex Chevalier, for your help about online gaming, and Leslie Hansford, for your help about sleazy perfumes for men, my grateful thanks.

To Patti Roberts of Paradox Book Covers, as always, my most grateful thanks for your wonderful cover art, your support and your friendship.

To Cindy Smeeton Chenhall, my Cover Queen. Cindy, your efforts in my behalf have been truly magnificent, and I am proud to have your pictures gracing my cover.

To Darrell Caruana of Glimmarpics

Dance of Chaos

Photography. You spent hours doing a professional photo shoot with Cindy for my cover pictures. You did not even know me at the time, and I am just in awe of your kindness and generosity.

To Kylie Browning of KMB Beauty. You generously gave your time and your enormous skills as a professional makeup artist for my cover shoot. You did this kindness for a total stranger. Thank you so much!

Finally, to my beta readers. Thank you so much for your help.

ೞPROLOGUEಚ

...common experience sheweth, that where a change hath been made of things advisedly established (no evident necessity so requiring) sundry inconveniences have thereupon ensued; and those many times more and greater than the evils that were intended to be remedied by such change...
Book of Common Prayer

The first big computer I ever saw was in a science fiction movie. It had kerzillions of flashing lights, and tapes going round and round. When it wanted to talk, it made a great booming voice come out of the ceiling, a bit like the Hollywood God. It talked freely, and even made jokes whenever it felt like it, without having to wait for anything as mundane as input.

I saw no reason to doubt the verisimilitude of this portrayal. After all, a horse on the movies looks pretty much like a horse in real life, doesn't it?

So that when I saw a notice in the tea room of my boring office, inviting applications for a job as a trainee programmer, I had a vague idea of a vast control room like a cross between the bridge of the Enterprise and Myers' window at Christmas, with me standing around looking commanding in a white miniskirt.

It is possible that I may have been slightly optimistic.

❧CHAPTER ONE☙

For promotion cometh neither from the east, nor from the west: nor yet from the south.
Psalm 75:7

I ambled back to my desk, spilling a cup of coffee over my boss in transit. This was such a common occurrence that he didn't even bother to comment; that's if he noticed at all – it was after lunch and, as usual, Clive Simpkin, or Retread as we all called him behind his back, was feeling no pain. Clive was a tall, vague, anaemic-looking yuppie type, who always looked as though he needed pressing; his chief interests were getting paralytic and stealing the credit for other people's ideas. He spent his mornings quaffing Dexsal, his lunchtimes in the pub and his afternoons in his office with the door closed, rising to ever greater heights of plagiarism and emerging only to visit the lavatory with clocklike regularity, and make cups of tea in which he often forgot the teabag. We always knew he was well plastered when we saw him going back to his desk with a cup of milk and water. He was okay to work for, because he was frightened of absolutely everybody.

Peter and Sean, the other members of my department, didn't bother to look up. Peter had his monitor switched off and was trying to pluck out his nose hair with a bulldog clip, using the darkened glass as a reflector. Sean was playing Dragons of Atlantis, his latest Facebook obsession. He played practically non-stop throughout the working day, and was always droning on about it, and trying to get me and Peter to join his alliance, or whatever it was called. I was just grateful that he was finally over Candy Crush.

'I'm going to be a Computer Programmer,' I announced.

My colleagues greeted my statement with wild enthusiasm.

'Have you tried that new pore-minimising toner from Clinique?' said Peter.

Sean didn't say anything except to mutter darkly about tail armour.

Dance of Chaos

***

They were somewhat more impressed when I rang up the I. T. Department and found out that I would have to sit a whole battery of aptitude tests to qualify for the job. Our department, which consisted of Peter, Sean and me, did credit investigations on companies that wanted to open accounts with us. There were not enough new credit applications at Marsh and Spacknall to require three people to do the investigations; in an average week there were generally enough to occupy two people, or even one person, if that person was really keen. When there wasn't enough work to keep us all busy, which was most of the time, Retread used to threaten to a) sack all of us and do the lot himself and b) sack all of us and get the credit investigations done by Dun and Bradstreet, who would do them both better and cheaper. It remained a mystery to us why he never did, but then logic wasn't all that notable as a driver for the management decisions at Marsh and Spacknall. It was more about who had more people reporting, who had the biggest company car, who had a corner office, and stuff like that. Probably Retread's boss, who would have had to approve any sackings, didn't want to reduce the size of his little empire. Anyway, the I. T. Department said the tests would take about three and a half hours, which basically meant a whole afternoon off work.

Peter was instantly seized with a spirit of emulation, and bustled off to Retread's office to put his name down for the test. 'Never mind the job, sweetheart, who cares what the job is,' he said. 'It's a bloody afternoon off, isn't it?'

Sean was kind and supportive, as always.

'You haven't got a hope,' he informed me smugly. 'You're too dumb. Besides, you're a woman. This company wouldn't hire a woman to do that kind of job, they're far too sexist. Look at Peter, he hasn't had a pay rise for three years.'

'Peter's not a woman.'

'Sexist, homophobic, it's all the same. Bigotry's bigotry, by any name. Hey, I'm a poet! But seriously, haven't you ever noticed how it's always the same people who're super sexist who're also homophobes? They go together. It's some kind of defensive thing by people that are insecure about their own sexuality. Or they're frightened of their own homosexual urges, or have a tiny dick, or something. Anyway, all that aside, can you seriously imagine them letting anyone as clumsy as you near anything more complex than a biro?'

I shot him a look of withering scorn, or what I hoped would pass for withering scorn. I had practised all the more unpleasant facial expressions in the glass for hours the previous year, when I was auditioning for Lady Macbeth in the Drama Club's production at Uni. Despite all my hard work, I never actually caught myself looking more threatening than a kitten. Being five foot two and having fluffy red hair doesn't really help one in the more manly arts. I didn't get the part. It went to a great strapping girl with hockey legs and a Scottish accent. Nor did I have any more success in subduing Sean now. I heard him snigger as I marched off to Retread's office.

***

Peter was just coming out as I went in. He didn't look happy.

'Ah, Fiona. What can I do for you?' Retread looked up as I approached his desk. His eyes didn't really look focused, and I suspected he only recognised me because of my red hair. I noted with satisfaction that there was a cup of milk and water on his desk. This was going to be a pushover; the only problem was, would he remember about it on Monday?

'I want to apply for a job in the I. T. section. There's one going now.'

Retread looked at me over the tops of his glasses. This wasn't difficult, because they were sliding down his nose. His eyes seemed to be going different ways.

'The I. T. section? Really?'

'Yes, why not?'

'Well, I mean, er... isn't that awfully boring? You've been doing excellent work here, Fiona, excellent. We'd really hate to lose you.' *I'd really miss getting the credit for all your ideas.*

'I'd really like to go for it, Ret– er, Clive. I think it sounds like fun.'

'Fun?' This seemed to be a concept with which Retread was unfamiliar. He fixed me with a slow, puzzled stare, and started to tilt sideways.

'Yes. I think I'd like it,' I translated. 'Anyway, I'd like to at least sit the test. There wouldn't be any harm in that, would there? After all, they might not want me.' I gave him my best smile.

Retread seemed to cheer up slightly at this thought. 'Alright, then. I suppose there's no harm in your sitting the test. After all, you probably won't even get the job.' Ten points for originality. No wonder we called him Retread. 'I'll call H. R. and put you down for it. I'll let you know when the test is.'

I threw him another Grade A smile, which was probably wasted, as I doubted he could see past his desk, and got out quickly before he changed his mind.

***

Peter was still fizzing when I got back. Sean was vainly trying to get him to keep his voice down; the whole office seemed vastly entertained, with heads popping up from behind partitions all over the place. As I sat down, he fixed me with the kind of spiteful glare that only a man with pierced ears ever seems to achieve.

'What's the matter with him?' I muttered to Sean. Sean looked superior.

'Retread won't let him go for the aptitude tests. He said he should spend more time doing his own work, and less frotting on everyone else's.'

'Retread never said "frotting"!'

'Well, more or less, apparently. Words to that effect. Can't say I'm surprised. Serves him right for being such a bludger.'

Peter was instantly on the defensive. 'Well I wouldn't have any trouble getting a lot done either, if I made all my reports up like SOME PEOPLE.'

This was pretty unfair, as if anyone was famous for fictional reporting it was Peter. On the few occasions that he did any work at all, he bore more relation to the Bullshit Fairy than Woodward and Bernstein. The only reason that Marsh and Spacknall's credit files weren't completely fictional was that most of Peter's work was done by me and Sean; we kept him as a sort of office pet, because he was entertaining to have around, he made us laugh all day and cheered us up, and because we all went out together quite a bit, and it would have spoiled things if he got the sack. As a result, both Sean and I were rendered speechless with outrage, particularly since we had just finished collaborating on a huge investigation of a vast corporate group with forty-two companies all knotted together in a big tangle, owning each other, or parts of each other, in endless circles, which had been assigned to Peter, and for which we were certainly not going to get any credit, since it would mean his job if anyone found out we'd done it. Sean howled with outrage.

'Alright, you fat bastard, that's the last time I do your balance sheets for you. Jesus, three hours this morning. I've got a massive headache, and that's all the thanks I bloody well get. You can bloody well do them yourself next time. Prick.'

'Well, Fiona can do them, then.'

'Me? I write half your reports as it is, and do all the interviews. I'm not doing it.'

'Well, I certainly can't.'

'Why the hell not?'

'It makes my eyes red, anyway I can never get them to add up.'

The three of us spent the rest of the afternoon in a pregnant silence.

***

'Not computers!'

My mother was drawn back against the kitchen sink, one hand clasped to her throat in a pose of outraged horror. It reminded me of *The Lair of the White Worm*, the bit where Mimi finds out her next door neighbour is really a giant maggot. By a massive effort, aided by my failed Macbeth training, I kept my face straight.

'Why not, Mum?'

'They're so dirty!'

That's my Mum. The woman who washes the driveway with White King, in case germs breed in the concrete. The only person in the human race who Estapoled the inside of the garbage can. My father didn't say anything; he was gazing out of the window in a professorial sort of way.

'Mum. Mum. Computer rooms are all white and sterile. Honestly. I saw a picture of one.'

My mother assumed her favourite expression, the one that resembles long-suffering Patience ministering to an imbecile.

'Darling, sixty percent of people who work with computers get Legionnaires' Disease. Everyone knows that.'

'Mum, that's air conditioning, and it's only about half a percent. Anyway, everyone took measures about it ages ago. Nobody gets Legionnaires' Disease any more.'

I escaped to my room and collapsed on the bed. Why was everyone against me? I only wanted to become a space-age genius and save the world. I imagined myself saying 'Battle computers online' in a stern voice, with a massive fleet of Klingons looming in the viewport. Bam! Biff! Zowie! Another Enemy of Democracy bites the interstellar dust. I am decorated by the Galactic President. 'General MacDougall, you have liberated the Known Universe from our hated oppressors,' he says, during a fly-past of the entire Galactic Confederation space force.

Dance of Chaos

Suddenly, a hairy alien flies across the stadium and lands on my chest. I opened my eyes. It was Moses, my cat, who had dived off the top of the wardrobe. By some freak mischance he had missed my solar plexus, so I was still breathing. I threw my arms around him and buried my nose in his fur. Some days I feel that Moses is the only person who really understands me.

He bit me.

CHAPTER TWO

...that no man might presume to execute any of them, except he were first called, tried, examined, and known to have such qualities as are requisite for the same...
Book of Common Prayer

By the following Thursday, the day of the aptitude test, I was feeling pretty down about the whole thing. Peter wasn't speaking to me, Sean had hardly opened his mouth except to deliver the odd crushing putdown, my mother did nothing but rave about germs and my father had evinced a total lack of interest. I couldn't even tell my brother about it, as he was spending the school holidays at our grandmother's house in the country, and she won't have the telephone put on in case it attracts lightning strikes. My boyfriend, Tim, had just given me the flick for about the nineteenth time, so I couldn't ring him up either. Gloria, my best friend, was off in Canberra, covering some political conference or something. Moses, the emotional mainstay of my life and the reason I was still living at home with my parents at twenty, had bitten me again, and had later killed and dissected a seagull all over my room, and even Arnold, my teddy bear, was somehow looking more moth-eaten than usual.

Nevertheless, I did my best to get into a positive frame of mind. After all, this was D Day, when I was going to Show Them All. I washed my hair and put on my most stunning outfit.

During breakfast I dropped my toast. A perfectly normal occurrence for me. And of course one expects toast to land honey side down. But did it have to land on Moses?

By the time I had given Moses a quick bath, and my mother had given me a slow lecture for eating the toast, I was half an hour late.

At the tram stop, the first tram in twenty minutes not only didn't stop, but the driver threw me the finger as he shot past. It started to rain. A ladder mysteriously appeared in my tights.

I arrived at the office in a horrible state at twenty to ten, and furtively sneaked up the back stairs to the ladies' room. I was damned if I was going to give Peter and Sean any more taunting material by appearing like a refugee from Hell House.

Fortunately, because this kind of thing is always happening to me, I carry a full makeup kit, spare tights, tissues, safety pins etc in my bag, so I was able to effect reasonable repairs. I dried my hair under the hand dryer. It went fuzzy. I fluffed it up with an afro comb and tried to convince myself that it looked deliberate.

I strolled into the office with my bag behind my back, trying to look natural and casual. There was a white envelope on my desk. My stomach went cold and crawly; had Retread sacked me for being late, right on the eve of my triumph? I didn't feel any easier when I noticed Peter and Sean studiously avoiding looking at me and pretending to work.

I ripped open the envelope. Inside was a card with a picture of a fluffy black chicken coming out of its egg. The card said, 'Good Luck'. It had been signed by the whole office.

I burst into tears.

***

The test was held in the sixth floor conference room. There were about eight of us sitting for it.

Some woman from H. R., whom I'd never seen before, gave us all name tags (why? No one was talking to anyone) and invited us to use the Café Bar. Big deal, it was just like the grotty one on our floor. I opened up the top and peered inside. It even had the same dead silverfish floating in the water. I made myself a strong cup of ersatz Yarra water; I've never been overly concerned about hygiene; with my mother about, worrying about germs is gilding the lily.

I checked out the other applicants. They all looked madly hostile; this was because word had gone around that there was only one programming position. It's a dog eat dog world at Marsh & Spacknall. I imagined myself as a corporate shark: 'Sell twenty thousand BHP,' I snarled, slamming down the phone and lighting a cigar. I curled my lip at the abjectly cringing department head fawning before my antique rosewood desk; he bore a strange resemblance to Retread.

I emerged from this pleasant reverie to find that the H. R. woman had handed out the first test paper and I had missed all the instructions.

***

The tests all seemed pretty easy. I didn't worry too much, because I had on the nicest outfit in the room. I had forgotten about my fuzzy hair, and filled in time between tests by furtively observing the other applicants. I didn't know any of them; they were all from other departments. By the absence of gold teeth and brass buttons, I could tell none of them was from Sales.

The most remarkable person in the room was a tall, pale, forgettable man in his twenties. At least, his face was totally forgettable, but he was noticeable enough just from the way he smelled. It was horrible, as if he'd rolled in a dead fish or something. I couldn't imagine how anyone could smell like that so early in the day. Sadly, I had allowed myself to be seated next to him.

Besides the Incredible Stinking Man, there was one girl who looked as if she shopped at Katies out of duty rather than pleasure, and various other nondescript people. I looked back at my test paper. Idly I turned the page over, and realised with an icy shock that there were five more questions on the other side, and only three minutes left. I grabbed my pencil frantically; the point broke off. I looked out of the sides of my eyes, praying for inspiration. Please, God, I prayed, give me something to write with, and make it fast.

God must have been in a good mood; Mr Stinky had a biro sticking out of his coat pocket. I eased it out gently; he didn't feel a thing. The biro was a bit smelly, but it did the job, and when the H. R. woman cleared her throat I was able to look just as smug as everyone else while I casually slid Stinking Man's property up my sleeve. I didn't really want to contaminate my silk shirt, but this biro was a fancy gold job with initials engraved on it, and I didn't want him letting out a scream of outrage and pouncing on it before the tests were over.

At the end of the final test, the H. R. woman gave us each an appointment with the I. T. manager for an interview the next day. Mine was at 11:00. The woman gave me a patronising smile. She wasn't troubling to hide the fact that she thought it was obvious I had no chance. I suppose if I had a figure like a matchbox, I'd want to patronise somebody, too.

I caught up with Stinky in the corridor.

'Excuse me, I think you dropped your pen. It was on the floor.'

'Oh yes, it is mine. Thanks very much, I'd hate to lose that.'

'Oh, it's my pleasure. It would be a real shame to lose a lovely pen like that.' I smiled at him nicely, holding my breath.

Dance of Chaos

***

I made it back to my desk on the stroke of four-thirty, just as Peter and Sean were packing up ready to go to the pub. We always went to the pub on Thursdays and also on Fridays, it was a sacred duty. Luckily the pub was just across the street from our building; if we'd had to go any farther, Peter and Sean would probably have swelled up like bullfrogs from sheer nosiness.

We settled into our usual table in the beer garden, and our usual argument about who would buy the first round. Considering the number of drinks we always got through in the course of the evening, this argument was pretty academic, but it was a ritual part of our week, and we all enjoyed it in a perverse kind of way.

'Fiona has to buy the first round because she's got something to celebrate.'

'No way. You'd better buy it if you expect me to tell you anything.'

'Get lost, I'm not getting it. I had to pay for your card.'

'God, Peter, you're such a stingy bastard. You probably wash your Kleenex and use it again.'

'That's nothing. I've been round his place and

seen toilet paper drying on the line.'

'Ooh! Don't you give ME a hard time, sweetheart! I can't even afford to get my teeth capped!'

Sean sniggered evilly. 'Why don't you Tippex them out?'

'Ooooh, you BITCH! I'd punch your face in if I wasn't so fat and cowardly!'

I got up and went to the bar. When I got back with the beer, Peter and Sean were still at it. I don't think they'd even noticed I wasn't there. They noticed alright when I put beer in front of them, though. Sean flashed me one of his darkly handsome smiles, that always made me wish a) that we didn't work together, and b) that I didn't already have a boyfriend. I wondered in passing why Tim hadn't rung me yet.

'Okay, Fiona, let's have all the bitchy details.'

'Well. There's only one programming position, and eight of us going for it.'

'Who are the others, there's no one from our floor, is there?'

'No, I didn't know anybody. There was this one guy that really stinks, I had to sit next to him, it was SO disgusto. Swear to God I nearly chucked.'

'Well, HE'S history.' One of the charming things about Peter is that he's always so utterly certain about everything. 'Who'd hire someone that stinks? I MEAN.'

'Who'd hire a fat lazy git with rotten teeth?'

Peter waved his cigarette at Sean. 'You want this out in your face?'

Sean and I both ignored the threat; we'd heard it several times a week for the last six months. 'So what else are you competing with?'

'Oh well, some blonde girl, she looked really bad-tempered, and some boring-looking clerical types.'

'Men or women?'

'They were all so boring I couldn't really tell. I was afraid if I looked at them too much I'd fall asleep and miss the tests.'

'What were the tests like?'

'Really easy, a breeze. Except my pencil broke right near the end of one. It was okay though, the guy with BO lent me a pen.'

'God, what a moron. I wouldn't help anyone

that was going for a job I wanted.'

'You wouldn't help your grandmother across the street. Anyway, he didn't mean to, I shoplifted it out of his pocket.'

'What, you mean you just took it out of his pocket? While he was sitting there ?'

'Sure. It was easy. He was probably half unconscious from his own BO. You've got to smell this guy, it was incredible. The yanks could use him in Guantanamo Bay instead of waterboarding. Anyway, we all have to go and see the I. T. manager now. I'm going tomorrow morning.'

Peter's eyes lit up. 'You know what you've got to do, don't you? Now listen, I'm going to tell you exactly what you've got to do to get this job. First you...'

I tuned out. Peter always knew how to go about everything, and his advice always followed the same format. Instead, I thought about cool, quiet rooms with lots of white tiles. By the time he got to the part about the fishnet stockings, I'd decided that if I didn't get the job life wouldn't be worth living. I'd simply have to end it all. Dressed in something black and flowing, I'd walk slowly along the Westgate Bridge, a lonely, tragic figure. My family, of course, would be distraught. I pictured my funeral, my mother sobbing uncontrollably, my father dry-eyed but agonised, my little brother Patrick silent and shivering like a frail orphan. Moses would wander round the house all night, crying and running to the door every time footsteps passed in the street. When I got to that part I found it so moving that I started to cry, and inhaled my beer.

***

I went home early, so as to get ready for the interview. Perhaps the I. T. manager's impression of me would be the deciding factor. I had decided on a very businesslike outfit. A crisp white shirt and navy skirt. Or would that make me look too much like a bank teller? Perhaps my mother would lend me her pearls. It was true that the last time I'd borrowed them she had had to get them restrung, but I was sure she'd forgotten about that.

❧CHAPTER THREE☙

I have not dwelt with vain persons: neither will I have fellowship with the deceitful.
Psalm 26:4

It was only seven o'clock when I let myself into the house. I fed Moses and wandered into the sitting room. It was empty. Further investigation revealed Dad in his study, marking assignments and muttering angrily about the degeneration of modern youth. He looked up in astonishment as I walked in.

'Fiona! What on earth are you doing here?'

'I live here, remember?' Sometimes Dad really worries me. 'Where's Mum?'

'Gone to the station to fetch Patrick.'

'Patrick! Is he coming home tonight?'

'No, Fiona, but your mother thought it would be interesting to go a day early, and spend the night at Spencer Street Station.'

I had walked right into that one. Dad is sudden death on inane remarks. I often wonder how he and Mum manage to get along, and yet I don't think I've ever heard them say a cross word to each other. Perhaps they fight secretly, in the night.

Dad fired a parting shot as I wandered out. 'Since you're home early, you'd better get dinner.'

Hell.

***

I went upstairs to change into my jeans. I couldn't decide whether I was ecstatic that Patrick was coming home, or furious that I had to cook dinner. Not that I would have begrudged the effort to cook Patrick a wonderful homecoming dinner with all his favourite things, it was just that I'm such an awful cook. What rotten timing, I thought miserably. I could just about manage something depressing, like sausages with mashed potatoes and peas. If I hadn't arrived home early, they probably would have taken him out to the Pancake Parlour or something.

Dance of Chaos

I went back downstairs feeling a tiny bit more hopeful.

'Dad? Why don't we go out to the Pancake Parlour for dinner? It's his favourite, we ought to do something special to welcome him home.'

My father looked at me mistily. 'You are a thoughtful child, Fiona. So few young women today would take the trouble to come home early for their little brother. I'll tell you what. Why don't you take Patrick out to dinner, and your mother and I can have a little time to ourselves.'

Better and better. I'd have to pay for dinner, of course, but I'd saved a fortune anyway, by coming home early from the pub. And I couldn't wait to get hold of Patrick. He'd been spending the school holidays at our grandmother's house, and I had missed him terribly. Also, I was dying to tell him about the new job. I knew he, at least, would be properly impressed.

'Gee, thanks, Dad.' I went back upstairs, relieved to be off the hook and wondering why all the dialogue in our house sounded like a nineteen fifties movie.

***

By the time Mum and Patrick got home I had

sorted out my clothes for the interview, all except the pearls. Everything I had chosen needed ironing, but I felt the decisions were the important part and the fine detail could wait. Patrick fell on my neck like the man in the Bible. He was very emotional for thirteen, which I didn't mind at all, and taller than me, which I did. I practically dragged him out the door, which surprised me rather, because usually it's more a question of not getting trampled in the rush if there's food going.

The Pancake Parlour was crowded as usual, but we managed to get a table right next to the fire all the same. On the way there I had found out why Patrick had been so uncharacteristically keen to stay and unpack his own bag; on his holiday he had somehow acquired a stack of pornographic magazines from one of his dirty little friends, and they were in among his shirts and socks, together with the packet of fancy condoms which another of his dirty little friends had dared him to buy. In a normal family, he might have been able to get away with it, but no doubt our mother was just slavering to pounce on the bag and disinfect the lining the minute we got out the door.

'Honestly, Patrick, you're so immature.'

'I can't help it if I'm sexually precocious.'

'Come off it, Patrick, this is me, Fiona. The

person who knows you sleep with your teddy bear.'

'Well, John reckons if you're not sexually active by the time you're fourteen, you break out in these massive zits.'

'Well, John should know, I guess. He must weigh all of forty kilos, and thirty-five of that would be pus.'

'Fiona, DO you mind. I'm trying to eat my dinner, if you could refrain from being so disgusting.'

I shrugged. 'Okay, then. I guess you don't want me to get you off the hook with Mum.'

That got to him. His eyes went all round and buggy.

'Oh, Fi. Do you think you could?'

I sat back and crossed my arms. 'If I get you out of this, you have to do all my share of the washing up until Christmas.'

Patrick nodded dumbly.

'And you can throw away those filthy stick books.'

'Oh, come on, Fi, fair go. What about the zits?'

'I'll give you some cream for those. Do we have a deal or not?'

There was a long silence.

'Yeah, okay.'

I stuck out my hand. 'Give us your mobile.'

Patrick went pale. 'Can't you pay for dinner? Is that why you made me promise to do your share of the washing up?'

'To ring Mum, stupid. Mine's out of credit. Come on, or it'll be too late.'

He handed over his phone, and I took it outside where it was quieter and dialled our house, hoping I looked confident. Actually I had no idea whether I could stop Mum from looking in Patrick's bag, but the opportunity of getting out of six months' washing up had been too good to miss.

'Hello, Mum?'

'Fiona, darling. Are you and Patrick having a lovely dinner?'

Good. She hadn't found anything yet.

'Fine. Ah, Mum, have you opened Patrick's bag yet?'

'No, I haven't quite got around to it yet. Um, your father and I had a few things to discuss.'

Great Scott! She actually sounded embarrassed! Could they have been Doing It? Our parents? I couldn't decide between relief and shock. But there was no time to be lost on this absorbing question, with the life and honour of my only brother at stake.

'Yes, well the thing is, Mum, I think you should leave it for Patrick to unpack it himself. Apparently he's got a huge tarantula or something in there that he brought back from Gran's. I thought I'd better warn you. Something about a science project, he said.'

My mother's voice came faintly back to me from a long way away. 'That was very thoughtful of you, Fiona. I'll just leave Patrick's bag where it is. Mind you tell him not to let it escape. And don't keep him out too late, will you? Remember he's a growing boy.'

Oh, he's that alright. 'Okay, Mum. You and Dad have a lovely time.'

'Oh, we're fine. We're just going to have an early night. Goodnight, dear.'

An early night. Sure. I swaggered back to our cosy fireside table, feeling vastly satisfied at having pulled off a fast one and discovered my parents' guilty secret.

'You're safe, this time. Just remember there's a tarantula in your bag, it's a science project for school, okay?'

My little brother gazed at me adoringly, and fell on the food with new relish. While he was busy stuffing his face I told him, at some length, about my new career opportunities. I could tell I had his rapt attention, because he only had one helping of dessert.

'It sounds great, Fi. How did you think you went on the test?'

I brushed aside this minor detail as unimportant. I knew the interview was the thing that counted, and I couldn't imagine Miss Katies having access to real pearls.

***

We got home around eleven. So much for my early night, and I still hadn't ironed my clothes for tomorrow. I set the alarm for six a.m., and fell into bed next to Moses.

***

When I woke up the next morning it looked

pretty light for seven o'clock. Then I saw my bedside clock; it was after eight-thirty. The button on top was pushed down, silencing the alarm. Had I really forgotten to set it, or had Moses learned a new trick? I decided on the former option; if Moses had wanted to shut off the alarm, he'd have been more likely to smash the clock.

I raced frantically down the hall to the bathroom, and skidded to a halt in front of the locked door. From within I could hear something like a cheap Niagara Falls and very loud, tuneless singing. I knew with a horrid certainty that Patrick was in there, using all the hot water and leaving piles of soggy towels all over the floor. I banged on the door. If he used my rubber duck I'd personally kill him.

'If you use my rubber duck I'll personally kill you,' I shouted, racing for the laundry to heat up the iron.

***

Scott Jenkins, the manager of the I. T. Department, was a short, flabby, pale man in his thirties. When I first saw him I had a horrible impression that he had no irises in his eyes, just little tiny pupils, but then I realised his eyes were just very, very pale, like the rest of him. I didn't get a very clear impression of his personality at the interview, perhaps because it was as colourless as his eyes. He asked me a few vague questions about my work background, and then he hit me with the biggie: why did I want to be a programmer?

This one threw me for a bit of a loop; I hadn't been expecting such a pointless question, and therefore hadn't troubled to prepare a sensible answer for it. After all, I hadn't really a clue what programmers did, so how could I even know if I really wanted to be one, let alone why? What I really wanted to be was General MacDougall, interstellar saviour of the Universe, but I realised I couldn't tell Jenkins that.

I had to say something soon. Jenkins had started tapping his pencil. I took a deep breath and let it out again.

'I think it will be fun,' I said.

Jenkins looked a bit startled. Perhaps, like Retread, fun wasn't a concept with which he was familiar. He cleared his throat nervously.

'Er, hm. Yes. You scored exceptionally high on the aptitude test.' He looked a bit dubious, as if the test had been supposed to screen out people who liked fun. I started to have second thoughts. 'Well, would you like the job?'

'Are you offering it to me?'

'Well, your transfer would have to be conditional on your own manager releasing you. Is there likely to be any problem about that?'

Damn right there was, but I wasn't about to tell Jenkins that. My second thoughts of a moment ago had vanished like the morning mist; all the petty little frustrations of my job came crowding in on me, and I thought I saw vistas of freedom opening out before me, like the starry deeps of space.

'Oh, I'm sure it would be alright. Clive Simpkin is my manager. I discussed it with him before taking the test, he was really supportive.'

'Good, good. Well, I think we can say that as long as there isn't any problem about your transfer, you could start with us some time next month. Would that be acceptable to you?'

I found myself grinning and nodding like an idiot. A cold little voice in the back of my head nagged that I hadn't quite told the exact truth about Retread, but I stored that thought for later. After all, 'Sufficient unto the day is the evil thereof', we have that on good authority. I felt sure God would let the matter pass, since I'd shown such filial piety the night before in cleverly saving my mother from so much unhappiness.

↣CHAPTER FOUR↢

Who shall ascend into the hill of the Lord: or who shall rise up in his holy place? Even he that hath clean hands, and a pure heart: and that hath not lift up his mind unto vanity, nor sworn to deceive his neighbour.
Psalm 24: 3 – 4

'I got it!' I shrieked, rushing into our kitchen. I skidded to a halt in front of the stove. The kitchen was empty. Feeling slightly deflated, I tried the sitting room. My father was there, reading *Pravda* and furtively smoking his pipe. I jumped up and down a bit to get his attention.

'Dad! Dad! I got it!'

My father looked up from *Pravda* and raised one eyebrow pointedly. He didn't seem impressed.

Moses glanced contemptuously at me from the windowsill and turned back to the garden. He didn't actually seen terribly impressed either. I looked around the room, but there were still no cheering crowds.

'Where's Mum?'

'She went shopping with your brother. She said you'd get dinner.'

Shit. Just what I needed. I mooched out again. As I went I could hear my father shouting after me.

'And don't come in here screaming. I get enough of that at work. You young people have got no respect. In my day...'

His voice had faded into the distance but I knew it all off by heart, we all did, even Moses. One day he flew into such a passion that he lost his voice, and Patrick said all his words for him. Dad was terribly unimpressed, especially as Patrick was only six at the time, but I thought it was adorable, and such a very Patrick thing to do.

Upstairs in my room, I checked my phone, but there were no new messages. Why hadn't Tim called me? I knew he would be interested in my news; he was always impressed by anything to do with money. It was true that he had dumped me, but he was always dumping me; I'd stopped taking it seriously after the fifth time, realising that it was just Tim being a drama queen. Perhaps I should call him? But no. It would only give him silly ideas if I started running after him, ringing him up and so on. Best to stay with my usual habit of not returning his first six calls after he dumped me. That was guaranteed to result in flowers, chocolates and a really good night out, usually to the ballet or opera. The Ring Cycle was coming up, I remembered. I wondered if I could get him to take me to all four operas? Perhaps I'd better ignore the first twelve calls.

I tried Gloria's number, but it was still going straight to voice mail. Really, I thought, irritated, what was the point of having friends at all? I didn't bother to leave a message, because I had already left one the day before.

I threw myself on my bed. I reckoned I had time for at least three quarters of an hour of sulking before I needed to start worrying about dinner. God, dinner. Why should I ever start worrying about it? Did I say I would? I'd just landed this massive new job, with no help from Them, mind you, and all they could do was piss off to Chapel Street and expect dinner to be ready when they got home, probably without even buying me anything. Stuff them, I thought. Let them jolly well eat cake. I drifted into a light doze.

***

I dreamed I was trapped in a crashed spaceship on the surface of Jupiter. Massive volcanic eruptions on the planet's surface were drawing closer and closer, and there was no rescue team closer than Alpha Centauri. One by one the life support systems were failing, and soon it would be dark. All of my brave comrades lay about the control room in various postures of death; the mission to terraform the outer planets of the solar system had met with a freak storm on entering the Jovanic troposphere. I started to pray, and then remembered that in my dream there was no God.

Suddenly a loud pounding on the airlock penetrated my black despair. I activated the viewscreen, gibbering with relief, and the ghastly monster out of Alien loomed at me. I screamed and raced for the door. My legs tangled in the sheets and I fell out of bed.

I crouched on the floor, shivering and clutching Arnold, my teddy bear. Bits of real life started to skitter back into my brain. House. Name. Cat on top of wardrobe.

Don't be such a baby, Fiona, said part of myself (a small part). Why not? said the other (much larger) part. Suddenly I realised the pounding at the airlock was still going on.

Dive under the bed and hide, said the major part of me. Or the wardrobe. Grow up, Fiona, said the little part. What if it's the Alien out there, said the big part, with tremendous logic. Aha, said the small part triumphantly. But what if someone catches you hiding under the bed?

Some arguments are incontrovertible. I suppose I'm not the bravest person I know, but I'd rather face the Alien, or even Fred Kruger, than be laughed at. I went and opened the door.

I won't say I wasn't relieved to see my mother. Then I remembered about dinner, and wondered if I hadn't been better off with the Alien.

'Er. Hello, Mummy.'

'Fiona, what on earth is the matter with you lately? I've told you and told you about going to sleep with your clothes on. You know perfectly well it breeds dust mites, and it's not a healthy kind of sleep when you sleep that heavily. I thought I was going to break my hand, have you any idea how long...' etc etc.

'...and you'd better put some blusher on before you come downstairs, you look terrible, all washed out. It's that dreadful job, with all those strange people...'

***

First thing on Monday morning, I went to see Retread, nice and early while he was still sober. I explained everything, my words falling like stones into a vast grave of silence. He looked at me over the tops of his glasses.

'So you see,' I finished, 'all you have to do is let me and Mr Jenkins know when I can move up there.'

Retread took off his glasses and polished them on his tie. 'I'm afraid it's not quite that simple, Fiona. Look, I honestly have to admit I never dreamed you'd pass the tests. There didn't seem any harm in letting you sit them, since you wanted to so badly, but as to releasing you from this department in the next year, I'm really afraid it's out of the question. You're one of the most experienced people I've got. You do see, er...'

'But, but they won't wait a year, Clive, they want me next month.' One of the most experienced people indeed, I thought furiously, when I'd only been there six months since changing my mind about Uni. What he really meant was that I had the cheapest salary, being under twenty-one.

'Well, I'm afraid you can't go.' Just like that. I couldn't believe this little creep was saying this to me.

Well, I gave it my best shot. I pleaded, then I argued, then when that failed I cried all over the place, but Retread seemed to have struck a deep and unexpected vein of fortitude. Nothing I could say or do seemed to make any impression on him at all.

***

I sat down at my desk and opened a few files, numb with misery. I hadn't really cared that much about the job until it looked as if I couldn't have it. I racked my brains, but couldn't think of anything I hadn't already tried. I tried to accustom myself to the thought that for the first time in my life, I couldn't have something I really wanted.

After twenty minutes or so, I noticed that both Peter and Sean were missing from their desks. It seemed artistically right that the two people on whom I most depended should be absent in the hour of my greatest need. I imagined myself dying alone and unloved, a poor old woman in a bedsitter, with newspaper stuffed between the dingy blankets to keep out the cold. Moses, of course, had abandoned me to go and live with rich people who had caviare for breakfast.

Peter and Sean reappeared from the direction of the tearoom, giggling. I regarded them crossly. What insensitivity. They didn't even ask me how my meeting with Retread had gone. Probably they already knew he wasn't letting me go. Probably the whole office had known before I did. What a bunch of creeps.

'Fiona, guess what?'

'Rack off, Peter. I'm busy.'

'You're not too busy to hear this.'

I ignored him and shuffled papers.

'Are you feeling okay, Fiona?' Sean peered at me. 'It's not like you not to be interested in a really good bit of goss.'

'Look, I couldn't give a toss. I'm too bloody miserable. Just leave me alone.' I slammed a few drawers to drive home my point.

'What on earth's the matter? You were okay this morning. Did you have some bad news?'

'Bad news, too bloody right. That bastard. He's not letting me go.'

'What bastard? Who?'

'Bloody Retread. He said I can't take the job in

I. T.'

Peter was his usual sensitive self.

'Oh well, never mind, I've got some excellent goss about him that you won't believe. You can cheer yourself up by spreading it around.'

I was so depressed that even the prospect of a juicy piece of gossip did nothing for me.

'Tell me later, I'm going for coffee now.'

Peter followed me to the café bar. As I was making my cup of rehydrated goat droppings, he prowled round the empty tearoom, checking outside the door and under the tables. Having satisfied himself that there was no one else there, he astounded me by actually lowering his voice, a thing I'd never seen before.

'You know the Clockwork Steam Palace, right? Where I go on Wednesdays?'

I did indeed, or at least I knew of it. The Clockwork Steam Palace was a reproduction Roman baths with a Steampunk theme, and I had heard about it *ad nauseam* from Peter, who went there at least once a week for a sauna and other activities. Apparently as well as the baths, steam rooms etc, there was also a bar, pool tables, and various private and semi-private rooms for the other activities. It was the mainspring of Peter's varied and adventurous social life, and he considered himself a social failure if he had intimate relations with fewer than four people on any given night there. He'd often tried to get me to go there with him, but somehow I just felt that it wasn't my kind of place.

'Look, Peter, I'm just not in the mood, okay?'

'Yes, you are. Guess who I ran into there, last night?'

'I don't care if it was Tony Abbott in a clown suit. Get out of my way, will you?'

Peter dodged in front of me again. 'Retread!' he pronounced with a flourish.

I dropped my coffee.

'OWWWW!' screamed Peter, forgetting all about being discreet. 'You clumsy bitch, I just had these pants dry cleaned.'

He rabbited on about the cost of dry cleaning for a while. I didn't listen. A horrible and shocking idea was taking possession of my brain.

'Peter, listen. Are you really sure it was him?'

'Of course I'm sure. I talked to him. He was

really embarrassed. I suppose he didn't want anyone at the office knowing what a big fat man-whore he is. They soon will, though, after I open my big mouth!'

'Have you told anyone else except Sean?'

'Of course not, you know I always tell you and Sean everything first.'

That was true enough. The three of us had a standing agreement to share all gossip with each other first.

'Look, Peter, I want you to do me a huge favour. Promise you won't tell anyone else about this until after I start in the I. T. Department.'

'But you're not getting the transfer, you just said.'

I smiled happily. 'Oh, yes, I am.'

෨CHAPTER FIVE☙

Prosper, we pray thee, the industries of this place; defend those who are engaged therein from all perils, and grant that they may rejoice in the fruits of thy bounty...
Book of Common Prayer

I could feel my heart pounding as I got out of the lift. My first day in the I. T. industry, awesome! (as Patrick would have said. We steely-eyed technical types didn't go in for such juvenile expressions, of course.)

The office was open plan, of course. All offices are open plan. But this one, like my old department downstairs, had the managers' offices actually built, I don't mean built from plywood like most executive offices are now, but really built, solidly part of the building. I knew from bitter experience downstairs that this made it virtually impossible to eavesdrop.

There were three men sitting at the desks. I thought I had seen one of them somewhere before, but couldn't be sure; he seemed to have no distinguishing characteristics at all. The second of the men was really ugly, and I certainly knew I had never seen *him* before; in fact, I had never seen anyone remotely like him before. He had enormous bright red lips in the middle of a totally spherical face, like one of those black goldfish. The rest of his body was incredibly tall and skinny; he looked a bit like a stop sign. There was also a third man sitting at a terminal in the corner, but he looked quite old, at least fifty, so I dismissed him as unimportant.

I tapped on Scott Jenkins' door and went in. He was crouched over his desk looking despondent. When he saw me, he let out an alarmed cry and jumped up, his glasses sliding down his nose.

'Is it today you're starting?' His tone was tinged with horrified disbelief.

I was struck dumb. I'd had this day circled in red for the past month, crossing off days on my calendar and generally focusing on it. Now this fat little creep hadn't even remembered that I was starting today. I didn't know whether to shriek with rage or burst into tears. I ground my teeth while I contemplated the alternatives; then I remembered that grinding the teeth gives you jowls, and stopped.

Jenkins came out from behind his desk. He was shorter and fatter than I remembered. 'Well, we'd better go and see Frank.'

We headed for the old guy in the corner.

'Frank?' Jenkins seemed even smaller and more timid than he had a moment ago. The old man swung around, snarling like a tiger disturbed feeding. A second later the snarl was replaced by an expression of suave urbanity. The transformation was so fast and so complete that I wondered if I'd imagined it.

'This is Fiona, our new trainee. Fiona, this is Frank Stevenson. You'll be reporting to him.'

'How do you do, Mr Stevenson.' Stevenson regarded me with an expression of horrified distaste. He had a big hole in the front of his jumper, which made him look even more fierce.

'We don't go in for those fancy manners up here. You can call me Frank. This will be your desk, right here next to mine. That's so you can ask me questions whenever you need to. That's my office over there next to Scott's, but I don't like to use it, I always sit here. That's the computer room in there,' he jerked his thumb towards a glass partition, in a lordly and dismissive sort of way. Suddenly, Frank stopped talking and looked at me expectantly.

'Er, why don't you like to use your office?'

'I need to be accessible. If I'm shut up in an office, people won't come in and ask me things. If people don't ask me things, they try to decide on their own and get screwed up, okay? So I stay out here all the time.' He ratted around in a drawer and produced a scuzzy-looking book with a torn, stained cover, which he slapped down in front of me as if it was the Holy Grail. 'This is your first course, okay? Work at your own pace. Any questions, ask me, okay?' Frank turned back to his terminal and appeared to forget I existed. I took a look at the book. It was a book about computers, big deal. I didn't come up here to read books.

'Ah, excuse me, Frank?'

'Yeah?'

'When do I actually get to see the, you know, computer?'

Frank swivelled around in his chair and looked me up and down. He sighed in a weary sort of way.

'Listen, kid, no one has time to give you a

guided tour, okay? Look, I don't know what Scott told you and I don't particularly care, but you had better get it through your head that a trainee programmer is several inches lower than the ground, okay? Which is a lot lower than a trainee operator, okay? So don't be expecting any red carpet treatment around here, okay? In case you were going to ask, a trainee operator is senior to a trainee programmer because it takes a trainee operator about six weeks to be useful, and it takes a trainee programmer about six months to be useful, okay?'

I thought I would be useful a lot sooner than six months. After all, hadn't I had the highest score on the aptitude tests, and won this job? But it just didn't seem like the time to say anything. I opened the book.

***

I looked at my watch. Six o'clock, an hour and a half past my usual knocking-off time. Since the extraordinary conversation I'd had with Frank, no one had spoken to me at all. Because the do-it-yourself computer concepts course, in spite of its filthy stained cover, was actually so easy that even a moron could follow it, I hadn't had an excuse even to ask Frank another question, and everyone else had completely ignored me all day. I supposed they all shared Frank's view that I was beneath contempt. Besides the two guys in the outside part of the office, there were a couple of carefree young people working inside the computer room, who I assumed were the operators. One of them was the Katies girl from the aptitude test. I felt absolutely shattered; I wanted to cry, but didn't, because I knew with a horrible certainty that no one would notice. I hated my wonderful new job. I'd looked forward to it for so long, and been so excited and proud about it, and it had turned out to be utterly horrible. Briefly I considered going to see Retread and asking for my old job back, but I knew I could never do it. Not after being so smug to everybody. I would just have to put on a cheerful face. I wondered how long I would have to stay before I could reasonably claim to have mastered the job and tired of it. I had a horrible feeling it would be several years. I felt like a trapped animal.

Well, at least today was over. I closed the book and collected my bag. I stood up. I walked to the door. Nobody said goodnight. I went out.

On the front steps of our building I ran into one of the junior clerks from my old department, Marjorie something.

'Fiona! How was your first day?'

I'd never paid much attention to her, she was a

bit dim, and generally looked as though she'd got dressed out of the rag bag with her eyes shut, but hers was the first friendly face I'd seen all day. I wanted to burst into tears and pour out the whole tragic story, but I couldn't face the sympathy of someone who looked like that. From somewhere I dredged up a smile and nailed it to my face.

'Fine. It's really exciting, I'm having a ball.'

'You look really tired. Do you have to work really hard up there?'

'Well, it's a bit more demanding. But it's terrific fun. Listen, I'm in a terrible hurry, I'm going out tonight, I'll see you later, okay?' I broke into a sort of canter till I got out of sight round the corner. At least my reputation was intact. Stunning new job, busy social life.

***

Of course it wasn't really as bad as all that, not after the first day, although I went through the whole of the first week without anyone actually speaking to me. By doing a bit of discreet eavesdropping while pretending to read the computer book Frank had given me, I discovered that there was a kind of cultural imperative that made everyone ignore me; they had a sort of elitist attitude which I began to absorb after a while. Once

I understood that as soon as there was another new trainee, I would be pretty well a member of the human race, I found it quite a bit easier to take; the only problem was that, as far as I knew, the department now had no vacancies, and I couldn't find out if anyone was thinking of leaving, because no one was speaking to me.

It was really Friday night that broke the ice, that blessed institution of Australian office life. Our office was especially social because of everyone being single (except Frank, who I found was regarded by everyone as a sort of god from Olympus) and all pretty much in the same age group, well, under thirty anyway, except for Frank and Scott.

What happened was that, having totally given up on any expectation of normal social intercourse in my new job after the first day, I simply continued my ordinary habits on Friday, and at four-thirty I sauntered down to the first floor. Peter and Sean were just packing up their desks ready for their weekly debauch (well, Sean was tidying his desk and Peter was primping), and pretended to be amazed to see me. They froze in mid-pack looking vaguely ridiculous, like cows in someone's back yard.

'Well,' I said, determined not to start crying,

although after the lonely, isolated week I'd just had I felt the strongest urge to break down and howl. I reminded myself firmly that it takes hardly anything to make me want to break down and howl. 'What are you staring at, gormless ones?'

Sean cleared his throat uncomfortably. They both shuffled their feet. 'Just wondering how much longer you were planning to keep us waiting. Let's go and get pissed, hey?'

Light dawned. They hadn't been expecting me back after I got the suave new job. For a second I wondered if I'd got things completely wrong. Was dropping one's old friends considered normal behaviour in office life? Would they not want to know me any more, and I'd just be replaced as their friend by whoever got hired into my old job? Nothing in my life had prepared me for such an idea. Then I decided I must have imagined the whole thing. The frightening crack that had opened for a second in my safe, comfortable world closed, and the day was bright again.

***

Settled comfortably in the beer garden at the Rat and Broomstick (affectionately known to us as the Dead Rat), with a cold, foaming pot in front of me and a familiar face at either side, I felt as if nothing bad had ever happened to me. Peter and

Sean were fizzing with curiosity.

'So come on, tell. What's it like?'

'Any prospects?'

By the depraved leer on Peter's face I knew he wasn't talking about career opportunities. What wasn't clear, however, was whether he was talking about sexual prospects from my viewpoint or his own. Although, now that I came to think of it, there probably wouldn't be a lot of difference. I wondered what it would be like if Peter and I both fancied the same person. Would it hurt our friendship? But then I realised that the situation could never arise, because the person we fancied would either be gay or not gay. Sort of like one of those problems in logic, really. Not (P and (not P)). I dragged my mind back to the present.

'Prospects for me or you?'

'For you, sweetheart. I'm too old and fat to attract any prospects.'

'Hell, no. There's Jenkins, I already told you about him. Terminal suburbia. Then there's my boss, Frank Stevenson. He's really old, at least forty. There's two programmers, Tony and Geoff. Tony's been there quite a while, he's a total horror head, though. He's really skinny with a head like a beach ball, and he's got these really huge lips. He looks like a road lollipop. And the other guy, Geoff, he only started about six weeks ago, so he's a trainee too. The training's six months. Then there's the operators, there's four…'

'Oooh, forget it, sweetheart. We don't want to know about the menials.'

I privately thought Peter was being a bit harsh. Menial the operators might be, but they seemed more promising than Geoff and Tony. For one thing, none of them was exactly ugly, and for another, one of them had actually said hello to me in the lift that morning. Compared to my fellow programmers this was a miracle of sociability. I let it pass.

'So, how's it been in Credit since I left?'

Peter looked woebegone.

'God, Fiona, it's been so tragic since you left. I had to do three reports yesterday, it's killing me, and I got a biro mark on my new shirt. I think I'm just going to have to go home, run a hot bath and slit my wrists.'

He really had something to bitch about. A normal day's output, when there was enough work to go round, was about ten reports. I noticed he was still wearing the shirt with the biro mark. It was pale green satin.

'You fat lazy wanker. You deserve everything you get,' Sean said spitefully. 'I'm not doing any more of your reports for you. I bust a gut to make sure you get your quota, I did six reports for you yesterday, that's on top of my own work mind you, and now you've got the bloody gall to bitch because you had to do three. Bloody do it yourself next week, see how far you get. Prick.'

'Oooh, you bitch!' Peter went into his Wronged Innocent routine. It was only convincing if you were far enough away not to be able actually to hear the words. Besides, it was awfully familiar. I let my attention wander around the crowded bar. Suddenly I froze.

'Peter! Shut up! Look over there.'

As usual, Peter demonstrated his mastery of social diplomacy by turning right around and extending his neck several inches.

'What is it?' he boomed out in his stentorian voice. 'I can't see anything worth the trouble.'

'Shut up. Sit down. It's Them!'

'What them? Them who?'

'The people from the office. See, that's Tony there, the really tall skinny one.'

'My God, they are huge, aren't they! What a prick, why doesn't he have plastic surgery?'

Sean was quietly cracking up.

'God, Fiona, don't tell me you're working with Crack Man.' He continued sniggering evilly while I gazed at him in bewilderment.

'What d'you mean, Crack Man?' Sean didn't seem to be able to stop sniggering long enough to draw breath, so I poked him sharply with my longest fingernail. Suddenly Peter gasped. 'My God! Is he the one who –'

Sean nodded helplessly through his giggle fit.

'Tracey in Accounts...'

Another nod.

'Oh my GOD!' I watched furiously as Peter followed Sean into the depths of hysterics. I obviously wasn't going to get any sense out of either of them for at least the next drink. I looked over to where my new colleagues had settled in around a big table near the door. They all seemed to be there except Frank and Jenkins. One of the operators looked over and waved. I waved back.

Good God. Was this a social overture?

Sean took a deep breath of beer and managed to become articulate for a few seconds.

'Fiona'd better start shopping at Maggie T. Clothes for the mature figure.'

This cryptic remark was evidently the last word in wit. Peter and Sean went into a fresh paroxysm. I wondered whether Patrick was free tonight for a game of Snakes and Ladders. Hanging around here was getting to be a drag. The one thing I've never been able to stand is being excluded from anything. The other one thing I absolutely cannot stand is being laughed at. I looked up and saw Penny, the operator who'd waved, coming towards our table.

'Um, hi, Fiona.'

'Hello.'

This civilised interchange was punctuated by incontinent sniggering from my so-called friends.

'We looked for you when we were coming over, but you'd already left. Listen, I just thought, well, I mean, why don't you join us? And your friends, I mean.'

'Well, um. Sure, why not? Come on, guys.'

Sean finally managed to stop his immature behaviour for a moment. He gave Penny an angelic smile.

'Hello. We've been looking forward to meeting Fiona's new friends. Of course, we know Tony Rockwell already.'

And he was off again. I looked from him to Penny in disbelief. I shrugged.

'I don't know what's got into him. Probably some new drug. We'd love to join you, wouldn't we, Peter?'

We all got up and started collecting drinks, jackets, etcetera. There was quite a bit of etcetera lying about the table. I furtively poked Sean again.

'Stop it or I'll kick you in the balls,' I whispered.

Sean fixed me with a dignified stare.

'Will you, darling? What makes you think I've got any?'

He picked up his drink and led the way to the other table in a lord of the manor sort of way, all traces of hysteria mysteriously vanished. Sometimes I could kill him.

We settled in at the new table, and introductions were performed. The operators were called Penny, Julie, Adam and Steve. I hadn't known all of their names before, since no one had been bothering to speak to me in the office. I was a bit apprehensive about Sean, but he seemed to have got a grip on himself, and remained calm even when introduced to Tony.

***

They seemed to be a pleasant enough crowd. I found out that Adam's parents ran a country post office, and Julie's mother made crocheted weasels for charity. I didn't like to ask why. Penny made several determined attempts to flirt with Sean, quite successfully in fact, as Sean will flirt with anything that isn't actually dead, and I wouldn't even count on that a hundred percent if the corpse was still warm. Peter and I both had a marvellous time embellishing the story about Retread in the Clockwork Steam Palace, now that I was safely transferred. Rounds of drinks were bought, and the evening slipped quietly towards closing time.

Around nine o'clock I noticed fuzzily that Tony had moved to the chair next to mine, and was staring at me intently. I narrowed my eyes at him. I don't like being stared at in an accusing way by people with huge lips. I think I may have mentioned before that I have this quite intense dislike of ugly people, it's so embarrassing, you never know where to look.

Tony regarded me soulfully.

'Let's go back to my place.'

I regarded him in total disbelief. Could overwork be producing auditory hallucinations? Doctor, I imagined myself saying, I have this terrible recurring dream that I'm being propositioned by a person with six inch lips. I'm afraid you are suffering from an extremely rare form of lymphatic disorder, replied Dr Kildare. You probably don't have more than six months to live. Fade to the usual deathbed scene; lying gracefully in a huge, antique four-poster with black lace curtains (black goes so well with my hair) I smile sweetly, an elegantly wasted shadow of my former self. I forgive you all, I whisper sadly. My family, beside themselves with grief, etc etc.

Tony hadn't gone away. I wished, rather desperately, that Tim (why hadn't he rung me?) was there. Playing for time, I blinked innocently.

'Sorry?'

'I think we should go back to my place. I want to make passionate love to you.'

Dear God. I didn't know whether to laugh or vomit. I couldn't decide what put me off more, his huge lips and general ugliness, or his pathetic soap-opera dialogue. I decided it was kinder to be really firm right away.

'Piss off, you creep.'

'No, really, I mean it. I can show you things you've never imagined.' That part of Tony's face not occupied by lips assumed an expression of sleazy cunning. 'It'll be a whole new experience.'

'I hardly think you're likely to know anything I don't,' I informed him frostily. Too bloody right, with a face like that it would be a wonder if he knew the elementary facts of life.

'You don't know what you're missing.' He shook his head pityingly.

'Okay then, you tell me. What am I missing?'

Tony looked triumphant, rather like Einstein announcing relativity.

'Golf balls.'

'WHAT?'

He looked smug. 'Golf balls.'

I could feel myself turning pale. I'd never met a

real pervert before. No wonder Peter and Sean had cracked up. I wondered if they'd been laughing about this or something different. I hoped it was something different; perhaps I was on the brink of discovering a new sex practice. I tried to think of anything sexy that could be done with golf balls, and failed. Obviously it was going to be something wildly perverse.

'What d'you do with them?' I half expected him to say it was a joke, but he answered me quite seriously, as if he were discussing the weather, or the stock market.

'You put them in your back passage. You'll love it.'

I couldn't believe my ears. This nerd actually expected me, or anyone else for that matter, to insert a golf ball, or perhaps several golf balls... One question seemed more vital than all the rest.

'How d'you get it out again?'

Tony smirked. 'Come home with me and you'll find out.'

'I don't believe you. Nobody could be that sick. D'you honestly expect me to believe you sit around shoving golf balls up your bum? How many d'you put up there at a time?'

'Oh, about six. It's really wonderful, you haven't lived until you've tried it. I could show you lots of other things, too.'

'Um. Excuse me a minute.' I had had about all I could take for the moment. I escaped to the ladies' loo.

ଛCHAPTER SIXଓ

Let his days be few: and let another take his office.
Psalm 109:7

Julie was in the lav, fixing her makeup. The lavatories at the Rat and Broomstick were quite posh, not like the rest of the place. There was a sort of sitting-room arrangement when you came in, with two or three nice comfortable armchairs and a low table. I collapsed into one of the chairs.

'You'll never believe what Tony's been telling me.'

'What, about the golf balls?' Julie didn't look too concerned.

'Well, yes. It was about golf balls. But he said he sticks them...'

'Up his arse. He's always on about it. Best not to take any notice, he's just picking on you because you're new. He tries it on with everybody.'

Well, at least I didn't have some special attraction for perverts. But I was consumed by curiosity. Somehow it hadn't occurred to me that a person with a weird habit like that would have told more than one person about it. I'd assumed he'd confided in me because I was discreet, although come to think of it he didn't actually know me, so it couldn't be that.

'Tell me, has anyone ever...?'

'Not as far as I know. I shouldn't think so, though. He's not exactly the most attractive thing, is he?'

'Yuk. D'you think it's true, about the golf balls?'

Julie shrugged. 'Could be footballs for all I care.' She sniggered evilly. 'It could be watermelons.'

A hilarious thought suddenly occurred to me.

'Maybe that's why he's got such big lips. It's a couple of golf balls forcing their way up!'

We both cracked up over this really suave piece

of wit.

***

Patrick's light was still on when I got home. Melbourne was having one of its occasional fits of perfect weather, and the air was still soft and warm. I meandered gently up the path, singing softly and tunefully. Suddenly a great crash rent the night. Mr Tucker next door had thrown an alarm clock out the window.

'For Christ's sake stop that bloody screeching!' he yelled. Lights went on in our house, and also in several other houses up the street.

I let myself in quickly, and navigated up the stairs without any worse mishap than a few bruises when Moses ran between my feet. I tapped gently on Patrick's door. He was sitting up in bed with an enormous textbook on his lap. I automatically checked for the stick book tucked inside, but hard as it was to believe, he seemed actually to have been studying. I looked at the cover. Latin. Yuk.

Patrick eyed me critically.

'You've been drinking.'

'No, really? How awfully pers– perspex– clever of you. You'll go far, young man, with deductive powers like that.'

'Look Fiona, bugger off, will you? I've got to learn this, I've got a test on Monday and I don't know anything. Baldy swore if I get zero again it'll be a Saturday detention.'

'Never mind that, I'll help you with it tomorrow. I've got to tell you about this guy tonight.'

'Fiona, some desperate clerk making a pass at you isn't really worth failing this test and having to spend next Saturday at school.'

'Patrick. A new sex act.'

'A new sex act? How could there be a new one?'

'This guy at work, he sticks golf balls up his backside. Honestly. He wanted me to do it too.'

'You went to bed with someone who sticks golf balls up his arse?'

'NO! He was telling me about it in the pub. Like, it was supposed to be the main attraction. He said it would be an experience I'd never had before, and all stuff like that.'

'I should bloody well hope so! So give us the details: how's he get them out again?'

'He wouldn't tell me. But I can't imagine how you could. Anyway, isn't it the most ghastly, disgusting thing you've ever heard?'

Patrick rolled his eyes. 'Did you say you're working with this guy?'

'He's the senior programmer in our office.'

'Better hope you can help me with this Latin, Fi, hadn't you?'

'What d'you mean?'

'Shouldn't imagine Mum'll be too rapt. Not very hygienic, is it?'

'You wouldn't!'

My little brother smiled angelically.

***

Next morning, Patrick and I settled ourselves comfortably on my bed with the Latin textbook. I had planned to go shopping, but assuring the safety of one's home base has to be a top priority. I think that's in Sun Tzu.

'It's the cases I can't really get.'

'What's so hard about cases?'

'I don't know. I don't really understand it.'

'Well, look. It's just like all the different ways you can use a word. In English you put words like, um, to, for, the, and like that in front. Latin doesn't have those words, so they use the noun. Look, it's easy. First, the nominative case. That means, to name something. From *nomen, nominis*, okay? So you might say, The ship sailed away. That's nominative. Ship, that is. Then vocative, that means the voice case. It's from *vox, vocis*. Voice case means you're talking to the thing. Like, Hello, ship.'

'Why would you want to talk to a ship?'

'The Romans were pretty weird. But are you getting the idea?'

Patrick nodded dubiously.

'Then we have the accusative case.'

A brilliant light of comprehension dawned over Patrick's face.

'Aaah, I get it. You fucking ship!'

***

Tony didn't seem embarrassed at all when I walked into the office on Monday morning. I settled back into the do-it-yourself computer course. I had finished the first one last Wednesday and expected to be shown the computer, but Frank had just sneered and tossed me another course book, in an even more grotty state than the first. This one was much longer and harder. I wondered if I'd finish it before Christmas.

About eleven o'clock, Scott came shambling out of his office, looking even more dreary than usual, and cleared his throat unhappily.

'Could you gather round, people? I have an announcement to make.'

Zounds! This was pretty assertive behaviour for Jenkins. Adam and Julie drifted out of the computer room. Steve and Penny weren't there, because they were the afternoon shift that week. We all pricked up our ears and waited politely. Scott cleared his throat again.

'We're getting a new manager. Some hot shot from South Africa. He'll be reporting directly to the G. M. His name's Godfrey Goebbels, hope he doesn't live up to it,' (a polite laugh) 'and he'll be arriving next week sometime, probably around the middle of the week.'

He wambled back into his office. I didn't blame him for wambling a bit, he must be pretty badly shaken up by something like that. It was pretty obvious that he, too, was going to be reporting to the new guy, which you had to admit sucked for him, however you dressed it up.

Everyone drifted into a little huddle around the Café Bar, standing closer together than usual.

'God. I just can't believe they'd do something like that.'

'Come off it, this is Marsh and Spacknall, you know.' Geoff assumed a superior expression. 'This is a classic case of what we call a shafting.'

'Wonder what the new guy'll be like.'

'Are you joking? A South African, with a name like Goebbels? Adam assumed a stage German accent. 'Vot do you mean your program is not finished? Avay to zee gas chambers mit you!'

'What about Jenkins? He looked pretty upset.'

'Wouldn't you, if you'd just had some foreigner brought in over your head? Especially when they just might decide to sack you.'

'They wouldn't sack him, would they?'

'Why not? He's not exactly Mr Dynamic, is he? This guy Goebbels probably sacks people like water. Look at what happened when Jacobs arrived.'

There was a long silence while we all pondered that one. Carl Jacobs, the managing director, had come out from Head Office in America a few months previously, not long after I'd started there myself, in fact. After spending six weeks getting all buddy-buddy with the salesmen, taking them to the races and encouraging them to get drunk and indiscreet, and generally being just one of the boys, he had suddenly come in one Monday morning and sacked three quarters of them on the spot, citing as cause all the drunkenness, promiscuity, drug abuse, gambling problems, etcetera that he'd witnessed. Obviously all foreigners were snakes in the grass who were just waiting to catch you in some failing of decorum and reduce you to the deadly dole queue.

Adam's voice, when he broke the silence, sounded like a funeral knell.

'Christ, we're going to have to be careful what we say in front of this guy.'

***

Over the next few days, more or less by common consent, everyone became a model of decorum.

Tony: Good morning Fiona. I trust you had an enjoyable weekend?'

Fiona: Quite, thank you, Tony. The Sunday School picnic was a great success. And you?

Tony: Wonderful. I discovered a Greater Spotted Midnight Warbler nesting above my garage.

Bit by bit, the office took on the atmosphere of a Quaker village. All the girls stopped wearing low-cut tops and scent. Geoff and Tony, who both smoked, got nicotine patches and stopped scuttling downstairs every hour. Someone removed the Playboy calendar. Only Frank and Scott didn't change. Scott got more and more depressed, but essentially remained his own droopy self, and Frank, as malleable as a Sherman tank, continued to say fuck all the time.

***

A week went by, and then another. The jokes about Sunday School picnics and stamp collecting grew stale. Geoff and Tony resumed nicking out the back to smoke every hour, and I gave back the demure grey wool skirt and cardigan I'd found at the back of my mother's wardrobe. I got promoted to a new course which was even more boring than the last two, all about something called JCL (job control language) and we heard from downstairs that Retread, no doubt shamed by the now public knowledge of his sinful debauchery, had resigned, and gone to work for the RSPCA.

***

Late afternoon sun streamed in at the window. A big shaft of it had trapped a kerzillion particles of dust. I could see it all swirling around like a tame nova. I yawned and turned the page of my magazine. The holy silence of total inactivity was broken only by the regular tapping of Geoff's keyboard.

'Hey Geoff.'

'Hey yeah.'

'Anything good on TV tonight?'

'Actually there is, a really brilliant documentary on the ABC, "*Pus Through the Ages*."'

'Are you serious?'

Suddenly the door opened. Sodden with laziness, none of us moved. Carl Jacobs walked into the room.

A bucket of ice water cascaded down my spine. I was leaning back in my chair with my shoes off and my feet on the desk, which was quite, quite bare except for a copy of Vogue and a bottle of scarlet nail polish.

'Good afternoon, Mr Jacobs.' I tried to sound cool, but my voice came out all squeaky.

Jacobs shifted his vast bulk around, glaring at us out of his piggy little eyes. He made a non-committal grunting sound, way down in his chest. No doubt he was eidetically registering all the incriminating details. Geoff and Tony looked marginally better than I did, but not all that much. Geoff had hit Alt/Tab as soon as Jacobs came in, so his screen displayed a respectable page of Cobol, but his red face and shifty expression gave him away, and Tony had been reading the kind of magazine that's sold in a plastic cover.

'Harrumph,' said Jacobs, apparently speaking to the air. 'Doesn't look as if Jenkins is in his office. Gorff, grumpph.'

'No, actually he isn't,' I said brightly, sitting up and casually sweeping the Vogue and Whore's Delight enamel off the desk. 'Damn poor show, what?' I could never resist sending Jacobs up, partly because he was such a pompous old fool, but mostly because he was so fat and conceited he never noticed.

Someone noticed this time, though. Too late I discerned a beady, watchful pair of eyes glinting out of a small mop at about Jacobs' waist level. The lurker in the coattails didn't say anything. In fact, for quite a long time no one said anything. Then Jacobs let out a final snort like an elephant on bath night, wheeled around and processed out, towing the shaggy little man along with him on an invisible lead.

Tony, off the hook, was baffled. 'What the Christ was that?'

'God knows.' Geoff, uninterested in absolutely everything as usual, went back to the ABC website.

Intrigued, I found I couldn't let it rest. Why on earth would Jacobs suddenly charge in here like that, unexpected, and then charge straight out again? I knew he had to have been unexpected, because Frank and Scott were both spending the afternoon at some business rort with free drinks. Usually we never saw Jacobs at all unless he wanted to show his spiffy new I. T. Department to some other big fat executive from abroad. Then he would come wallowing in and insist on being introduced to everybody as if he'd never met them before.

Wait a minute. Executive from abroad. Oh no. I became aware of a cold sensation in my foot.

Nail polish was dripping into my shoe.

ಐCHAPTER SEVENಡ

O God, the heathen are come into thine inheritance: thy holy temple have they defiled, and made Jerusalem an heap of stones.

Psalm 79:1

I walked through the door into chaos. The whole front wall of Frank's office, and a good part of Scott's, had apparently been lasered out of existence. There were great piles of rubble where the walls had been, and clouds of concrete dust hung in the air. There were vibrations of solemn disaster quivering about the place. Someone was really going to get it. Maybe someone had already got it.

I took a closer look. There didn't seem to be any bodies lying about; perhaps the bomb had gone off very early this morning, before anybody was in. I noticed there was a little frill of bricks running along the ceiling where Frank's wall had been. I caught a flash of movement among the rubble. Going by the general ambience of the place, it ought to have been a rat scavenging among the debris, but as I moved closer, a thicker section of dust resolved itself into a large grey man in large grey overalls.

Moving slowly, so as not to attract attention, I got over to my desk. Geoff and Tony were standing around in an interested kind of way. The air was clearer in our part of the office, and I realised you could hear voices coming out of the Stinking Cloud.

'It's a load-bearing WALL, for Chrissake!'

'Don't be so bloody stupid. No one asked you to knock the whole thing down anyway.'

The second voice sounded foreign, a kind of foreign that I couldn't identify. I nudged Tony.

'What's going on?'

Tony sniggered. 'That's our new boss, sweetheart. Arrived last week from South Africa.'

'Is that the little hairy guy that came in with Jacobs on Friday?'

'Sure is. As you would know if you hadn't

snuck off to the hairdresser. They came back about three-thirty. Scotty and Frank were both really out of it; they'd been boozing since lunch at that pseudo seminar thing. Jacobs didn't look too impressed.'

'Did anyone notice I wasn't there?'

'Scott asked where you were, but don't worry, your secret is safe. I said you were in the loo, and you'd eaten something that didn't agree. So you owe me one.' Tony's fat face took on an unpleasant, leering expression.

Actually, I had not been to the hairdresser. I had been into town to the magic shop, to buy Patrick a rubber spider. After our mother had accused him of cruelty for keeping it, as we had claimed, in a glass jar, he had realised that the fictitious tarantula would, if properly nurtured, enable him to keep our mother out of his bedroom forever, and to this end he had negotiated with our neighbour's little boy for an old glass fish tank and a piece of masonite to go on top, and with me for the *piece*, as it were, *de resistance*. I had made up the hairdresser story because I felt the truth was just too sordid and infra dig for public consumption. As, of course, truth nearly always is, and that's why we have manners, as my grandmother always says.

'God, thanks so much, you deadshit. Thanks for making me look like a dork in front of our new boss. I think I'd rather you told him I was having my hair done. So what's he like?'

'You'd know if you'd been over the pub Friday, wouldn't you?' The smugness of the creature was unbearable, especially as my noble act of self-sacrifice in going straight home with the rubber spider, and the other things I'd bought, had been totally wasted, since I had forgotten that Patrick was spending the weekend with one of his nasty little friends. I looked around for something I could smash Rockwell with. There wasn't anything; the decks had evidently been cleared for the sinister action now taking place in the corner.

'Oh, come on, Tony.' I batted my eyelashes hopefully. Tony responded with all the subtlety of a used car salesman, moving even closer and almost suffocating me in a cloud of Axe.

'Well, we didn't really see too much of him until Pub Time. He just sort of grunted at us and went into Scott's office, but then he came out and went over the pub with us. He seemed okay. You know, friendly and everything. Not up himself at all.'

'So what did he say?'

'What about?'

'Anything, dickbrain. Did he say what he'd been closeted with Scott about?'

'Oh, that. Yeah, he was trying to get a secretary hired. Seemed really pissed off that he couldn't just order one for immediate delivery, like a pizza. Kept going on about how things were different in "Sairth Efricaw".'

'A good thing, too. Is he a total fascist, d'you think?'

Tony shrugged. 'No idea. I mean, we were hardly going to ask him, were we?'

'So anyway, what's going on here?'

Tony did his best to look enigmatic, and succeeded in looking like a dead toad. Geoff rolled his eyes.

'It's called Getting Ready for the New Secretary. See where all the wall's gone, well he wants to have his office open off the secretary's office, like in those really posh places, then he can hide in there and play golf or whatever, and she tells everyone he's in conference. A bit much for this place, I reckon.'

'Hang on a second. What d'you mean, his office and the secretary's office? That's Scott and Frank's offices.'

Geoff and Tony both shifted their feet and looked uncomfortable.

'Well, Frank doesn't really need that office, you know how he never uses it.'

'Scott uses his.'

There was an uncomfortable silence.

'Well where's he going to sit, out here with us?'

More silence.

'Look, where is Scott?'

Geoff cleared his throat.

'Well, he isn't. That is, he left on Friday.'

'You're kidding! Goebbels sacked him, just like that?'

Like the devil, his name mentioned, Goebbels appeared out of a cloud of smoke. He was indeed the tiny, shaggy person we'd seen with Jacobs. He looked us up and down, especially me, with his beady little eyes.

'Get on with your work.' he snapped.

I could feel myself turning pale. No one, not

anyone, had ever spoken to me like that. After all, I'm cute. People are nice to me. Even when I do something truly awful, it's always a case of sorrow rather than anger. I gasped feebly, opening and closing my mouth like a fish. Geoff and Tony were bustling around at their desks, rattling papers convincingly. I opened my mouth to deliver a stinging retort.

'Well, don't stand there with your mouth open. Get on with it. This isn't a bloody rest home.'

Goebbels walked away, leaving the stinging retort I hadn't been able to think of forever unborn. I sat down numbly. The man was evil, there was no doubt of it. He had sacked our boss, for no reason at all, and then he had spoken harshly to lovely me. I couldn't believe it. Digging frantically in my top drawer for some work to pretend, I vowed to make him pay for his insulting behaviour. I would stalk into his office, my black cape swirling lavishly around my ankles. 'Prepare to die, thou caitiff.' I drew my rapier with one black-gloved hand. Goebbels staggered backwards, his crabbed little hands feebly warding as, with a single mighty blow, I pierced his vitals.

***

At home, Patrick and I set up the tarantula. It was just like decorating the Christmas tree, squabbling about where everything should go. Overcome by a fit of filial piety, I had not only bought the biggest, fiercest rubber spider in the shop, but had also gone to Petworld for some of those cute little multicoloured pebbles to put on the bottom of the tank.

Patrick wasn't impressed.

'What the hell's this?'

'Coloured stones, for the bottom of the tank. You want him to look nice, don't you?'

'No. I want him to look scary. Not like bloody Home Beautiful with all his multicoloured rocks.'

'Look, it's got to be realistic. If you had a real spider in there you'd have to have sand or whatever.'

'What for?'

'To soak up his little droppings, of course. You wouldn't want him just weeing everywhere.'

'Spiders don't have droppings, you moron.'

'They do so.'

'Do not.'

'Do so.'

'Do not.'

We carried on like this until it was time to start hitting each other with pillows. Then it was time to discuss the other little matter.

'Fiona! What the hell is that?'

'I got it at the pet shop. Isn't it cute?'

'Fiona. In science projects, we do not put little china divers in with the subject.'

'Ah. But it's all part of the Master Plan, you see. You put the spider next to that human figure, subconsciously it looks even bigger and more terrifying.'

Patrick looked suspicious.

'No it doesn't.'

'Ah, but it does subconsciously. We did it in Psych 101.'

Patrick deferred to the higher authority of tertiary education. I sniggered to myself; I had made the whole thing up. I hadn't even done Psych 101.

'Okay, put him in.'

I gently lowered the huge rubber spider into the tank next to the diver, arranging its legs artistically in a pose which I felt suggested temporarily satiated ferocity. We admired the effect in silence.

Presently there was a tap on the door.

'Oh, God. Quick, get rid of this stuff.'

I shoved the magic shop bag under the bed, and stood in front of the tank while Patrick opened the door. Our mother was looking flustered.

'Darlings, don't forget Father Simpson's coming to dinner. Please try not to discuss anything vulgar at the table, and Patrick, please put on a tie.'

***

Dinner with Father Simpson was always pretty slow. Dad used to invite him about once a week, and after dinner they'd disappear into Dad's study to discuss whatever anthropologists discuss. This one started out pretty average, as follows:

7:30: Patrick and Fiona place themselves respectably in the sitting room, Patrick in a white shirt and tie, and Fiona in a modest blue dress and no makeup, pretending to do something respectable like play Scrabble or help Patrick with his Latin.

7:35: The doorbell rings. Patrick and Fiona stop whispering dirty jokes over the scrabble board. Mrs MacDougall bustles, beaming, to the door. The vicar is shown into the sitting room. He is dressed in his dusty, moth-eaten clericals and smells faintly of incense. He eyes Patrick and Fiona with a vague and tolerant expression tempered by slight nervousness (he still hasn't forgotten the time ten-year-old Patrick put the caterpillar down his back.) He makes a vague movement as if he were going to pat us on the head and thought better of it. He does this every single time.

7:37: Mrs MacDougall bustles in with dry sherry on a tray. I can have a drink but Patrick, who normally has wine at dinner every night like the rest of us, can't. I furtively pass him my glass after I've drunk half.

7:45: Mr MacDougall ambles in from his study, dropping pipe ashes on the carpet and looking almost as moth-eaten as the vicar in his tweed coat. They shake hands in a manly way reminiscent of the nineteen-fifties, when one supposes they were dashing young bucks in the 47th armoured light somethings.

8:00: Everyone proceeds into the dining room, where all the silver, and for that matter everything else, is freshly polished. Moses has been banished upstairs because last time he tried to do something embarrassing to the vicar's leg.

8:05: Mrs MacDougall brings in the roast beef.

Mr MacDougall cuts himself with the carving knife.

8:10: We finally get something to eat. Polite conversation is made by all. Patrick, deprived of his usual glass of wine, sulks into his milk.

On this particular evening, however, fate had something else in store for us. All proceeded as described until halfway through dinner, when Dad and Simpson's enlivening discussion of betrothal customs in ancient Greece was interrupted by a terrible crash, and eight kilos of tomcat landed squarely in the centre of the table, skidding to a halt nose to nose with the vicar. We all sat stunned for a moment.

Then Hell broke loose.

'By Jove,' said the vicar. 'What's that he's got in his mouth?'

'EEEEEEEEEEEEEEEEEEEEEEEEEEE!' said my mother.

'Everybody just stay calm,' said my father. (Some hope.)

'OMGWTF!' said Patrick, who had been Carefully Brought Up.

I didn't say anything.

***

Patrick was the first of us really to regain the use of his faculties. He lunged across the table and grabbed at Moses, who arched his back kittenishly and pranced out of reach. Patrick landed with a splash, on his stomach on top of the roast beef.

'Here, kitty kitty,' said the vicar, without much hope. Moses shot him a look of pure loathing and sprang to the sideboard, hairy rubber legs trailing from his mouth like a mandarin moustache. I seized the opportunity to stand up and interpose myself casually between him and everyone else, blocking their view of the incriminating evidence.

'My God, it's still alive!' I said.

'EEEEEEEEEEEEEEEEEEEEEEEEE!'

'Look, Mary, just calm down.'

'By Jove, what a ratter!'

'Fiona, get the spider. Don't let him kill it, whatever you do!' Patrick had picked up my cue right away, bless him. I allowed myself a small flicker of hope. I reached behind me, groping.

'Napkin!' I snapped, just like I'd seen on *Shortland Street*.

Nothing happened.

'Come ON, quick, someone pass me a napkin.'

'Patrick! Don't you dare, with my best table napkins.' I heard vague scuffling sounds.

'Use your hanky,' Patrick shouted despairingly.

'Blow that. What if he piddles in it?'

'Spiders don't pee.'

'They do so!'

'Do not!'

I recalled what we were there for, and that the spider wasn't real. In all the excitement I had forgotten that. I took out my nice clean handkerchief, and grabbed Moses by the scruff of the neck in the other hand. I quickly wrapped the spider in my handkerchief, gathering up the corners. Safe at last! I turned around; my family and the vicar were frozen in an insane sitcom tableau. I shook the handkerchief unobtrusively to make it look as if the spider was struggling against his bonds.

As Patrick and I left the room, I heard the faintest whisper from my mother.

'Oh Fiona, you're so brave.'

⊰CHAPTER EIGHT⊱

Deliver me, O Lord, from the evil man: and preserve me from the wicked man. Who imagine mischief in their hearts: and stir up strife all the day long. They have sharpened their tongues like a serpent: adder's poison is under their lips.

Psalm 140:1–3

The office, a couple of days later, resembled the interior of a coal mine. Huge steel rods, wedged on a slant, propped up the ceiling around the edges of what had been Frank's office. Three large men in grey overalls were crouched on the floor, muttering and stirring something, like the witches in Macbeth. Unlike the witches, however, they hadn't bothered with the cauldron part of it; a heaving mass of wet concrete rose from the carpet like Venus from the waves. Goebbels danced wildly round the edges of the little group, shrieking and waving his arms, no doubt casting an incantation. I tried to sneak past unobtrusively (it was half past nine) but he looked up and gibbered faintly at me.

I buried myself in the stock control programs Goebbels had set me as a training exercise. Geoff and Tony both had their heads down. Under the new regime it seemed safer to work all the time. Goebbels had actually set deadlines for Geoff and Tony. I thanked God I was still a trainee, when I wasn't wishing I had enough experience to get a job somewhere else.

***

'Holy shit!' Tony's voice was low and reverent. I looked up from the flowchart I'd been struggling with.

A tall, dark woman was picking her way delicately through the rubble and splashes of cement. She wore a white blouse and a bright red skirt, sharp and straight as a pencil. Scarlet patent leather sandals with matching toenails stepped unerringly on the clean patches of our floor.

She was as out of place as an orchid in a cesspool.

'Excuse me. I'm looking for Mr Goebbels.' Her

voice, when she spoke, was light and clear, and I realised she was only about my own age. I wasn't surprised to find she had a slight foreign accent.

'That's him over there. The one not in overalls.'

'Thanks.' She smiled at me, a cool benediction. I watched her walk towards Goebbels with her terrifying confidence. I wanted to jump up and down with curiosity. Tony was already jumping up and down for other reasons. Geoff, who was hardly ever interested in anything except weird documentaries like *Pus Through The Ages* and *Fermat Unchained*, still had his nose in the Cobol manual.

'Mr Goebbels? I'm Jane Edmonds, your new secretary.'

Goebbels actually seemed to swell up like a bullfrog. I had to admit I was pretty surprised myself. Our H. R. department weren't exactly famous for being quick off the mark.

'YOU?' Goebbels' voice was charged with malice, spite and other awful things. Tony and I exchanged a glance. Obviously he knew her from somewhere, and equally obviously, the memories weren't pleasant.

Goebbels got marginal control of himself after a brief struggle.

'Well, you can see your desk isn't ready yet. Come back after lunch.'

That was it? Not even how do you do, welcome aboard, thank God you've arrived? I couldn't believe my ears. Jane Edmonds, however, seemed to take it all in her stride. Perhaps she was from a temp agency. 'Okay, I'll come back at two then,' she said, and walked calmly out without a backward glance.

Goebbels jittered over to us in a state of horrible disarray. He reminded me of the people in the bible, moaning and gnashing their teeth.

'Jesus, ken you believe it? I cawn't bleddy believe it.' Under stress, his accent was even thicker than usual. I was at a bit of a loss what to say.

'Did you know her before?'

'Know her? Jesus Christ, how could I bloody know her?'

'Well. I mean, you don't seem awfully pleased, I thought...'

I trailed off as I noticed Tony was shaking with silent hysteria. If possible, this made him even less attractive than usual.

'The woman's a bloody KAFFIR!'

'What's that?' I asked, reasonably, I thought. Goebbels shot me a look of utter loathing and stomped into his office. He must have been really disappointed that there was no door for him to slam. We heard him banging around with the telephone, muttering imprecations.

'Tony? What's a kaffir?'

'Well, you know.'

I reflected on all the physical reasons why a five foot two person can't pick up a six foot four person and shake them. I took a deep breath.

'No, I don't know, that's why I'm asking.'

'Well, you know, a black person. That's what they call black people, in South Africa.'

Geoff looked up. 'You mean that's what people like Goebbels call them.'

'Yeah, well.' Tony showed signs of relapsing. 'He certainly isn't too happy, is he?'

Faint howls drifted over from the open office. 'I don't care what the law says, I'm not having a bloody kaffir. There aren't any facilities...'

'What's he mean, facilities?'

Geoff shrugged. 'Maybe he expects separate lavatories and things. That's what they used to have where he comes from.'

'We have separate lavatories.'

'God, Fiona. Hey Tony, what's the difference between Fiona and a dumb blonde?'

Tony snorted. 'Easy: Fiona's got red hair.'

They both found this witless remark highly amusing.

***

By lunchtime the three witches had raised a waist-high wall of bricks all around the collapsed bit. They went off to have their lunch, presumably at the Dead Rat. I envied their simple life. I passed a few minutes reflecting on the virtues of manual labour. I imagined myself in a Benedictine monastery, clothed in black wool (so flattering to my hair) and leather sandals, rising before dawn to chant psalms before going off to a day's untroubled labour in field and vineyard, returning at night to a simple meal of milk and vegetables.

I emerged from my contemplation of the monastic life to find that it was already one-thirty.

There was no sign of the workmen, but Geoff and Tony were both just arriving back from lunch. I noticed Geoff was looking smug.

'What are you looking so smug about?'

Geoff looked even more smug.

'I found out what Goebbels was on about this morning.'

'Really? Well, come on, hurry up and tell, before he gets back.'

'I don't know if I should give you this valuable information.'

Tony cleared his throat and moved very close to Geoff. He was such a wimp most of the time that one tended to forget how tall he actually was. He put both hands on Geoff's desk and leaned over it menacingly.

'Yes, well. Apparently Goebbels rang up H. R., breathing fire and brimstone, and he absolutely refused to have what's-her-name as his secretary, because of being black.'

'Yeah, we heard that part.'

'That's not all. Apparently, he said it wasn't prejudice, and that we didn't have the facilities to have black people working here, and when John asked him what facilities he thought we needed, he said separate lavatories!'

Light dawned. 'What, you mean like black lavatories and white lavatories?'

'Yes, and when John told him she could use the same loo as the other women on this floor, he said it wasn't hygienic!'

We were all silent for a while, contemplating this.

'So what did John tell him?'

'Well, from what I gather, he sent him off with an absolute flea in his ear and said he could have her or no secretary at all. So I guess she's here to stay.'

Tony breathed a sigh of ecstasy.

***

At exactly two p.m. Jane Edmonds stalked back into the office. Goebbels glared at her in a resigned way.

'I don't know why you bothered coming back so soon, you can see there's nowhere for you to sit.' Bloody Kaffirs.

'Well, Mr Goebbels, why don't you leave me to arrange that? I'm sure you have far more important things to do than worry about the builders.'

Goebbels shot her a look of pure loathing and stormed out of the office.

This was getting embarrassing. 'I wouldn't worry about Goebbels,' I told her, doing my best to sound convincing. 'He's like that all the time. Why don't you just go ahead and organise the builders, someone needs to. They still haven't come back from the pub.'

Jane Edmonds looked worried. It was the first sign I'd seen that she was merely human. I wondered how much of the impossibly perfect facade was just that. Then her face lit up in a huge grin and she shrugged.

'What the hell. He can only sack me, right? I can always go back on the dole.'

Wow. She'd really experienced the raw edges of life. The Dole. Far out.

'How did you get it, the dole? I thought you had to be an Australian citizen. Are you naturalised?'

The brief rapport evaporated. Edmonds shot me

a look of contempt and scorn to rival the one she'd received earlier from Goebbels, stalked into Goebbels' office and sat down at his desk, picking up the phone. I looked at Tony in utter bewilderment. What had I said? I'd meant to be friendly to the new arrival, and she'd looked at me as if I'd made a mess on the carpet.

'Jesus, Fiona. Tact really isn't your middle name, is it?'

'But what did I say?'

'God.' Tony raised his eyes to heaven. 'What a thing to say to an Aboriginal person. I mean, for fuck's sake, Fiona.'

'Well, I don't see what's so bad about that. Lots of people aren't Australian citizens. Look at Mia Kondopoulis in Sales.'

'Fiona, it's a bit of a sore point,' Geoff chimed in, in his usual know-it-all tone. 'Australia was colonised under Terra Nullius, which means that officially, the Indigenous people didn't exist, the place was empty. There's one section of British law for colonies in inhabited countries, and one for uninhabited places. Australia was considered uninhabited. So, when they had the referendum in 1967, Aboriginal people were made citizens of Australia, but before that, they officially didn't exist.'

'You're kidding. What did they put on their passports?'

'Tell me something, Fiona. Did you actually go to school at all, or an institution for the retarded? I'm really interested.'

'What's the difference between Fiona and a French poodle?'

'Dunno, what?'

'You can teach a French poodle to do tricks.'

'Oh, very funny. You drag up all this ancient history and expect me to do twenty questions. What's it got to do with her, anyway? She's not Aboriginal.'

'Yes, she is.'

'No, she isn't, she's got a foreign accent.'

'Aboriginal people sometimes have a slightly different accent than us. Jesus, Fiona, how can you be so ignorant about your own country?'

The penny dropped. 'Oh, God, and I asked her if she was a citizen.'

'Tacky, Fiona. Very tacky.'

***

Having branded myself as a racist bigot second only to Goebbels, I spent the rest of the day in a sort of haze of embarrassment. I'd never given much thought to Aboriginal people, probably because I'd never met any. I hadn't realised that they had been targets of monstrous injustice like what one reads about in foreign countries; I'd always thought of racism as mainly an American thing.

Goebbels did not return to work at all that day. Presumably he'd gone home to his wife who, being South African, would understand all about Kaffirs having Facilities, and not marrying one's sister or moving into one's neighbourhood. Jane Edmonds remained in his office and spent nearly an hour on the telephone, after which the workmen filed back into the office looking bootfaced, and toiled away like the seven dwarves until five-thirty, without even a tea break. I stayed late out of sheer curiosity, and they actually finished laying the bricks all the way up to join the little frills that remained of the original brickwork.

They were packing up, finally, to go home when Jane Edmonds, who hadn't gone home either, came out of Goebbels' office and cleared her throat pointedly. Instantly the men zoomed back to work and swarmed all over the place, sweeping up dust and taking down the steel poles that had supported the ceiling.

The office was transformed. Now that the walls were back up, you couldn't see the big splotch on the carpet where they'd mixed the mortar.

'That's amazing,' I said to her. 'How on earth did you get them to work like that?'

She smiled mysteriously. 'It's easy when you know how.'

I was fascinated. She seemed to have the real world at her fingertips in a way that I couldn't even imagine.

'Look,' I said. 'I'm really sorry about what I said earlier. I thought you were foreign.'

She sighed. 'It doesn't matter. It happens all the time. Like, if you're a Koori you're supposed to have bare feet and live in an old car.'

We walked down the corridor together. At the lift she turned around and looked back towards the office. She looked very tired, and somehow smaller.

☙CHAPTER NINE☙

Assuage, we humbly beseech thee, all strife and contention between those who are engaged in the labours of industry and those who employ their labour; deliver both masters and workmen from all greed and covetousness; and grant that they, seeking only that which is just and equal, may live and work together in brotherly union and concord, to their own well-being and the prosperity of this realm...
Book of Common Prayer

I spent the whole of that evening locked in the bathroom, having facepacks and things. If there's one thing I can't stand, it's women who look better than me. There ought to be a law against it, I thought crossly as I painted my freckles with lemon juice. Moses cried and scratched at the door. I opened it for the forty-third time. As usual, he stood half in and half out, looking aimless. I knew it was only an exercise of power, and that he didn't really want to go anywhere. It's really humiliating to be emotionally dominated by a cat. On the other hand, most things are okay as long as no one else sees them. Cheered by this reflection, I turned back to the mirror and picked up my glass of skim milk. My friend Gloria had recently lost eight pounds in six days by living entirely on skim milk and vitamin pills. I went over the sum again in my head. Eight divided by six is one and a half, so I was guaranteed to be almost two pounds thinner by morning. But Gloria had already been really thin anyway, so perhaps I'd lose even more. Perhaps as much as three pounds.

Patrick suddenly appeared in the mirror behind me, and I nearly dropped my glass. Milk flew about the place.

'Dammit Fiona, milk all over me. Why are you so clumsy?'

I shrugged and turned back to the mirror.

'Go and find Moses, he'll lick it off.'

'Licked by a cat is not what I call clean, Fiona.'

Why does the name Fiona always sound so disapproving when uttered by any of my family or friends, I wondered. Perhaps I'd change my name.

'Go away, Patrick, I'm busy.'

'I don't care. You got me into this mess, now you can get me out of it.'

'What mess?'

'It's Mum. Now that she won't go into my room because of Harvey, she's making me do it. I can't even miss bits, she stands at the door watching me. I had to vacuum in there for an hour this afternoon. You know what she's like.'

'So what's that got to do with me?'

'It was your idea. I reckon you ought to do it.'

'Ha ha, Patrick. Very funny.'

'It's not funny. You've got no idea what it's like. She stands there like Attila the Hun, armed with a can of Baygon in case Harvey makes a dash for freedom. And she said I've got to scrub out his tank with Domestos because of the droppings.'

'Droppings? What droppings?'

'Harvey's droppings, dickbrain.'

'Harvey's fake, remember? He doesn't have droppings.'

'Yeah, well, I raked up the gravel a bit in there to make him look like he'd done his little poos and covered it up. Just in case she ever does nerve herself up to come in, I thought it'd look suspicious if nothing ever moved in there. Anyway, now she says I've got to scrub out the tank and change his litter every day. She got some of that Kitty Flakes stuff from the supermarket. If we don't do something soon she'll be wanting me to give him a bath and spray under his arms with deodorant.'

'We'll just have to make him look even more savage and terrifying. I'll give it some thought. But I am not cleaning your room. Not, of course, unless you want Mum to know about those cigarettes you've got under your mattress.'

Impasse.

***

Examining my features in the cold light of morning, I couldn't see that my freckles, or anything else, had changed at all. Ah well. At least I'd be thin. I went to the bathroom and weighed myself. I had gained a pound.

***

The office was lovely and quiet without the workmen around. I arrived quite early, about half past eight. Normally this would have meant a quiet half-hour to sip my coffee and read Harpers, but Goebbels was always in. He claimed to drive in at seven to avoid the peak hour traffic, but I always felt it was more likely that he had no home to go to, and slept standing up in the coat cupboard. This morning I apparently wasn't even to have the limited peace of my desk; Goebbels accosted me at the café bar and ordered me to his office. As usual, he dispensed with any polite formalities.

'Frank tells me you've finished all the basic courses.'

I saw no harm in admitting this.

'So it's time for you to go into the machine room. Frank thinks trainee programmers should complete the operators' training as well, and we might as well try it, you're not much use around here anyway. You made a right bloody cock-up of that stock control program.'

'Okay. When...'

'You'll start on Monday, with the day shift. They start at seven sharp. Perhaps that will teach you some punctuality. I want you to remember that you're not on flexitime. Alright, that's all.'

He looked dismissively down at the listing in front of him. What a pig. I resolved never to go anywhere near Africa, if that was what they were like.

As I left via Jane's new office, I bumped into the doorway. With a little sigh, the new brickwork subsided into a bowed shape, leaving a foot-wide slit along the top. I got out fast.

***

Goebbels roared out of his office about three to examine the repairs. The builders, who had returned in force with more bricks within an hour of Jane's single telephone call (how did she do it?) were standing around drinking tea and looking baffled, like policemen in a Sherlock Holmes movie.

'What's this bloody rubbish?' screamed Goebbels, dancing with rage. I had to admit he had a point. Instead of ripping out the, now gracefully curved, new wall and starting again, they had added more bricks to the top of it, until only a narrow slit remained near the ceiling. The head workman shrugged apologetically.

'I guess they must be different sized bricks,' he said, with an air of gracious acceptance of nature's phenomena.

It didn't end there, of course. For a while I hoped Goebbels might lash himself into such a frenzy of rage that he'd drop dead with a stroke, but alas, God was not on our side to that extent. He dashed about the place for a bit, yelling 'You're fired' at the workmen, but since they were subcontractors they weren't unduly worried by this, and Jane eventually managed to get everyone calmed down. Soon they were whistling cheerfully and posting pieces of wooden planks into the slot, covering up the outside with mortar. We all got back to work, keeping one eye on Goebbels' door.

About an hour later they ground to a halt, having run out of boards. The head workman, a large person in a grey overall, ambled over to my desk, glancing furtively towards Jane's door.

'Listen love, have youse got any cardboard boxes around the place?'

'Sure. You mean like this?' I showed him the one I kept under my desk for waste paper. We threw out dozens of these small cartons every day, the computer paper came in them.

'Yeah, that'd be perfect. You got any more like that?'

'We always have stacks. I'll get some from the operators. How many d'you want?'

He turned and eyed the remaining slit

speculatively. Surely they weren't going to nail cardboard boxes over the hole?

'Oh, I reckon about six'd do the job. Ta.'

The plan actually turned out to be slightly more sophisticated than I'd thought. They ripped up the boxes and posted the pieces, the way they had the planks. When it was all covered up with nice fresh mortar, you could hardly tell the difference.

***

Back at home, I changed into my jeans and took my coffee into the back garden, to get away from the too-tempting smell of the chocolate chip biscuits my mother had baked. I sat down on the back step, feeling drained and peaceful. Moses came running out of the shrubbery, chirping in a welcoming sort of way. He had caught a mouse, and was carrying it proudly by the neck. He curled up against my feet and started to gnaw on it; it was already dead, so I let him get on with it unmolested.

Time passed in a pleasant haze. The house was unusually quiet because Mum and Dad had gone out for the evening, and it was Patrick's day to play Dungeons and Dragons. He wouldn't be home until at least seven, and if he had known our parents would be out, it could be much later.

But it was not to be. All too soon I heard the front door bang. Moses, who had been chased with a broom the last time Mum caught him with a mouse, whisked off under the house, leaving his mangled prey. I automatically moved my foot to cover it as the screen door opened behind me.

Patrick sat down beside me.

'How did your game go?'

'Terrific. We so kicked butt.'

'Great.' I had to change the subject, or I'd be hearing about hit points and portable holes all night. I nudged the mouse, which now consisted only of hindquarters and tail, with my toe. 'Look what Moses caught.'

***

Since Mum and Dad were out, we had pizza, and Patrick didn't do his homework. Instead, we watched Game of Thrones with all the lights out, and drank rather a lot of Dad's whisky. Moses came swaggering in at about midnight, and we all went virtuously to bed and slept the sleep of the just and the righteous.

The next morning, I noticed the mouse was gone.

***

I went to work very early the next day, hoping to get into training ready for the seven o'clock starts next week. I had never woken up before seven before in my life, and I approached this perverse undertaking in the light of, say, climbing Everest. So effective was this stratagem that I actually arrived at eight a.m. (well, nearly) and caught Goebbels and Jane Edmonds having a massive row.

'Excellent!' I thought, sliding noiselessly over to my desk and cowering behind my computer so as to be able to eavesdrop unnoticed for as long as possible. If there's one thing I really love, it's eavesdropping on other people's fights.

'Don't be so bloody stupid, you stupid woman!' screamed Goebbels. 'How could it just be gone?'

'It bloody well is gone. Just take a look for yourself. Go on, just look!'

'Get a grip on yourself. These things don't just disappear. I think you're seriously unstable, Jane. This is an office, not a bloody mental ward. If you're having your period or something just go home, will you, don't hang around here causing trouble.'

Dance of Chaos

'CHRIST! I don't believe this! I'm telling you the bloody thing is gone, vanished, kaput, and you just want to turn your back on the whole bloody thing and pretend it isn't happening! Well go on, go and sit in your fancy new office and read your bloody stick books or whatever the hell it is you do all day, after all, you've got a window, I'll just sit here in the dark until it's time to go home. God, why should I care?'

Jane turned her back on Goebbels and marched into her office, slamming the door with great effect. This left Goebbels, who had obviously met his match at shouting, at a bit of a loss, since the only entry to his new office, according to his strict instructions, was now via Jane's office. He marched unsteadily off to the café bar, muttering about Kaffirs under his breath.

Reasoning that he would have to stay away for at least ten minutes to save face, I sneaked over to Jane's office and opened the door. She was sitting in the dark all right, it was pitch black in there except for a faint bit of daylight filtering through from Goebbels' window.

'What was all that about?'

In the dim light, I couldn't tell whether Jane was glaring angrily at me, but she certainly sounded like it.

'Those bloody workmen. They've taken away the light switch.'

'You're kidding.'

'See for yourself.'

Which, of course, was exactly what I couldn't do. But I ran my hands over the walls for several feet on each side of the doorway, and could feel nothing.

'Here.' A match flared in the dark. By this tiny fire I could see that both walls were, indeed, without switches.

'They couldn't have put it in his office, could they?'

'Go and look yourself. I'm not saying anything, I'm not being accused of insanity again, once a day is quite enough, thanks very much. Go on,' she added. 'Just look yourself. See if you can find a light switch. After all, you're white. White people can always find a light switch when they want one. It's just us bloody KAFFIRS that have trouble.'

Her voice sounded harsh and uneven, as though she was crying. Being a master of tact and diplomacy, I wisely refrained from embarrassing her by mentioning this.

'You're not crying, are you?'

'Of course I'm bloody not. If you must know, I've got a cold. Or maybe I'm getting my period, that's what makes women get emotional and not be able to find light switches, isn't it? Especially black women. Jesus Christ.'

There was a bit of a silence.

'He's like that to everyone, you know.'

'No, he bloody isn't. It's me, because I'm black, Aboriginal, a fucking KAFFIR.'

There was quite a long silence.

'He's from South Africa, you know.'

'No shit, Sherlock.'

'Yes, and actually, he really is horrible to everyone. Just because you're, well, you know, that's just something else he can use. It wouldn't matter what you were, he'd find something.'

It was starting to get on my nerves the way we kept having these long silences. I was embarrassed as hell about Goebbels saying all those racist things, although why I should be embarrassed when he wasn't was beyond me. I suppose it's just that we never talk about those things. Anyway, I nearly went through the roof when Jane blew her nose. It's amazing how being in the dark can get to you. So I screamed and that startled Jane and she started screaming too and we blundered about in the dark and someone knocked Jane's computer off her desk. I don't think it was me.

We got out into the light and I saw Jane had gone a horrid grayish colour. She squinted at me.

'God, you've gone an awful colour,' she said.

***

Goebbels came back after lunch, reeking of gin. By this time, Jane had spent another hour on the phone, and the head workman had returned in a sort of procession with the two junior workmen, two electricians and a young boy whose main function seemed to be getting out of people's way. 'Get out of the way, Ratso,' said one electrician. 'Pass me the drill. No not that one, you idiot. The one on your left. No, your other left.' No doubt feeling a quiet satisfaction at having accomplished this complex technical task, Ratso would stand back to admire his work. 'Get out of the way, Ratso,' said the other electrician, and so on. They drilled holes all over the walls and ceiling of Jane's and Goebbels' offices. They knocked all over the ceilings with the back end of a hammer, looking for a manhole. There was no manhole. At this point Adam came out of the computer room and helpfully pointed out that there were lots of manholes in the computer room floor. This was not well received. The workmen then created a manhole of sorts (well, if there isn't a manhole, we'll just have to make one) in Goebbels' office, by removing part of the ceiling. It was a pity no one thought to cover his desk with newspaper first, but at least, Jane pointed out, his desk was now well and truly white.

By the time Goebbels arrived, they had installed two new light switches (buy one, get one free) on the wall next to Goebbels' door (so useful for Jane to have the opportunity to practise her night vision each morning) and withdrawn in triumph.

We all gathered round for the unveiling. Having observed the professionals at work, no one wanted to be the first to touch the new switches.

'I wonder why there's two?'

'One for Goebbels' office and one for Jane's.'

'Maybe it's one for on and one for off.'

'Hey, maybe this is the separate facilities Goebbels was after.'

'Nah, they're both white.' Snigger snigger.

At this point Goebbels arrived, snapping 'Get

back to your work,' automatically right and left, like a wind-up toy. He inspected the new switches, growling in the back of his throat like a guard dog on the leash. I wondered if Jane had been vaccinated against rabies. There was a brief silence as he pressed the switches. We all held our breath, united in a single hope. Would Goebbels be blown up, or fried to a crisp?

No such luck. Neither of the switches had the slightest effect, on Goebbels or on the lights.

☙CHAPTER TEN❧

It is but lost labour that ye haste to rise up early, and so late take rest, and eat the bread of carefulness...
Psalm 127:3

I arrived home to a scene straight out of one of those old black and white Gothic horror films. My mother was draped over the couch like a vampire's victim, my father was hovering solicitously over her and my younger brother was standing in a corner, looking furtive and sinister. Moses added a touch of the more earthy side of life to the tableau; he was sprawled in the middle of the floor, licking his bottom. And in my father's hand, was that – yes, actually a bottle of smelling salts.

I edged over to Patrick and muttered out of the side of my mouth, as I'd seen them do in that old prison film, the one where Robert Redford ate a maggot.

'What have you done?'

'Me?' Patrick looked as innocent as the day, so I knew that whatever it was he'd done was far worse than usual. If he'd really been innocent, he'd have been looking guilty, as he wondered which of the things he'd done last week had been found out.

'Come on, out with it.'

'Well, it's Harvey.'

Harvey was the name we'd given the rubber spider.

'What happened?'

'He caught a mouse.'

I raced up the stairs two at a time and burst panting into Patrick's room. The half-eaten mouse that Moses had discarded on the back step yesterday was artfully arranged between Harvey's front claws.

***

After that, it was decided unanimously, or at any rate unanimously by Mum and Dad, that Harvey had to go. Patrick, tears, pleading and sulks ignored, was dispatched with a can of Baygon to do the fell deed. I went with him to supervise the

Dance of Chaos

operation.

In his room, with the door safely closed, we turned Harvey onto his back. He looked quite convincing, except for having Made in Japan on his stomach.

'Wait on. Don't they curl all their legs up when they die?'

Patrick bent Harvey's feet up to the middle. As soon as he let go, the rubber legs sprang back into their original wild sprawl.

'We'll have to stick his feet down. Have you got any glue?'

Patrick shook his head.

'We'll use nail polish. I've got some clear. Wait a sec.'

Carefully checking that the coast was clear, I darted along the hall to my room and grabbed the bottle of Sally Hansen, hoping it wouldn't look too shiny. Probably no one was going to examine the corpse too closely, anyhow.

'Here it is. I'll paint his tummy, then we'll stick his little feet onto it. You'll have to hold them while it dries.'

'Will that stuff really work?'

'Who knows? Worth a try, isn't it?'

I painted Harvey liberally with Sally Hansen, but couldn't get all his feet up at once.

'Here, hold these four. We'll have to do it in a couple of goes.'

'Why don't you hold it yourself?'

'Because it'll wreck my nail polish if any gets on. Come on, d'you want him to look dead or don't you?'

I timed it on my watch, allowing five minutes for it to set.

'Okay, you should be able to let go now.'

Patrick raised his finger from the tank. The corpselike Harvey rose with it, like Venus from the waves.

'Hell. It's stuck to my finger.'

'Just pull it off gently.'

Patrick grabbed the spider's body in his other hand and wrenched it away. All the legs sprang out and waved around gaily. 'See! I'm not really dead!' Harvey seemed to be saying.

'Bloody hell!'

'Here, let me do it. You're too clumsy.'

There was a gentle tapping on the door. I grabbed the Baygon and frantically squirted it about. 'Look out! He's getting out of the box!' I shrieked.

'Don't worry, Fi,' Patrick shouted at the door. 'I'll bash him with my shoe.'

He started thumping the walls and floor with an old running shoe. Footsteps beat a swift retreat down the hall. Gasping with relief, I nearly choked on the fumes.

'God, you're a fumblefoot,' I panted, opening the window. 'We could have been nearly finished by now. If she walks in and catches us sticking him up with nail polish, I'm leaving you to do the explaining.'

'Why don't we just leave him? It's not like anyone's going to be doing an autopsy. We'll just bung him in the rubbish in a paper bag or something.'

'He just doesn't look dead with his legs hanging out all over the place. What about pins?'

'Too long.'

'Yeah, you're right. Well, let's have another go.'

We finally managed to get Harvey's feet stuck to his underneath, although we were painfully aware that it wouldn't stand up to close scrutiny. His feet were all glossy from the nail polish.

'You should have used one that wasn't shiny.'

'It's all shiny, they don't make flat nail polish. It's supposed to be shiny, dickbrain.'

'Maybe we could paint a red one over it, make it look like he bled to death.'

'Great idea, Patrick. Why don't we use a nice glittery pink one, make it look like he was manicured to death by a rogue stylist?'

We arranged him carefully on the sheet of Masonite which had covered his tank.

'Okay, let's go.'

'Wait a sec. Why don't we give him a little funeral in the back yard?'

Patrick rolled his eyes. 'Not again, Fiona.'

'Yes! It'll make the whole thing even more realistic, and if we do it straight away, we won't have to worry about Dad maybe taking a close look at him.'

'Alright then, but I'm not being the priest.'

'You can dig the hole and carry the coffin.'

I dashed back to my room again and grabbed a black silk scarf and my old Book of Common Prayer. When I was a little girl I wanted to be a priest, and was always holding funerals for dead moths and things, so I knew my way around the funeral service pretty well, despite never having been to a real one.

We went down to the bottom of the garden, behind some trees where we were out of sight of the house. Patrick started digging.

'Not there, you can't bury him there, right in the open like that.'

'Why not?'

'Someone might walk on him. You mustn't walk on a grave or your teeth fall out. Besides, it's not respectful.'

'Jesus, Fi, it's only a rubber spider, for God's sake. It doesn't matter where he goes.'

'Well you can't bury him there. His little cross might get caught in the lawn mower.'

'What little cross? He doesn't need a cross, he isn't even alive. Jesus.'

'Don't be blasphemous. Put him over in the corner there, by the fence.'

Patrick rolled his eyes long-sufferingly at heaven. I've often noticed what a common gesture that is, I've hardly ever known anyone that didn't do it. He dug a small, cross hole in the corner by the fence.

'Come on then, bung him in.'

'Wait on. Man that is born of woman hath but a short time to live, and is full of misery. He cometh-'

'Oh come off it, Fiona. You're not going to do the whole funeral service for a rubber spider. Anyway, he's not man born of woman. He's a fucking rubber spider made in a factory.'

'Don't be disrespectful, anyway it's not the full service, it's just the graveside bit. He cometh up, and is cut down, like a flower; he fleeth as it were a _'

Patrick was fidgeting; I fixed him with a steely glare, as I'd seen Father Simpson do in church.

'He fleeth as it were a shadow, and never continueth in one stay. In the midst of life we are in death: of whom may we seek succour, but of thee, O Lord, who for our sins are justly displeased?'

Patrick was now glaring at me and muttering about suckers. I hurried through the next bit as much as I could; he looked as though he was running out of patience, and I didn't want to be stuck filling in the hole myself. I hate gardening, bits of earth always get under my fingernails; anyway, that's what other people are for, as my grandmother always says.

'...for any pains of death to fall from thee. Okay, start casting the Earth upon the Body. Forasmuch as it has pleased Almighty God of his great mercy to take unto himself the soul of our dear brother here departed, we therefore commit his body to the ground; slow down, it's got to last through this whole bit. Earth to earth, ashes to –'

Patrick had finished filling the hole and was walking away. He has no idea about doing things properly.

***

In the end I gave up on getting up early for the morning shift, and decided instead to stay up all Sunday night. This way, I reasoned, I would also have no trouble getting to sleep early on Monday night, and therefore could easily wake up early on

Tuesday, etc etc. I prepared for my vigil by taking a long nap on Sunday afternoon, annoying my mother who had been expecting me to help her scrub out the garage (I can't think why), and laying in a stash of chocolate chip cookies.

I had to wait until after dinner to put the second part of my plan into action. Piece by piece I sneaked the coffee machine upstairs. I knew I would have all hell to deal with if my mother found out I was planning to stay up all night. You keep on getting older all the time, but somewhere around fourteen, parents just seem to stop noticing it. I suppose I really shouldn't have been still living at home at twenty, but the one time I tried moving out (during my few weeks at university, when I went to live in college) it was a disaster. Moses just didn't take to it, and it didn't take to him remarkably well, either. In fact we were both asked to leave, although how on earth I should have been expected to know that you weren't allowed to have animals is beyond me. They seem to expect you to be psychic in these places. I didn't like the university anyway, it was noisy and crowded, and I was always getting lost trying to find my way to lectures.

***

In the event, my plan worked so well that I got to the office at twenty-five past six. I couldn't ever remember being up so early before. Everything looked very sharp and clear, and the air smelled very clean, and seemed to tingle on my skin. I felt as though I could see and hear five times more acutely than usual. Why don't I do this more often, I asked myself.

The door to the office was shut, which surprised me. I'd never seen it closed before; perhaps I was the first to arrive. Well, that's good, I thought. I'll show them I'm super keen and efficient. I turned the handle.

The next moment I nearly jumped through the ceiling. An incredible cacophony assaulted my ears. 'Fire,' I gasped weakly, 'Police.' Was it a bomb attack? The American Consulate was next door, and they often attracted crank calls and demonstrations. Oh, God. Could it be a nuclear attack? I remembered air raid alerts on old war films I'd seen. They sounded like this. Was the Axis of Evil bombing us? Or the Americans? God knew they were capable of anything. I'd better do something practical. What was practical? Bandages and cups of tea, I seemed to remember from my brief time in the Scouts. I ran into the tea room, noticing on the way that the phone on Frank's desk was ringing. It was a good thing I'd thought to check; the café bar was indeed switched off. I filled up the water and switched it on. Right, what next? Bandages. I was sure I'd seen a first-aid cabinet somewhere. But where? It was hard to think with the klaxon blaring all the time, and the phone had started again, too.

I was still searching for the first-aid box when the police arrived.

CHAPTER ELEVEN

Lord, how are they increased that trouble me: many are they that rise against me.
Psalm 3:1

The police station was really grotty, I didn't think much of it at all. I expected at least they'd have a sign that said Police or something, but it was just this really manky old building. There was all kinds of junk lying around the entrance, I noticed an old wooden chair with a nasty-looking stain on the seat as if someone had been incontinent in it, and there were several half-full buckets of water standing around the door. One of them had something floating in it that might have been a dead rat. There was a strong smell of disinfectant, mixed with something else I couldn't identify. I could hear someone singing from inside the building. Whoever it was sounded drunk.

Inside, it was really warm, quite hot in fact. I could feel my nose getting shiny as we walked around miles of narrow little passages, up and down stairs. By the time we stopped, I wasn't even sure what floor we were on. We went into a tiny little room with just a little table and some chairs. I didn't think much of it; the paint was all flaking off the walls and the curtains were filthy. There was a funny smell, too.

'What's that funny smell?' I asked.

'Don't worry about the smell, just have a seat there.'

They definitely weren't friendly, although since they'd just arrested me for breaking and entering I supposed that wasn't really surprising. I comforted myself with the reflection that as long as they didn't know who I was they couldn't charge me with anything, and also that an innocent person has nothing to fear from the police. I knew the first fact from Tim, who was at College of Law (why hadn't he rung me?) and the second from primary school. I sat down and looked out of the window. We seemed to be on the first or second floor, although it was difficult to be sure, as we had been both up and down various flights of stairs. The taller of the two policeman started doing something to a big machine that was on the table, and the short fat one sat in the chair opposite, glaring at me. He had put my bag down on the floor, out of my reach.

'Um, excuse me?'

The short fat policeman raised an eyebrow.

'Could you pass me my bag, please?'

'You'll get your bag, don't worry. Now we want you to answer a few questions. You can start with your full name and address.'

'Look, I really need my bag. I've broken a nail.' I didn't feel it was necessary to point out that it was Their Fault.

'Never mind about your fingernails, you're in serious trouble, young lady. Now please state your full name and address.'

'No. I want my bag.'

'All in good time. State your name and address.'

The tall policeman sat down and leaned forward.

'You realise that if you refuse to state your name we are empowered to hold you indefinitely? In the cells? I don't think you'd find it very comfortable down there, Miss...?'

I had seen this on TV, I knew one of them would pretend to be really nasty and the other one would be sympathetic so as to win my confidence. I just had to keep my nerve and not crack. I reminded myself cunningly that they didn't know I'd already been up all night without any sleep.

The tall policeman sighed.

'Okay. Well, I'd rather not have had to do this, but if you refuse to co-operate. Let's have the bag, Steve.'

I smiled to myself. You just had to be firm. The next minute I was reeling with shock. They had opened my bag and were systematically removing the contents.

'What are you doing? That's my handbag!'

'I'm sorry, but since you refuse to co-operate to the extent of identifying yourself, we are empowered to conduct a search of your personal effects in order to establish your identity.' The tall policeman looked at me sourly. 'You know, you could make this a lot easier on yourself.' He shook his head and started reading out the contents of my bag, like some kind of demented checklist.

'Lipstick. Mobile phone. Powder compact. One pair of pantyhose, still in the packet. Eighty-five cents in loose change. Three safety pins. What's this? Oh, a manicure set. I must say you seem to be equipped for every contingency. Five tampons, unused. Can't see a purse or wallet anywhere yet. One packet of tissues. Handkerchief, lace edges. Very nice. Initialled FM. Those your initials, are they?'

'Of course they're mine, d'you think I carry other people's handkerchiefs about?' I was trying desperately to think what awful things might be at the bottom of my bag.

'It's not for me to say what you might or might not do.' He looked bootfaced, and went on investigating my bag. 'Photograph in a silver frame. Your boyfriend, is it? No, it's of a cat.'

The short fat policeman shifted in his chair and muttered something about fruitcakes. I thought about Tim, who still hadn't rung me. Perhaps I should use my one phone call to ring him. I knew from the movies that I would be allowed one phone call. On the other hand, it would be better value to ring someone long distance.

'One bottle of perfume. No, here's another. Two bottles of perfume. One bottle of nail polish. She's a walking chemist's shop. Aha! What's this, a purse? No, it's got makeup. Three eyeshadow, two mascara, another lipstick. One bottle of liquid foundation. Pretty messy in there, you should be more careful screwing the cap on. Eyebrow pencil. Hairpins, eight, no nine. What's this stuff? Ceramic Glaze. Looks like some kind of nail polish. Call it nail polish, that makes two. Okay, that's everything in the purse. Shit, it's all over me.' He carefully extracted a handkerchief from his trouser pocket and wiped his fingers. I could get to hate this man, I thought.

'God, what the hell's this? An apple core. Jesus. And a biscuit. Christ. Another bottle of perfume. Two muesli bars, peanut flavour. Good God! One pair of knickers, black lace. One religious picture. Three biros, two blue one red. That seems to be all. No wallet, pity about that. She can cool off in the cells until she decides to co-operate. I'll take her down, Steve, you can check her stuff in.'

The fat policeman started shoving everything back in the bag. Good, I thought, I'll get my hands on my nail file at last.

'Okay, Sunshine. Walk this way.'

They didn't give me my bag after all. Instead, I was marched up and down endless miles of corridors until we arrived back where we'd come in. On the way, we stopped at a kind of counter where the tall policeman was given some keys by a young pimply policeman, who looked about seventeen. On the radio, someone was angrily demanding an IVR. Whatever it was, evidently nobody was giving him one, because he kept demanding it over and over.

'What's an IVR?' I asked the tall policeman. He looked at me contemptuously.

'Don't you worry about that.'

I went back to wondering uneasily what I'd done with my wallet.

***

The place we'd come in seemed even more depressing than before. The tall policeman showed me into a room and slammed the door before I had a chance to say anything. I wanted to say plenty when I got a look at the room, I'd never been anywhere so disgusting in my life. There was actually a lavatory, right in the corner without even a screen around it. Most of the floor space was taken up by two benches with ghastly-looking plastic cushions on them. One of them had a pile of filthy grey blankets. The drunk I'd heard earlier was apparently right next door. Presently he finished singing *I'll Take You Home Again Kathleen*, and started shouting a string of meaningless obscenities. I walked around the room, looking for somewhere to sit down. I was exhausted, all the coffee seemed to have worn off at once, but I didn't want to sit on the plastic cushions, they looked so dirty, and that only left the lavatory, which I now noticed didn't even have a seat anyway. The only window was about ten feet up and covered with fine steel mesh. Even when I stood on the bench, I couldn't see out. Someone had tried to see out before me, I could see the despairing fingermarks clawed into the dust on the sloped sill. Perhaps it was the same person who'd kicked all the paint off the wall in a big patch near the floor. I could practically feel his rage and despair, but other people had apparently adjusted quite well to captivity, and had left a number of cheerful messages graffitied on the wall. I wondered where they'd got the biros from.

***

'Miss MacDougall?'

It was the tall policeman again. I glared at him.

'We've spoken to your employer, you're free to go. Here's your bag, I'll drive you back to your office.'

He lectured me all the way back to Marsh and Spacknall about the trouble I'd caused by not telling them my name. I thought that was a bit much, after all I hadn't asked them to arrest me. And he wouldn't even put the siren on.

Dance of Chaos

***

You would think that after an experience like that, Goebbels would have given me the rest of the day off. You would think that, wouldn't you? I certainly did, thereby proving that I had no conception of the depths to which a truly evil and vicious person can sink. Not only did he not give me the rest of the day off, but I had to work late to make up the time I had spent at the police station.

Both Penny and Steve were laughing when they let me into the computer room.

'What's the big joke?' I asked crossly.

Those two morons just went on giggling like maniacs. I knew they were laughing at me. However, I also knew that I was a Trainee Programmer, and they were destined to remain operators. I also knew that Penny was constitutionally unable to hang onto a boyfriend for more than six weeks, despite (or perhaps because of, I personally thought) buying them all expensive presents, and that Steve had acne scars and still lived with his parents in Wantirna, for God's sake. I mean, nobody lives in Wantirna.

So I just smiled nicely and said nothing. Presently, the giggles died down, and they both started glancing furtively towards Goebbels' office.

'We'd better look serious. Goebbels gave us both a hell of a rocket for not locking the door last night.'

'But aren't Adam and Julie on evening shift?'

Penny rolled her eyes. 'Since when does a little detail like that matter to Prick Features? He's got to have someone to scream at, we were here and they weren't. I'm sure there'll be plenty left over for them when they get in. Slack mongrels.'

'Yeah,' said Steve feelingly. He looked as though he'd been crying. Steve was well known around the office for being over-sensitive.

We all sighed, thinking about working somewhere else, knowing it was hopeless.

'Well, come on,' I said brightly. 'What about this computer?'

'Yes, right! Bloody old obsolete heap of junk. Let's start with the printer. It makes most of the work.' Penny walked over to one of the nondescript blue boxes and nonchalantly threw up a lid on top. The noise level increased by ten million decibels. I could see the paper jumping around inside. She touched a button and it stopped.

'Watch and learn, Fiona. This must be the only working impact printer left in the world. Frank has to service it himself because no one even supports them any more. You press this button to stop it when it comes to the end of a job. Then you can take the paper out.'

'How do you know when it comes to the end of a job?'

'Because it stops.'

'Well why press the button then? If it's already stopped.'

'That stops it from starting a new job. Then you start it again and it goes on printing whenever there's something to print. Or you might want to change the stationery. A lot of the production jobs print on special stationery, sticky labels or cards. Oh, and you're not supposed to wear bracelets or scarves, either, when you're working in here, or anything that hangs off.'

'Why not?'

'In case you got it caught, you might get your hand ripped off or something.'

'Like Isadora Duncan.' Steve sniggered. 'I wish we could get Goebbels in here to change the paper, he might get his beard caught.'

'Yeah, rip his face off.'

'His wife'd probably thank us for improving his looks.'

Penny swung the lid down and flicked the START button.

'I'll show you how to change the paper when it stops. We have to vacuum it all the time, too.'

'Vacuum it?'

'Yes, it's got its own little vacuum hose built in. The paper dust clogs it up. You vacuum it every time it stops, or when you change the paper, or if it's been going more than an hour you stop it and vacuum it. It's not so bad, it only takes a minute. This big one behind it is the air conditioner.'

'Hang on a sec, I want to see the little vacuum cleaner.' I moved closer to the printer and peered inside, expecting a miniature Hoover. Suddenly an icy gale shot up my legs and ballooned my skirt to waist height. Unfortunately I don't have legs like Marilyn Monroe. 'What's happening?' I shrieked, frantically trying to hold my skirt down, and no doubt looking as utterly stupid as Monroe did in that movie, although hopefully not as slutty.

Penny and Steve were all creased up again.

'Get off the vent. He-he-he-he...'

In fact I was standing on a little grille in the floor which I hadn't noticed. It was right in front of the printer.

'What a stupid place to put a ventilation hole. Why don't you move the printer?'

'Sorry, I should have warned you. Frank set it up like that, he sits out there and watches our dresses blow up. It's really better to wear trousers.'

As she was doing, the smug bitch. Looking out the plate glass wall I saw Frank, Tony and Geoff leering horribly. Even Jane seemed to be sniggering through her open door. Goebbels was fortunately out of sight; that was the only good thing about him, that sometimes he wasn't there.

The air conditioner was about ten feet high and ten feet wide. I gazed at it in wonder. No wonder it was freezing in here.

'Why don't you turn it down a bit, then?'

'The machinery has to be kept at a constant temperature, or everything goes wrong. You know the disk platters are made of metal, they can't afford to expand or contract even a tiny bit. If the air conditioner broke down, we'd have to shut down the whole machine until it was fixed. Anyway, we don't do anything to it, it just stays on all the time.

The engineer comes and adjusts it every now and then. Okay. These are the tape drives. We have to clean them once every shift. We haven't done it yet today, so I'll show you when one's free. You generally do them when you've got a bit of free time, it doesn't matter when, as long as they get done once during every shift.'

The tape drives were tall and narrow, like refrigerators. The tapes didn't rotate smoothly, but in a series of jerks. I peered into the glass fronts, looking for the vacuum hoses.

'Where are the vacuum things?'

'The vacuum goes down the middle, see where the loop of tape is? That makes the tape go at an even speed past the heads, even though the reels stop and start all the time.'

'Well, if the vacuum goes all the time, why do you have to clean it?'

Penny looked at me in a slow, wondering way.

'What's the vacuum got to do with it?'

'Well, doesn't it vacuum itself?'

'Oh, I see. No, we clean the tape drives with tape cleaning fluid and cotton wool.'

Dance of Chaos

Steve became animated. 'It's great stuff, the tape fluid. You'll love it. Excellent for sniffing.'

'Shut up, Steve. These are the DASD devices. These two are removable packs and the others are all fixed pack devices. You have to be very, very careful with the removable packs, there's no way they'll survive being dropped.'

I nodded wisely and tried to look like the sort of person who never drops things. Perhaps by careful manoeuvring I would be able to avoid ever handling the disk packs. Luckily, I remembered just in time what a DASD was from the course. It's really a Direct Access Storage Device, but IBM like to call everything by cute little four-letter acronyms (FLAs).

'...and this is the CPU.'

This was it, the moment I'd been waiting for. The CPU (Central Processing Unit – when IBM haven't got enough words for a FLA they make it a TLA) was really pretty, with lots of red and green lights flashing on and off, and some really impressive looking dials and switches. Next to it, a cute little typewriter chattered merrily away, spitting continuous paper out the back. You could type things in on it yourself, and the computer also wrote on it. The computer's words all came out in capitals, and the person's words were all in little letters.

Penny was still rattling on. '…the console typewriter communicates with it. The most important thing to remember is to never, ever let it run out of paper. See, it just feeds the continuous paper like the big printer. If it runs out of paper the whole thing stops, so you have to keep an eye on it all the time, especially when there's a lot happening.'

'hello,' I typed furtively, when Penny and Steve weren't looking.

***

I had never been so exhausted in my life as when I finally dragged myself home that night. Quivering with ecstasy in anticipation of a hot bath and fourteen hours' sleep, I crawled upstairs and collapsed through my bedroom door.

Moses was gambolling happily around the room, tossing something dark brown into the air with his claws. Showers of dark powder seemed to be coming out of it. Must be a pretty dried-up old rat, I thought to myself. Then I caught sight of the overturned coffee filter thing behind my bed. A great puddle of coffee had soaked into the pale green carpet, and Moses had evidently been killing the filter bag for some time; a fine layer of damp coffee grounds coated every surface, especially the bed, which seemed to have been nested in by a wet bear.

By the time I got it all cleaned up, I never wanted to see a cute little Hoover again.

☙CHAPTER TWELVE☙

Prosper with thy blessing the work of all who labour for the instruction and upbringing of the young in virtue and true godliness…
      Book of Common Prayer

Of course the telephone had to ring just as Moses and I got settled down in front of the television. I sighed and hit pause. 'Hello?'

'It's Miss Peemoller from St Bedivere's. I'd like to speak to Mrs MacDougall, please.'

The voice on the phone sounded strict and severe. I wondered what Patrick had done now, and whether I could get him out of it. Might as well give it my best shot, I decided.

'This is Mrs MacDougall speaking. How may I help you?'

'I'm afraid it's about your son, Patrick. I wonder if I could come over and see you this evening?'

Oh dear. No way could I pass for Patrick's mother. Also, our real mother would doubtless be home soon.

'Well, I'm awfully sorry, but I'm afraid it's my bridge night tonight. Couldn't you tell me about it on the phone?'

'I really don't think that would be the best thing, Mrs MacDougall. What if I popped around now, and we could have a chat before you have to go out?'

'Look, I really don't think you should come here. Um, we've got measles. You wouldn't want to carry it to all the kids in your class. Why don't you just tell me what it's about? I suppose Patrick's got up to some mischief again. I'll have a little talk to him, shall I?'

I seemed to be getting deeper and deeper into this web of lies. My grandmother always says that truth is the enemy of kindness, but it just didn't seem to be working for me today.

'Mrs MacDougall, I don't think–'

'Sorry, I really must go. Thank you so much for

calling, and you may be sure I'll have a few sharp words with Patrick. Goodbye.'

Faint squawking sounds issued from the receiver as I hung up. I felt rather pleased with myself – that 'few sharp words' had been a really authentic touch.

***

'Battle computers online,' purred Zen. I sniggered to myself. I knew how unrealistic it all was. All the same, I wished our computer was more like Zen and Orac. You could only talk to it in maniac statements like ROD, or CANCEL F3,PARTDUMP, and if you got even one letter wrong it couldn't understand anything. I wished I had a space cruiser and could go anywhere in the galaxy, especially with a sexy creature like Avon aboard, even if he was a bit fat. On the other hand, Servalan was catching up fast and it looked as if Blake & co were about to meet a very sticky end.

The doorbell rang. Immersed in my favourite vintage show, I paid no attention. I paid attention all right a minute later, when I heard the voice of that afternoon's caller.

'Oh, hello, Mrs MacDougall. I hoped I'd catch you before you went to your bridge game. I've already had measles, you see, so it's quite alright.'

Oh, God.

'But I don't play bridge,' said my mother in her slow, puzzled voice. Laser beams cannoned across the screen unnoticed. I was frozen in shock.

A second later they entered the room, and I lost my chance of bolting out of the window. Firmly I resolved to deny everything. I sneaked a look at Miss Peemoller. She wasn't at all what I had expected; she was actually quite pretty, and didn't seem to be much older than I was. Patrick had occasionally mentioned her in terms which had led me to expect a warty old hag on a broomstick.

'Fiona, this is Miss Peemoller, Patrick's form mistress. My daughter, Fiona.'

'How d'you do,' I mumbled, trying to make my voice as different as possible.

'Mrs MacDougall, I confiscated a magazine from Patrick this afternoon, and that's why I thought we should have a little chat.' Miss Peemoller fished around in her bag and produced a magazine. Out of the corner of my eye I noticed she was holding it delicately between two fingers, by the extreme corner. 'I cannot have such filth in my classroom. I really think Patrick is a boy in need of severe corrective discipline. Good heavens, Mrs MacDougall, he's only thirteen now, what's he going to be like in a few years?'

My mother fished around in her pocket and found her glasses. Leaning forward, she peered at the magazine. Then she started gasping like a landed trout. By the time I came back with a glass of water she had recovered her breath, and she and Miss Peemoller were nose to nose like two tomcats on a fence.

Miss Peemoller gathered up her bag as I handed the water to my mother. I hovered over her solicitously like Florence Nightingale, trying to give the impression of a person who would never, never pretend to be someone else on the telephone.

'Well, I must be going. Oh, and Mrs MacDougall, I haven't said anything to the Principal. As long as there's no recurrence, I don't see why this should have to go any further.' She included me in her bright, professional smile. Beautiful, I thought. Just in case there was any doubt, it's now perfectly clear what will happen if there *is* a recurrence. They headed for the door, cooing affectionately. On the television, the final credits were rolling.

***

At work the next day, I found the computer room door hanging off by one hinge. Steve was in the store room, hunting around frantically. Penny wasn't in yet.

'What happened to the door?'

He shot me an anguished look. 'Adam and Julie were practising Judo on the night shift. Julie rang Penny about one a.m., that's why she's not in yet. She rang up to warn us to be really careful. She threw Adam into the door and it just broke off. They stuck it up with sticky tape, but it's already come off. I'm just looking for some of that packing tape, it'll hold better. We'll just have to be really extra careful with it.'

'Why not just get it fixed?'

Steve gave me a look of scorn and contempt. 'Oh, sure. Excuse me, Mr Goebbels, I just popped in to tell you that the night shift operators broke down the computer room door playing Judo. You can go and tell Goebbels if you like. I'm certainly not.'

'I see your point. But what about a screw?'

'Sorry love, you're not my type.'

I gathered the subject was closed. We would stick up the door with packing tape, if we could find any, and be very very careful with it for ever.

'Um, Steve?'

'Yeah?' his voice echoed faintly from behind a cupboard. 'I think it might have been on the top shelf and fallen down back here. Could you just pull it out a bit? It's really dark back here.'

'No, I couldn't. Why were they doing Judo?'

Steve's bottom appeared, with cobwebs. 'Something to do, I guess. You know how it is after midnight. Come on, help me find it before Gobble-guts gets in.'

'Look, it's nothing to do with me. I'm not involving myself in any of it.'

'Your funeral, sweetie. Don't forget he hates you more than anyone. He'll probably convince himself it was all your fault.'

I couldn't really say anything to that, as Goebbels' hatred of me was a byword in the office. He couldn't even pass my desk without his beard standing up on end. I imagined his reaction to seeing the door hanging off the bottom hinge, with little bits of sticky fluttering gaily from the top.

I chucked my bag on the desk and started on the nearest filing cabinet.

An hour later, we had found the packing tape,

sworn at each other several times, got covered with dust and cobwebs, and stuck up the door, cleverly keeping all the tape on the inside so that it would look normal from the outside. It was after eight o'clock. Goebbels would be here any moment, in fact it was a wonder he wasn't here already. We both sighed with relief.

'Let's go and get some coffee.'

On my way out, carefully closing the door, I thought something looked odd about the computer room.

***

When we got back from coffee, Penny was sitting at the main console. It took me a second to recognise her, she looked so unlike herself. Penny was usually a relaxed, languid sort of person; this Penny was quivering with tension. She watched the silent typewriter like a cat at a mousehole. She jumped tremendously as we came in.

'Steve! What the hell have you been doing?'

'Just getting a coffee. What's up?'

'You didn't IPL the machine. How could you just forget? How could you forget to IPL the machine?' Her eyes narrowed in suspicion. 'You've only just got in, haven't you?'

'Oh, God. The door came unstuck and we couldn't find the tape, I guess I just forgot, sorry Pen.'

IPL, a TLA meaning Initial Program Load, is what you do to start up a computer. It takes at least half an hour to IPL and get everything up and running, which is why the morning shift had to start at seven o'clock. It was now eight thirty-five, since Steve and I had lingered over our coffee somewhat, feeling, with some justification, that we had something to celebrate.

'Don't you sorry Pen me, you little–' she broke off as the typewriter chattered. We all leaned over to read the message.

F3 DFH1500 LOADING CICS NUCLEUS was Greek to me, but seemed to comfort Penny and Steve. A whole bunch of other stuff followed, and we maintained a holy silence. I got a terrific cramp in my back from bending over like that, there was only one chair at the console, but somehow it didn't seem the right thing to go and get another chair. Finally the flood of gibberish ended with F3 DFH1500 CONTROL IS BEING GIVEN TO CICS. It looked a bit sinister to me actually, but Steve and Penny were both laughing and making thumbs-up signs, so I didn't say anything.

***

Because of getting off work at half past three, I managed to get the front seat on the tram going home. I amused myself by pretending the tram was a massive space cruiser and all the oncoming cars were hostile alien fighters. By the time I noticed the tram was already past my stop, I had notched up an impressive forty-eight kills, and a number of the enemy craft were careening blindly off into space with one wing sheared off, navigation systems shot out, etc. As I reached our house, wishing I were three inches taller and didn't have to wear stiletto heels all the time, Patrick was just letting himself in. Suddenly I remembered with a guilty shock about Miss Peemoller.

'Patrick! Don't go in!'

'What's the matter, Fi?' Patrick stood on the front step looking stupid. I gestured frantically from the front gate, hoping our mother hadn't already heard him. She has ears like radar.

Finally I managed to get Patrick a little way along the street, out of firing range from our front windows.

'Miss Peemoller was here yesterday with a stick book she said she took off you in her class. She showed it to Mum, she's furious.'

Patrick rolled his eyes. 'Oh, hell. No wonder

she was so nice to me today, she probably thinks I've already been flogged within an inch of my life, the old bat. She wouldn't have known I was at John's for the night. Well, thanks for the warning.' He started back up the path with a martyred air.

'Anyway, I thought you promised to get rid of all those stick books.'

'Gimme a break, Fi. I didn't say I wouldn't get any more, did I?'

***

Our mother was in the kitchen, viciously polishing the underneath of the table. She was obviously still mad with rage. Patrick dropped his bag on the floor and headed for the fridge.

'Hi, Mum,' he tossed over his shoulder cheerfully.

'You sit down here, Patrick. I want a word with you.' Her voice dripped with dark forebodings. I supposed I should make myself scarce, but I couldn't miss seeing how Patrick would attempt to weasel out of this. For once, I thought to myself virtuously, he'll have to take what's coming to him, having been caught red-handed.

'Mum, there's something I have to talk to you about.' Patrick looked serious as he sat down at the table. 'I think I've got a vocation for the priesthood.'

I was speechless with admiration. Our mother was also speechless, but not for long.

'Patrick Aloysius MacDougall, how dare you sit there and tell me you want to be a priest when only last night I had Miss Peemoller in here showing me that filthy magazine she caught you with.'

Patrick look amazed and hurt. His eyes went big and liquid, and was that a tear glinting in the corner? I thought it probably was.

'Oh Mum, how could you think that? One of the other boys passed it to me, and I was going to burn it at recess. When Miss Peemoller saw it, I had to pretend it was mine or I'd have got him into trouble, what else could I do? How could you think I'd want to look at disgusting stuff like that when I'm going to be a priest?' He paused, sorrowfully shaking his head. 'I thought you trusted me.'

Our mother melted. 'You poor boy. I should have known you wouldn't do a terrible thing like that. Of course you protected your friend. I'll ring Miss Peemoller tomorrow and explain.'

⳼CHAPTER THIRTEEN⳽

An unwise man doth not well consider this: and a fool doth not understand it.
Psalm 92:6

For several weeks Patrick could do no wrong in our house. Our mother, Anglo-Catholic to the core, was thrilled at giving her only son to Holy Mother Church (sic). She rang up Miss Peemoller:

Mother: Miss Peemoller, I just wanted you to know that our suspicions about Patrick were unfounded. The poor boy told me the whole story, he was terribly shocked that anyone could have thought he'd read a dirty magazine.

Miss Peemoller: Mrs MacDougall, I assure you Patrick was definitely reading that magazine when I took it away from him. He was leering like a dirty old man, and whatever story he may have told you, I can assure you there is no doubt whatever about it, and I absolutely cannot tolerate such behaviour in my classroom...

At this point I heard Dad coming upstairs and had to hang up the extension. But there was no escape the next time Father Simpson came to dinner.

'So here is our young Candidate. It's a fine decision you've made, my boy.'

And later, to our mother:

'You know, Mrs MacDougall, I had fears at one time that young Patrick might be a little unsteady, but all is clear now. The struggle with his vocation must have been going on for many years, and it's a heavy burden for a young boy, and often leads to wildness in his early life. The blessed St Francis himself...'

***

Neither of us could get out of going to church every Sunday, either. Now that Patrick was going to be a priest, the whole family had to turn out in force for Sunday Mass. This meant that we both had to come up with a whole array of subsidiary excuses for not being available to teach in the Sunday

Dance of Chaos

School, polish brass, sell jam at stalls, etc etc. Patrick got out of it reasonably well (I have so much Latin homework, etc etc *ad nauseam*), but I got roped in quite a lot; old ladies are so forceful. After I spilt a bottle of Brasso all over the altar, my services weren't in such demand. Actually they weren't very nice about that, which I thought was a bit unfair; how was I supposed to know you were supposed to take the candlesticks out the back to clean them? They looked heavy, and I had my fingernails to consider. The Brasso ate a big hole in the curtains that go round the front of the altar, but they weren't very nice ones anyway, sort of a mouldy olive green colour. I found some super red ones which I put up instead, they were much nicer and went well with the carpet. I don't know why Father Simpson wasn't more pleased, I suppose he must be colour blind.

Anyway, what with dodging the church ladies and Father Simpson, who seemed to have moved in with us, half the time and watching Patrick being revoltingly pious and reading stick books wrapped in Lives of the Saints the other half, the office started to seem like my only refuge.

***

I finished vacuuming the printer and straightened up with a sigh. In order to avoid

Frank's nasty little pervert vent, I had to lean right over sideways in an unnatural position. I had already been caught a number of times by this horrible device, and had been forced to spend a fortune on fancy new underwear. After all, if you have a job where your dress is going to keep blowing up around your waist, you can't very well have tatty old knickers. It was a bit of a strain, though, because in spite of having this fantastically challenging high-tech new position, my pay hadn't gone up at all. If Gobble-guts had his way, it would go down, I reflected gloomily.

I cheered up, reflecting that I had been left alone to run the computer all by myself. Only for a couple of hours while everybody else went out to lunch, but there I was at the helm, just like Blake. I sat down at the console.

'g 00e,' I typed. The printer resumed its mindless chattering. 'Battle computers online, prepare for evasive action,' I muttered to myself. Enemy craft swooped in from the Alpha sector. All systems were on amber alert. I shot fourteen Klingon fighters without pausing, then KABOOM! I took a direct hit amidships. Quickly I scanned the controls. Power systems OK, navigation systems OK. I checked the life support indicators. They were edging towards the red zone. Swiftly I grabbed the intercom, getting off a couple more telling shots with the other hand. 'Now hear this,' I boomed. 'This is your captain speaking. We are now on Red Alert, repeat Red Alert. Chief Engineer to the bridge at the double.' The life support warning klaxons blared into life, hooting and squealing. The noise was deafening.

Suddenly I realised the squealing noise was actually coming from the computer, in real life. Oh God. I remembered that we must always stay calm and look up the appropriate manual. I looked up the messages manual, but couldn't find anything under 'Squealing'. I tried Whistling, Hooting and Shrieking with no more success. The noise was really getting to me; it had a forlorn, unhappy sound, as if the computer was crying for its mother. I cried a bit myself, out of sympathy. I looked up 'Crying' in the messages manual, but there wasn't even anything close. I tried typing in 'msg bg' and found the console keyboard was locked. That was when I really got scared.

Presently there was an awful banging at the computer room door. Jane was outside making gestures and pointing to her ears. I went and opened the door.

'Who is it?' I had to shout over the racket the console was making.

'It's me, Jane, stupid, who did you think it was,

Father Christmas?'

'No, I mean, who is it on the telephone?'

She looked behind her nervously. 'What telephone?'

'Wasn't there a call for me?'

'No. Were you expecting one?'

'Not really. Hey, what are you doing here anyway, why aren't you at Gobble-guts's lunch?' Goebbels, in a rare fit of humanity, had taken the whole department out to lunch. Being the most junior person, I had remained behind to look after the computer.

Jane made a face. 'If I ate anything provided by that bastard, I reckon I might turn to stone. Anyway, what's that awful noise?'

'I don't know, I can't find anything about it in the manual.'

'Well, can't you talk to it, find out what the trouble is?'

I shook my head. 'I haven't got a clue what to do. The console isn't taking any messages, the keyboard's locked up and it just keeps screaming like that.'

'Why don't you turn it off?'

'You can't just turn it off.'

'Why not?'

'Well, bringing it down's really complicated, you have to stop all the partitions and stuff, anyway you need the keyboard and it's not working.'

'Well there's plenty of keyboards around, stick in another one.'

This suggestion seemed to have some merit. I took Frank's keyboard, as it was nearest (well, except for mine, but I didn't want to use mine in case something happened to it), and substituted it for the console one. It didn't make any difference. Jane was still standing at the computer room door, glaring at me.

Jane knocked on the door again. I sighed and went to open it.

'Sorry, it didn't make any difference.'

'Oh. Well, do something, hey, it's giving me a shocking headache. Could you turn down the volume, at least?'

Jane stalked back to her office. Normally her confidence that I would be able to do something would have given me a nice warm glow of confidence myself, but now I miserably realised that that was just Jane. Life held no surprises for Jane; she expected the worst, often got it, and always prepared for it with the meticulousness of a field marshal preparing to invade Britain. She had checklists for all of the things she did, and even wrote her grocery list in the same order the shelves were in in the supermarket. Each season she planned her wardrobe, and never, ever bought anything on impulse.

I sat back down at the console. I had to do something or the noise would drive me insane. I went over every inch of the keyboard looking for a volume key. There didn't seem to be one, but perhaps it was one of those combinations, like CTRL/S for save. But then, I reasoned, I wouldn't be able to use it anyway, since the keyboard was locked. But wait – this was Frank's keyboard, not the computer's own one. Perhaps the computer's own keyboard had special keys? I plugged it back in and examined it. Nothing looked remotely like a volume control.

Perhaps the volume knob was on the box itself? But a detailed search of both the front and back of the CPU failed to turn up anything except the earring I'd lost last week, half hidden under the edge of the unit. Of course, that was nice to have. I wondered what I'd done with the other one.

Jane was back knocking at the door again. I sighed.

'Look, why don't you ring Frank? Get some help, he can probably tell you what to do over the phone.'

I considered her suggestion. Really it had a lot of merit, but then I would have to admit that I didn't know how to fix the problem myself. Wouldn't it be far, far more stunning to fix it myself, and then just sort of casually mention it when they all got back? I'd be a hero.

'Let me try a couple more things first, then if I can't fix it I will.'

I looked about for inspiration, but didn't see anything except a grubby bit of paper sticky-taped to the front of the CPU. It seemed to have a list of telephone numbers. Messy, I thought, chucking it in the recycling bin. On my watch we have a clean computer room. Then I resumed looking for a volume control.

An hour later I had been over every inch of every device in the room, even the tape drives, and had also looked up 'crying', 'screaming', 'squealing', 'whistling', 'hooting' and as a measure of desperation, 'hissy fit' in every manual that we had. It was time to admit I was stuck, I realised sadly, and ask for help.

But I didn't have Frank's mobile number.

I thought briefly about leaving the computer room to get away from the noise; there didn't seem to be much point in staying, since I couldn't do anything about it. Then I thought about what Frank would say if he came back and found me in the tearoom ignoring a crisis. I read the log up to the point of failure. It all seemed perfectly normal, routine messages about jobs starting and finishing. There was no apparent cause for the problem. I looked underneath. There was an empty paper box. Well, at least I could keep the place neat. I took the box to the recycling bin and chucked it in.

Time passed. I started dismally out the window. The city looked happy and peaceful in the sunshine. Every time I glanced towards the rest of the office I could see Jane glaring at me. I knew that, in my place, Jane would not have had this problem. I examined the main CPU panel bit by bit, hoping for a clue to what to do next. What a wimp everyone would think I was, just sitting here and waiting for the problem to go away.

Then I saw the red button. It was large, about an inch and a half across, and it sat on the side of the panel looking masterful. A button that big must do something really important, I thought. I couldn't remember anyone ever using it or mentioning it. I peered at the little letters underneath the button.

They said 'EMERGENCY STOP'.

∞CHAPTER FOURTEEN∞

...nor can we expect that men of factious, peevish and perverse spirits should be satisfied with any thing that can be done...
Book of Common Prayer

It is not correct procedure to press the emergency stop button when the console typewriter has run out of paper. Goebbels explained this to me at some length:

'...You haven't done a stroke of work since you got here. You spend all day gossiping to Jane and expect the rest of us to carry you. If you ever bothered to pay the slightest attention to anything you're told you wouldn't have done such a stupid, wanton, destructive thing. Have you got any idea how many hours it's going to take Frank to get everything cleaned up and get the machine back up?

Do you even know how to change the paper on the console? Do you?'

'Well, not exactly –'

'If you ever bothered to grace us with your presence before eleven a.m. you might have found out. If you weren't always in Jane's office gossiping and going out for long lunches. I expect punctuality and discipline around here, young lady, and let me tell you –'

'Oh now, hold on. If you hadn't all been out boozing –'

Unfortunately that really made Goebbels hit the roof. If I'd thought he'd lost his temper before, I was wrong. The new explosion made Mount Vesuvius look like a dripping tap. In fact, Goebbels became totally incoherent, thereby justifying his nickname of Gobble-guts. What he did, actually, was gobble, very fast and loud, like a turkey with a South African accent. It sounded like this:

'...gobble gobble gobble lazy kaffirs gobble gobble gobble gobble gobble swanning in here like Lady Muck gobble gobble gobble gobble useless gobble gobble idle destructive gobble gobble gobble gobble pretty damn smartly.'

I didn't really know what to say to this.

'You people make me sick, do you hear me, sick, you think the world owes you a living. From now on I want you in on time every morning and you get exactly one hour for lunch, and by God don't let me catch you taking sixty-one minutes. If there is any repetition of today's effort you will be instantly dismissed. And I don't want to see you gossiping in the office, other people have work to do too, you don't seem to realise that. I'm going to be watching you every single minute of the day, and you'd just better bloody well pull your socks up, or you'll be out on your backside, do you understand?'

'...'

'Right. Get out of my sight.'

***

'Ha! Don't worry about it.' said Frank. 'An operator that hasn't done a bloody silly thing like that is an operator that's going to do a bloody silly thing like that some time in the future. When I was a trainee operator and got left alone in the machine room I staggered back from a liquid lunch and initialised the SYSRES pack. That was a hell of a lot more trouble to recover from than your effort, don't you worry.'

'Did you get the sack?'

Frank snorted. 'Not bloody likely. Course, I was pretty pissed, but you don't get the sack for a thing like that. Least, not unless you did it twice. See, it's their fault for leaving an inexperienced person in charge.'

'Goebbels didn't seem to think so.'

'Yeah, well he's got to explain to Mr Jacobs why all the users didn't have CICS for four hours. But when all's said and done, it was his decision to leave you there by yourself, and he's not going to like having to admit that to Mr Jacobs. He can't sack you for it, you're not worried about that, are you?'

'Well, yes, actually. He was sort of threatening to already. I mean, he can if he wants to, can't he?'

'This is 2010, Fiona, you can't just go around sacking people for no reason. You have to be able to show a good cause, and in your case he hasn't got one. You could sue the company for thousands if you were sacked unfairly, and Goebbels knows it. He was just blowing off steam. Leave him alone and he'll be right as rain tomorrow.'

Frank fished around in his desk drawers and produced a can of deodorant, which he thrust up under his jumper. He wriggled around, squirting both his armpits thoroughly.

'Don't you worry, kid. He's not gonna sack you.' Then he stumped off to help Goebbels explain the unexplainable.

All the same, I couldn't imagine Goebbels ever being right as rain.

***

'Just what you'd expect from that fucking arsehole,' said Jane.

***

'He's a bastard, he's always picking on you,' said Tony. 'I'd like to see him try that on with a man. Listen, why don't you come out with me tonight and I'll make you forget all about him?'

***

'Poor Fiona. Let's go over the pub,' said Steve and Adam.

***

'Christ, what a bastard,' said Patrick. 'I'd like to excommunicate the fucker.' We were in my room. Patrick had a copy of See, and was drawing moustaches on all the photographs of priests.

'You'd better not let Mum hear you using that language,' I said primly. 'Anyway, you couldn't excommunicate him, I'm sure he's a Satanist.'

Patrick started to give Bishop Huggins a goatee. 'You really ought to leave, Fiona, you can't stay working for a creep like that.'

I sighed. 'I wish I could, but who else would hire me? I've got to finish my training, then I can get a decent job. Never mind, I'm going onto afternoon shift next week, he won't be there most of the time.'

***

Afternoon shift started at three o'clock in the afternoon and went till eleven-thirty at night. I had been looking forward to it like anything because of getting away from Goebbels. I wasn't cherishing any hopes that absence would make him like me any better, but the prospect of only being around him for two hours a day, instead of eight, was like manna from heaven.

The first day, I made sure I got there at two-thirty, just so Goebbels couldn't accuse me of anything. I hung around in the machine room so he couldn't come near me. I could see him through the glass, glaring and bristling his beard. At three o'clock Steve arrived, and we went through the plan for the day. We would operate the machine as normal until five-thirty, when we would run the backups, which copied all the production files onto magnetic tapes. After that, the machine would be available for testing until ten o'clock, when we would bring down CICS, restore the production files from the backup tapes, and shut down for the night. We had to do all this because the company was too stingy to buy enough extra DASD to have a set of test files. Anyone who had testing to do had to come back to work after seven or so and do it in the evening, because of the risk of corrupting production files. They were not paid anything for doing this. Sometimes we could skip this step, if nobody was doing any testing, but at the moment, Geoff was doing something to the General Ledger Update, and would be coming back in after dinner to carry on with it.

Around four o'clock Goebbels rang up and barked at me and Steve to get into his office, slamming the phone down in my ear with his usual winning charm. We lined up at attention in front of his desk, braced for trouble. Nothing particular had gone wrong, but Gobble-guts was always trouble. If he felt like ripping into you and you hadn't done anything, he was quite capable of making something up.

'Penny's called in sick again. Claims she's got stomach trouble.'

Penny really had been having vicious stomach trouble for several weeks, and had seen the doctor about it a number of times. I opened my mouth to say something, but Steve kicked me sharply in the ankle. I closed my mouth, and concentrated on standing at attention on one foot.

'Now you two might think that because your supervisor is away it's going to be all beer and skittles.'

Working for Goebbels wasn't even tap water and tiddlywinks, but one hardly liked to say so.

'Now I will be reading every bit of tonight's log tomorrow morning, and if there is any hint of the slightest unusual thing happening, you'll both be out on your backsides. There's been far too much playing at funny buggers around here lately, and I'm perfectly well aware that you two are the ringleaders. You'd just better bloody well remember that you're both on probation. Now get out, the pair of you. You make me sick.'

As we left his office we made the mistake of looking at each other and were called back for another go.

'And you can cut out all that pulling faces and miming at each other. This is an office, not a bloody pantomime show.'

Dance of Chaos

Safely back in the computer room, we stood in front of the console with our backs carefully to the glass.

'What the hell was all that about?'

'Search me. The man's a maniac.'

The phone rang again. I picked it up on the first ring.

'Computer room.'

'What the hell are you doing standing around idling. This is an office not a bloody rest home. Get cracking and clean the bloody tape drives if you've got nothing else to do.' Click.

I got cracking and cleaned the bloody tape drives.

***

One of the really fun things about afternoon shift was the shredding. Each afternoon, all the discarded confidential documents from the various departments were delivered to us in huge sacks, and we fed them into the shredding machine during the evening. It was particularly good if you got a big continuous listing; we fed one end in and the shredder sucked in the whole listing at amazing speed, like a kid eating spaghetti. The other thing we did was draw Goebbels on the backs of the papers before feeding them in.

We were enjoying ourselves so much at this game that the time just flew by, and before we knew it, it was time to kick the programmers off the system and bring down CICS. Everything went smoothly, thank God; we were both uncomfortably aware of the going-over Goebbels would be giving the logs in the morning. Happily I started to set up for the final task of the night: restoring the production files from the five backup tapes.

'Steve?'

'Um?'

'Where are the backups?'

'I thought you were taking them.'

***

After spending some time in increasingly heated recriminations, during which Steve demonstrated his total incompetence as a man by failing to respond to tears, we rang Frank. He wasn't too pleased about being woken up at one a.m. (so what the fuck have you been doing for the last two hours?) but he did seem to be on top of the problem (well, I'll come in now and fix it, and you two can fucking well hang around and operate for me.) He said goodbye nicely (Fucking pisswits. Jesus!) and hung up.

It was a long night. There wasn't really anything for us to do, but Frank wouldn't let us go home. We had to stand around in the computer room while he swore and muttered and pounded his keyboard. Then he called us out for an interminable lecture about something called Dataset Forward Recovery and how lucky we were. I couldn't see it myself, my idea of luck is when something good happens, like winning a raffle or something. I suppose at least we had a good view out of the computer room window, you could see half Melbourne spread out like a kids' train set. I didn't think that was what Frank meant, though. What he probably meant, now that I thought of it, was that we were lucky we had him to fix everything so that we wouldn't have to tell Goebbels we'd forgotten to take the backups. I reflected happily on that thought all the way home in the taxi, and it comforted me as I fell asleep.

***

I was still tired when I arrived for afternoon shift the following day, but at least, I congratulated myself, Goebbels wouldn't be able to find fault with anything. I was even a quarter of an hour early, despite the previous night's extended effort.

It didn't really surprise me, though, that Goebbels was jumping up and down and bristling. He didn't really need a reason to be angry, he was like that all the time. When he saw me his eyes came out on stalks and his beard stood up on end.

'Get into my office!'

Ah well.

Steve was already in Goebbels' office, sitting hunched over and looking like a mouse after ten rounds with Moses. I couldn't imagine what Goebbels had found to bully him about, since our shift hadn't even started yet. I sat in the other chair while Goebbels slammed the door; he had to slam it several times, because it kept bouncing open again.

'Right. Now that you're both here I have something to say to you.' He wasn't shouting, I noticed with interest, but muttering intensely over the desk.

'Your performance last night was the most shocking piece of unprofessional behaviour I have ever seen. Let me tell you, if it weren't for the bloody decadent socialist customs in this country, you'd both be looking for another job this minute. As it is, I have to give you three written warnings before I can dismiss you. And don't start getting bloody cocky about it, either of you. Your work has consistently been of such a low standard that it won't give me any trouble at all to find reasons for another couple, believe me. Here are your written warnings about last night's effort, you are to read them and sign at the bottom. They will then be entered into your H. R. records.'

He handed us one each. I looked cautiously at mine. It was full of words like 'negligence' and 'attitude problem'. I wanted to ask what would happen if we refused to sign it, but my courage failed me at the last minute. We both signed our warnings.

'Right. Steve, get on with shift handover. Fiona, you stay back.'

Oh, shit. What else had I done? I searched my memory, but couldn't find anything he hadn't already shouted at me about.

'Right. This is your second written warning.' He handed me another piece of paper. I couldn't believe my ears, surely he couldn't give me more than one for the same thing? I looked at it. It was about last week's emergency stop.

'One more of these, just one more, and the next wrong move you make I'll have you out of here so fast you won't even touch the ground. Now get out.'

༂CHAPTER FIFTEEN༃

Thus were they stained with their own works: and went a-whoring with their own inventions.
Psalm 106:38

'Who was that on the phone?' Geoff had banged it down quite hard, which wasn't like him; he was usually so laid-back that you couldn't always tell if he was awake.

'Oh, just another one of Tony's birds. They all come crawling out of the woodwork when the warm weather hits.'

Several weeks had elapsed since the unfortunate incident in which I had received two written warnings in a single day. For some time I had lived every day in the expectation of immediate sacking, but as time went by, and Goebbels did nothing beyond his usual angry shouting fits, I came to think he'd made his point and I could safely forget it. Probably written warnings expired after a time, like the black marks the police put on your licence for speeding.

We were sitting in our new office, a tiny space just big enough to hold three desks jammed together. Or rather, two and a half desks, as I only had what appeared to be an old kitchen table rescued from the rubbish tip. I didn't have a proper chair, either, but an old dining-table type chair with one broken leg. The chair was much too low for the table, so that when I sat on it, the top of the table came to just below my chin. I could either kneel on the chair and lean over the table, which gave me a backache, or sit on the chair and hold my work on my lap, which gave me a crick in the neck, and was impossible anyway. Generally I sat on the floor.

None of us knew why we were now in this tiny partitioned-off island in the middle of the Sales department, three floors away from the rest of our own department. We generally assumed it was the start of some empire-building manoeuvre on Goebbels' part, but we were so grateful to be away from him that we didn't really care. Life had assumed a glorious calm, like a long sea voyage. This was chiefly because a new computer had been installed, and as so far Frank had not succeeded in getting CICS up for more than half an hour at a time, nobody could do any work. This was just as well, as we were averaging two dozen calls a day on our one shared phone, mostly all from Tony's various girlfriends, all of whom seemed to be pregnant, suicidal or both. Geoff and I spent our days reading novels, Facebooking, playing Dragons of Atlantis, going out for lunch, and taking tearful messages for Tony. Since he never bothered to read or reply to these messages, we gradually stopped bothering to write them down. Tony spent most of his time out of the office, doing God knew what.

'Hello, Tony Rockwell's answering service.'

'No, I'm afraid he's out of the office at the moment. May I take a message?'

'Right, right. I'll make sure he gets your message.'

Click. Ring.

'Your turn, Fiona.'

'Okay. Hello, Fiona speaking.'

'May I speak to Anthony, please.'

'I'm sorry, Tony isn't here just now. Any message?'

'Yes, could you just remind him he's got a two-year-old son.' Click.

'Right, that's it, Geoff. That is absolutely the last time I'm answering this phone.'

'What'd she say?'

'Oh, it was so embarrassing. She said to remind him he's got a two-year-old son. I suppose she must be his ex-wife. I felt terrible.'

The phone went again. It was Geoff's turn.

'Hello? Oh, they just hung up.'

'God, I hate it when people do that.'

Ring. Ring. I sat resolutely in my ghastly chair and wondered whose nerve would break first. Mine did.

'Hello?' I wondered what ghastly psychopath I was about to encounter this time.

'Fiona, you horrible bitch. Where the hell have you been?'

Dear God, it was Peter. I'd totally forgotten about him.

***

I hardly recognised Peter when I got to the Dead Rat. His hair was about half an inch long all over his head, and was marbled in shades of pastel pink, blue and mauve. His shirt was open nearly to the waist, and he was wearing a cubic zirconia necklace to match his cubic zirconia earrings.

'Dragon Woman!' he shrieked as I reached his table. 'Look at the new Pierre image, isn't it stunning?'

It was stunning alright. I was so stunned I couldn't think of anything to say.

'All those jealous queens in the office just hate it. They're so jealous, the bitches.'

'Um. Are you sure you're not going a bit far?'

'Oooh, I'm going too far and loving it!'

Sean arrived. 'Hello, Fiona. Listen, Peter, you'd better watch it. I saw Jacobs giving you a pretty strange look today. If I were you, I'd dye my hair back to a normal colour before I got the sack.'

'Oooh, don't YOU start, you bitchy queen. That old queer wouldn't dare sack me, I know too much about him. Anyway, who are you to talk, you're practically busting out of those pants. One deep breath and you'll be history, sweetheart.'

'Well at least they're men's pants, not like yours.'

'Ooooh, I'm such a poofter, aren't I?'

It was same old, same old. Everyone else was over any novelty that had ever attached to Peter's being gay (if he even really was, he was quite capable of making it up as an excuse for the weird outfits, or just for attention), but to him it was a new day every day. Idly I scanned the room for someone else I could go and talk to. Suddenly I froze.

'Hey, you two. Look who's here!'

It was Carl Jacobs, our Managing Director. He was leaning against the bar in a lordly way, surrounded at chest height by a group of sycophantically adoring salesmen. I watched in fascination as he went through his 'just one of the boys' routine. No doubt half of them would get pink slips on Monday. You'd think they'd learn. I looked guiltily at my watch; leaving the office at four o'clock probably had been pushing it a bit.

Peter and Sean gave him a cursory glance.

'Stupid old fart,' said Sean dismissively. 'Look, why don't we go on to Dirty Nellie's? This place sucks, I'm sick of it.'

'Yeah, let's blow this joint.' Snigger snigger. I realised suddenly that there comes a point when heavily emphasised double meanings lose their charm, and that Peter had long ago passed this point.

'It's too early for Nellie's, it's only six o'clock.'

'Oh shut up, Fiona, you're so depressing.'

God, the injustice of it all. I looked at my watch again. It really was only a few minutes after six.

'Look, you can't go to Dirty Nellie's at six o'clock, it's probably not even open. If it is it'll be full of salesmen. Why don't we have a couple more drinks here, have dinner somewhere and then go?'

Peter let out a screech of outrage. 'Dinner! I'm not wasting money on food, I had to pay my gas bill this week. I can hardly afford a couple of dim sims. I've only got fifty bucks left, and I've got to make that last till Thursday.'

'He's got a point, you know, Fiona. I'm not all that flush myself this week. Hey, you live around here, don't you? Why don't we go to your place for dinner?'

You would think any normal person would be delighted to entertain two friends for dinner. You would think that, wouldn't you? Except that in my case, there was a small problem. Several small problems, in fact. I spared a moment to congratulate myself on being sober enough to remember them all.

First, there was my mother. Of course, she knew I had friends at work, but she didn't actually know they were both men. Sean was no problem, he was very presentable, but Peter, especially with his new hairstyle, was guaranteed to provide material for a month of nagging and general hysteria. Then there was Patrick. He was at an impressionable age, and was already causing plenty of trouble, and I just didn't think it was a good idea bringing him and Peter into the same room; the potential for some kind of unholy synergy, or for a kind of behavioural critical mass being reached, was so enormous that I shrank from contemplating it.

These two problems were potentially solvable. My parents were going out tonight, so as long as we didn't get there until after they'd left, and were out again before they got home, the mother problem could be eliminated. As for Patrick, a sufficiently large cash bribe would certainly induce him to make himself scarce for the night. On second thoughts, all I had to do was threaten to blow the whistle on him about any of half a dozen things, and I could save my money. The third problem was far, far worse.

I didn't think I had actually told Peter and Sean that I still lived at home with my parents.

'Wake up, Fiona. I said, why don't we go to your place for dinner?'

I tried frantically to remember what I actually had told them about my living arrangements, but couldn't. Was it really obvious from looking at our house that a family lived there? I was afraid it was. On the other hand, I couldn't think of an excuse for not having them, and perhaps I would be able to think of something on the way there to explain the house. At least that would postpone my problem for a couple of hours.

'Sorry, I was just thinking what I've got in the fridge. Alright, we'll go to my place for dinner and then go on to Dirty Nellie's, okay?'

We had several more beers after that. I was playing for time; I knew my parents wouldn't leave the house until around seven-thirty. After three or four pots, Sean and Peter became less tedious, and soon I was having a great time, except for that niggling little worry about how I would get Patrick out of the house. Life took on a rosy glow, and even Goebbels didn't seem so bad. I was telling Sean and Peter about some of his wilder excesses when Carl Jacobs loomed over our table.

'Evening, Fiona. Sean.' Dear God, he actually knew our names. I thought about the four or five times I'd been introduced to him on his little tours of the department, wondering uneasily if he knew anything else.

'Peter, either get your hair back to a normal colour by Monday or don't bother coming back to work.' Jacobs strode off, looming as he went.

After that, we forgot about dinner and concentrated on getting seriously drunk, with rather notable success. By the time the pub closed at eleven, we were all having trouble walking straight, and had to hold onto each other to get to the tram stop. We went to my place, because it was closest, and had whisky.

We had fun on the tram. Peter got into a terrific argument with the tram driver and taunted him through the glass all the way home. It was a bit unfair, since everybody knows you're not allowed to stand on the seats and hang out of the windows, and all the driver had wanted was for Peter to sit down and behave himself, but then the tram driver couldn't speak English, so he wouldn't have been able to understand any of the awful stuff Peter was saying. Sean and I did, though, and were in fits all the way. It went something like this:

Peter: You motherless cretin. Your sister roots pigs for a living.

Tram conductor: blah blah blah (in a foreign

language).

Peter: Oooooh! Eat dirt and die, pus-bucket.

They kept this up until I suddenly noticed our house.

'Shit! That's our house! Quick, get off!'

Unfortunately the tram driver was offended with us, and spitefully let the tram go on for another two stops. None of us was in a condition to pull the cord, we kept grabbing for it and missing, and Peter fell over and bruised his knee. He kept on about it all the way back to the house, and it was only with the greatest difficulty that Sean and I restrained him from taking off his pants to show us his injury.

I had a bit of trouble getting my key into the keyhole, but I eventually got the door open, and we all cascaded into the hall. I looked carefully at my watch; it seemed to be nearly midnight, but with any luck at all my parents would have come home and gone straight to bed.

'Ssssssh!'

'Why?' screeched Peter. 'Are you afraid we'll wake up your secret lover? I know you've got one stashed in here somewhere.' He opened the hall closet.

'Well, he's not in there. Come out, come out, wherever you are!' He skipped gaily off down the hall, chanting. Sean started to giggle, and started up the stairs. I wondered frantically which one to follow.

'Shush, shut up, for Christ's sake, you'll wake the neighbours.'

'Oh my God! It's the creature from the Black Lagoon!' Sean erupted back down the stairs, howling, with Moses in hot pursuit, all fluffed up and swiping playfully at his ankles. 'Quick, Fiona, put the light on. There's a monster chasing me!'

'It's already on, you twit. Will you shut up?'

Peter came mincing back down the hall, bellowing in his great booming baritone. 'Where is he, Fiona? I bet you haven't got a lover at all. I bet any minute I'll open one of these doors and find a big fucking DILDO!'

He had opened the door to the sitting room as he spoke. The light was on in there, and so I could see inside quite clearly. My parents, and Father Simpson, were poised around the coffee table, frozen in motion like cattle surprised in someone's garden. Attracted by the silence, Sean came bustling over. He hesitated for only a split second, and made a bee-line for the vicar.

'Oh, good evening, you must be Mrs MacDougall. Fiona's told us so much about you.' He turned to my mother. 'And this must be little Patrick.'

☙CHAPTER SIXTEEN☙

The words of his mouth were softer than butter, having war in his heart: his words were smoother than oil, and yet be they very swords.
                                      Psalm 55:22

After turning up drunk in front of Father Simpson, there was no way I was going to get out of going to church on Sunday morning. Sulking and grumbling, Patrick and I crouched in the back of the car wearing unspeakable clothes chosen, and no doubt disinfected, by our mother, who was not currently speaking to either of us, or at least not in affectionate terms; as always, she had plenty to say about hygiene.

'Hey, Patrick. D'you think we could persuade her that churches are unhygienic?'

'Shit, no.' Patrick glared out of the window. He

was sulking even more than I was, because before our mother had forced him into a tie and frog-marched him out to the car, he'd been planning to spend the day in the city with some of his friends. I tried to think of something to say to cheer him up.

'Well, it doesn't go for more than an hour and a half, does it? We should be out by eleven-thirty.'

'Don't you believe it. Simpson's got one of his bloody airhead theological mates coming as a guest preacher. He was on about him for hours the other night. Simpson reckons he's God's gift.'

'God's gift to who?'

'To whom, Fiona.'

Bloody hell, a father never sleeps. I lowered my voice to a whisper.

'God's gift to whom?'

'God, I suppose. Who cares?'

'Shit. Guest preachers go on for ever.'

***

Sunk in boredom, I slouched in the pew, reading the list of people you're not allowed to marry. Who'd want to, I wondered for the kerzillionth time. I nudged Patrick.

'Hey, imagine marrying your grandmother's brother.'

'Shut up, Fiona.'

'No, really, look at this, look, you must be allowed to marry your grandmother's brother. You can't marry your granny, but you can marry her brother or sister. How sick is that?'

'Shut up, Fiona.'

'Lucky Gran was an only child.'

'Shut up, Fiona.'

'You can't marry your aunt or uncle, though. But you can in real life, Tim told me. I suppose it'd have to be a civil ceremony.'

'What d'you mean, you can in real life? How else could you marry someone?'

'I mean, it's not against the law. Tim told me, you're legally allowed to marry your aunt or uncle.'

'No way! So you could marry Uncle Mike?'

'EEEEWWWWWW!'

At this point, several people, including both parents, turned around to look at me reprovingly.

'Shut up, Fiona,' said Patrick, whose fault it was.

Why did everyone always blame me for everything, I wondered. Even my own brother was against me. God, it was a long service. We already seemed to have been there for hours, and they were only up to the Gloria. Father Simpson must have pulled out all the stops to impress his guest. I wondered vaguely where he was.

'Psst. Patrick, where's the other priest?'

'Shut up, Fiona.'

We sat down for the readings. I was pleased to notice that the first one was about me, although I've never been sure that I'd be totally above rubies if someone offered me a really big one. Emeralds are nicer with red hair, though. I peered around the sanctuary, looking for the visiting priest. He didn't seem to be there. Perhaps he hadn't come. Then Father Simpson would have to preach after all, and he wouldn't have prepared anything, so it would be really short.

'Patrick. D'you reckon he's not going to turn up?'

'God, Fiona. That's him over on the left side.'

'What's he all in white for? Everyone else is

wearing green robes.'

'God, Fiona. He's a Dominican, that's what they wear.'

'Aren't they Roman Catholic?'

'Sssssssh!' Mrs Davies turned round from the pew in front. 'You young people have got no respect,' she boomed out in a massive stage whisper, causing Father Simpson to jump furtively and lose his place in the Gospel.

***

We remained standing as Father Simpson conducted the Dominican to the pulpit. Heavens, I thought, he can't be all that stunning if he can't even find the pulpit by himself. Then he switched on the pulpit light, and I got a good look at him.

'My God, he's gorgeous!'

'Shit! That's bloody Joe Morelli. He's one of the teachers at St B's.'

'He's divine! I want to go back to school!'

'God, Fiona, will you shut up?' Patrick's mood didn't seem to be improving. I thought this was a bit unfair, considering why we were there at all.

'Shut up yourself. We're only stuck here

because of your filthy stick books.'

We seemed to have been waiting for rather a long time. I took another look at the Dominican. He looked uncomfortable, as though he had a spider crawling up his robes. I wondered why he didn't get on with it. Perhaps he was waiting for total silence. A minute passed, or several hours. I started to develop a cramp in my left foot. I nudged Patrick again.

'Why doesn't he start?'

'Dunno. He looks like he's waiting for something.'

The congregation was getting restive. Feet shuffled, cellophane rattled, a few people coughed. The Dominican's perfect marble features seemed a few shades paler.

'Oh, shit.' Patrick started giggling.

'What? Come on, what?'

'Roman Catholics don't bless the congregation at the beginning of the sermon. He's waiting for us to sit down!'

I got the giggles myself.

'We'd better sit down, then other people

might.'

'No way, it's funnier like this.'

Patrick burst into a fresh explosion. I poked him in the ribs again.

'Shut up, everyone's looking at us.'

'They might as well, looks like they're not getting a sermon.'

Just then our father cleared his throat loudly, and sat down. Bit by bit the congregation followed his example, some of the older and less flexible people pointedly crossing themselves as they did so.

I have never seen anyone look so relieved as the Dominican did when we all finally sat down. You could see all the tension drain out of him. The sermon wasn't bad either, quite hot stuff, actually. It was all about the value of sin in one's spiritual life. I couldn't quite follow all of it, because I kept getting sidetracked, what with the priest being such a total spunkrat, but apparently you can't be really good unless you've committed lots of sins and experienced God's redeeming grace. Bugger, I thought. I've hardly ever done anything bad. I wondered if the Dominican would be interested in helping me commit a really big one.

The rest of the service was quite an anticlimax.

***

After Mass, we all went into the church hall for tea and sherry. I generally lurk in a corner at these things, desperately trying to avoid catching anyone's eye in case I get press-ganged into fêtes or spiritual encounter groups, but today I had a Higher Purpose.

The Dominican was even better close up.

'Hello, I'm Fiona. Welcome to St Arnulf the Lesser.' What a bloody silly name for a church, I thought for the kerzillionth time. Why not just call it St Arnulf the Utterly Too Trivial To Be Worth Mentioning? What happened to St Arnulf the greater, anyway? Perhaps the Anglican church thought he was a bit ostentatious. I hoped I had struck the right note with the Dominican, informal but not too casual. In his pristine white robes, he didn't look as if he'd ever heard the word casual. They'd have been even better in black velvet, though, I thought. Although velvet attracts a lot of cat hairs. You'd think if the cat was the same colour as the clothes that they wouldn't show, but they always do.

I realised with a guilty start that the Dominican had been saying something, and was now waiting for a reply. The poor man, it seemed to be his lot in life to be always waiting for a response from other people, and not getting it. I settled for my all-purpose answer.

'Yes, isn't it?'

That seemed to satisfy him, anyway. I hoped I hadn't agreed to anything too stupid.

'My little brother wants to join your order, you know. That's him over there, in the blue shirt.'

'How nice. He looks very young, though.'

'Fourteen next June. That's not too young, is it?'

'Well, we usually like people to be around twenty-one or so.'

'Patrick's actually very mature for his age. He's always reading –' I caught myself just in time, '– the Bible, and Lives of the Saints, and all stuff like that.'

'Yes, well, there is a bit more to it than that. Actually. You seem very keen to get rid of your brother.'

'Oh, no, it's just that he's so frightfully keen on the Dominicans. I just want him to be happy.' I was starting to sound fake even to myself. Fluttering my eyelashes was not having the usual effect, either. I wished I'd taken the time for a second coat of mascara.

'I'm surprised he hasn't spoken to me about it himself.'

'Well, you see he's convinced himself he couldn't get into your order, apparently it's got incredibly high standards, so he just won't talk to anybody or do anything about it.'

'I shouldn't concern myself too much, if I were you. We get a lot of enquiries from young boys; generally they get a bit older, discover girls, and we never hear from them again.'

'Oh, I'm sure that won't happen with Patrick. He's not a bit interested in girls.' Just like you, I thought sourly. I was getting sick of the Dominican; here I was going to all this trouble to chat him up, and he was behaving as if I were one of the old church ladies, for God's sake. How dare he not fancy me? I wondered how I could extricate myself from this boring conversation. Aha, I thought.

'Come and I'll introduce you to him. He'll be thrilled, he was raving about your sermon.'

The Dominican looked modestly gratified, as presumably his order considered appropriate to the situation. I could just imagine the entry in their

Procedure Manual: Upon receiving a compliment, the Dominican shall assume an air of modest gratification. He is under no circumstances to leap into the air and click his heels.

Unfortunately, whatever procedure manual my brother was operating out of was not quite so suave. As he saw us approaching, his face assumed an expression of naked terror, like a cornered rat.

'Ah, Father Morelli! I want you to meet young Patrick MacDougall, a very keen member of our little flock. We believe he may have a vocation...'

At the sight of Father Simpson, the Dominican actually became quite animated. They moved off together, robes flapping like great bats. I heaved a sigh of relief and headed for the sherry.

***

Patrick was not very pleased with me. I heard about it all the way home.

'...an utter bloody bitch. You get the hots for some dreary bloody priest and then you expect me to –'

'Don't be disgusting!'

'Well, what else could you call it? I saw you letching all over him, batting your false eyelashes and undoing another button of your shirt.'

This remark hurt me more than anything.

'My eyelashes are not false, you take that back.'

'Bloody Simpson had Morelli all convinced that I want to go in the bloody Dominicans. Jesus. They're a celibate order, for Christ's sake. He wants me to go to their stupid monastery for some drippy bloody encounter weekend or something. How the hell am I going to get out of that? He teaches at St B's, for God's sake, it's not like I can avoid him, I've got him for Divinity.'

'Serves you right. If it wasn't for you I wouldn't have got stuck going to church all the time anyway. I already got you out of one lot of trouble with those stick books. Why can't you be normal, play football or something?'

'Christ, you call that getting me out of trouble, all that with bloody Harvey?'

'It worked, didn't it?'

'Christ.'

CHAPTER SEVENTEEN

Blessed is the man that hath not walked in the counsel of the ungodly, nor stood in the way of sinners: and hath not sat in the seat of the scornful.
Psalm 1:1

I knew it was going to be a bad day as soon as I got into the building and saw Peter with his hair unevenly dyed black. I just knew it.

As I crossed the foyer I had an uneasy sense of foreboding, even more than was usual on Monday mornings. I racked my brains, but couldn't think of anything bad that I had done, or anything necessary that I had failed to do. No, my conscience was clear for once. I got into the lift in a more relaxed frame of mind.

This relaxed frame of mind lasted all the way up in the lift. Then it left, without even saying goodbye. Our office was gone. I couldn't believe it. Where there had been a grotty little corral of partitions enclosing our bashed-up old furniture, there was now a grotty little expanse of empty floor. I wandered around in circles for a while, and then decided to go upstairs and see if the computer had gone, too.

The computer was still there; so were Frank and Jane. They were screaming at each other. There was no sign of Goebbels. I waited for a break in the action. After a while, I decided I'd better interrupt.

'Um, excuse me...'

Both Frank and Jane whirled around, snarling. Perhaps interrupting hadn't been such a good idea.

'...our office seems to have, um, disappeared.'

Jane sneered. 'Oh dear, Fiona. How lucky for you that I always carry a spare office in my handbag. Jesus.' She raised her eyes to heaven, in that way she had.

I didn't know what to say. If anyone had a spare office in their handbag, it would be Jane.

'God, Fiona. Down the hall, where Acme Finance used to be.'

I could hear them resume screaming as I closed

the door.

The offices at the other end of the hall were a shambles. It looked as if the finance company had left in a hurry; there were cardboard boxes all over the place, and a few desks were scattered at random in the middle of the floor; there didn't seem to be any chairs. It was a nice big office, though, with plenty of natural light, and a proper tearoom in one corner, with little round tables. The coffee machine wasn't any better, though; just the standard café bar with the standard dead silverfish floating in the water tank. Geoff and Tony were squatting on the floor in a corner, sniggering over something they'd found in one of the boxes.

'What've you got there?'

'Aha, it's not for your chaste young eyes, Fiona.'

'Bullshit. Gimme that.' I snatched the magazine, then wished I hadn't. Did people really do things like that, and with pigs? I felt faint.

Just then Goebbels came roaring in, foaming at the mouth. When he saw me, his eyeballs nearly popped out. For a second I thought he was going to have a stroke, but it was just a beautiful dream. Then he noticed the magazine, which I was still clutching in nerveless fingers, and snatched it out of my hand.

'So this is what you spend your time on when I'm not here. Reading some trashy women's magazine.' He glanced down and froze, I suppose he'd noticed the pig. My life flashed before my eyes. He thrust the magazine at me with an expression of utter contempt, turned on his heel and strode off.

Geoff and Tony were both beside themselves with hysteria. Personally, I couldn't see what was funny about it. I had just been branded a deviate of the blackest stamp, a filthy red-eyed pervert, what was so amusing about that? God, I could probably be prosecuted just for having seen something like that. I imagined spending the rest of my life in a maximum security prison, shunned by all the other inmates, who would mutter sullen insults out of the sides of their mouths as they passed me in the exercise yard. That's if I wasn't in solitary confinement. Papillon was in solitary, after all, and all he did was kill a few people. I wondered if I could ever eat a cockroach, and decided I would starve to death first. I was almost certain I wouldn't be able to take Moses to prison with me, either. Perhaps I should leave the country immediately, before the Vice Squad got on my trail. Cloaked and masked, I would be rowed out to a waiting frigate at dead of night and proceed to the French coast, where I would live it up in Paris in satin knee breeches, returning occasionally to hold up a few coaches. Then I remembered that they don't have coaches or satin knee breeches any more.

While I remained sunk in my gloomy reverie, Tony had grabbed the best spot for his desk. Not that it looked very comfortable sitting right in front of what was presumably going to be Goebbels' office, but it had a terribly strong implication of being second in command which I didn't like to see. Geoff had taken the only other decent position. I was left with the spot facing directly into Goebbels' new office, which was glass from the waist up. Terrific, I thought. Imagine seeing both of them every time I look up. Especially knowing all the time that Gobble-Guts thinks I'm a pervert. I wondered if I could get another job, then remembered that I'd have to give Goebbels as a reference. God, I was stuck in this job until he retired, or dropped dead or something. I stood behind my new desk, wondering what to do next. I didn't even have a chair to sit in. I didn't have any of my stuff from my old desk, either, because all our furniture from last week's office had mysteriously vanished. I wondered where all the stuff had come from that Tony and Geoff were now busily loading into their desks.

Presently I had a brainwave, and sneaked off to

the stationery store, where I loaded up with everything I could think of; fortunately no one was around. On the way back I passed a pile of discarded printouts, so I grabbed a couple of nice big thick ones. By the time I had spread it all around my new desk, which I had to admit was beautiful, a huge L-shaped one in lovely pale pine, you couldn't tell I wasn't hard at work. Except for not having a chair, of course. The really annoying thing was that, while I'd been looting the stationery cupboard, those two sleazy creatures had got chairs from somewhere. I suddenly realised how much I hated them both. I just knew that if I asked them where they'd got the chairs and other gear from, they'd be making patronising jokes at my expense for the rest of the day, if not the week. Sexist creeps. I had to get a chair from somewhere.

***

The twelfth floor of our building was executive country. I'd never been there before. It all seemed very quiet and spacious, the carpet was nicer, too, and even the occasional ringing telephone had a muted, discreet sound, and could I smell... yes indeed; in a little alcove near the lifts was a real espresso machine! I made myself a cup, and prowled around a bit, doing my best to look inconspicuous, although I really needn't have bothered; there was hardly anyone around.

Presumably all the executives were out playing golf.

I found what I wanted in the boardroom. There were dozens of chairs, well a lot, anyway, around the table, nice big squashy-looking ones. I was about to grab one and race back to my desk when I noticed the one at the far end. It was a king, an emperor, among chairs, with a great high back that loomed above the rest of the furniture and dominated the whole room. I took a closer look. Yes, it was, real leather upholstery. I sat in it and leaned back, it even reclined. It was so big you could just about curl up and take a nap in it. This is the one, I thought. And even better, no one would even miss it, since it didn't match the rest of the chairs in there.

My new chair was surprisingly light. I had no trouble at all getting it down in the lift.

***

Patrick was still incredibly cross with me when I got home. Apparently Father Morelli had rung up to confirm that he was going on some training weekend thing for boys who wanted to be priests, and it was All My Fault. I often think it's unfair that I get the blame for so many things; after all, I don't run the world. I had gone totally off Father Morelli. Why did he have to come interfering in my life, causing trouble and making my brother hate me? I curled up on the sofa with Moses and racked my brains for a solution. Some time passed.

'Patrick?'

'What?'

'I'm sorry, I just can't see any way out of it. You'll just have to be a priest.'

'Fiona, I am not going to be a priest. No way. You'll just have to think of something, I can't keep this up much longer. Jesus, all this Latin and crap, and this bloody sandal-wearing loser weekend thing, there's no way I'm going on that.'

'You might enjoy it. God, I wish that Joe Morelli would ask me away for the weekend.'

'The kind of weekend you'd like to go away for, Fiona, is hardly what I'll be getting up at bloody Saint Dominic House, or whatever it's called.' Funny how he could sound so much like our father. 'I heard all about these deals from Tony DiAngelo. All these little R. C. jerks get together and talk about their wet dreams and play the guitar. Jesus.'

'Don't you talk to me about wet dreams, you little pervert. You wouldn't be having to worry about wet dreams if you didn't read all those filthy stick books all the time. That's what got you into this mess in the first place. And anyway, you were the one who started it, about being a priest, when Miss Peemoller rang up Mum. So it's all your own fault.'

'Shit.'

***

It took several days to get settled into our new office. First there were no connections for our computers, then there were no tables to put the computers on. Even though there were five computers and only three of us, Goebbels refused to allow us each to have one on our desks in the normal way. He seemed to feel that we would be corrupted by such sinful luxury, and lie about eating chocolates all day. Then, when we had got all the computers neatly installed on a line of tables down one side of the office, we discovered that there were no powerpoints to plug them into. By the time Goebbels had exhausted himself screaming at Frank, and Frank had exhausted himself screaming at Jane, and Jane, who had for some reason not accompanied the rest of us into the new premises, but remained with Frank in solitary splendour at the other end of the building, had shouted herself hoarse letting off steam in the ladies' room (which, we must remember, is a Separate Facility) we were all nervous wrecks, jumping at our own shadows and nicking off to the Dead Rat every lunchtime.

I was more of a nervous wreck than anyone, because as well as being naturally sensitive, I kept going home to the Cold War, with Patrick glaring and sulking from behind every corner, and my mother, who also seemed to be stressed, doing extreme Parkour-type cleaning activities such as disinfecting the downpipes and polishing the television antenna, and as if this weren't enough to cope with, Moses developed a Neurotic Complex, and started spraying in the bathroom every evening at precisely seven-fifteen. It cost me a fortune for scent so our mother wouldn't find out.

❧CHAPTER EIGHTEEN☙

Why do the heathen so furiously rage together: and why do the people imagine a vain thing?
Psalm 2:1

The one good thing about our new office, apart from the nicer furniture, was that none of Tony's girlfriends had our new direct telephone number. Apart from that, it was dreadful. I had finished all the stupid trainee programs that no one would ever use, and had been assigned to real work. At first this was quite exciting, but after the third program I realised they were all exactly the same, printout formatting programs to be run at the end of jobstreams, after the interesting stuff had all happened. I had a look at what Geoff and Tony were doing. It looked much more exciting. The next time I went to Goebbels for more work I brought this up, which was a mistake.

'I'm sick of these print programs, they're all the same. Why can't I do one of the updates?'

'You can learn to do a good job on the print programs first,' said Goebbels, contorting his face horribly. He wasn't shouting, so evidently his strange facial expression was meant to be a smile. It was the first time I'd ever seen him in anything approaching a good mood, so I thought I could probably persuade him to see things my way; most people generally do after a while.

'I already did a good job on three of them. What's the difference if I do twenty more? It's not fair, Geoff's been doing all the interesting stuff and I get stuck with all the print programs. He's only been here a couple of weeks longer than me, you know.'

Goebbels' face darkened with rage, bringing him back to his normal appearance.

'Geoff has applied himself, he has a good attitude. He took all the update programs home and studied them over the long weekend. He doesn't swan in here at half past nine and vanish out the door at four-thirty, or spend two hours painting his nails every lunch time. I don't want to hear any more complaints out of you, young lady. When you can do a fast accurate job on one of these print modules, we'll see about something more challenging, but the way you've been going that's going to be a hell of a long time. Now take this spec and come back and see me when you've read it thoroughly.'

***

'Bloody sexist pig,' said Jane. 'It's only because you're a woman.'

'I'm afraid he's right, Fiona,' said Frank. 'You made a right balls-up of the last one.'

This is how I knew Frank was a sexist too.

***

'Shit, Fiona,' said Patrick, gobbling the last Mint Slice. 'I don't know why you don't leave. It's not like you're the chairman of the board or anything, I mean it sounds even worse than your old job, and you're not getting paid any more, are you?'

'Because it's a career opportunity, moron. In a few years' time I'll be making squillions, and I won't give Gobble-guts the time of day. Do you realise you've just scoffed a whole packet of those things?'

'So what, I don't have a weight problem like some people.'

'You're going to have a hell of a zit problem in

a couple of days. Heard from Joe Morelli lately?'

'Bitch.'

***

I had the last laugh, because Patrick was going on his encounter weekend thingy at the end of the week, and was getting more and more depressed about it. Our mother, on the other hand, was getting more and more enthusiastic; she bought Patrick new underwear to take on the camp, and drifted about the house humming the Angelus all day.

'Shit, Fiona, what am I going to do? I can't let anyone see me wearing these fucking things.'

These fucking things were y-front underpants, with little green stripes around the top, the kind you see old men buying in Target.

'Honestly, Patrick, your language is getting so bad. I don't know what kind of example you're going to set your parishioners one day.'

He threw the underpants at me.

***

Back at the office, I comforted myself by reflecting that Patrick was far worse off than I was. At least I had nice underwear. I concentrated on the latest print program, determined to produce a miracle of speed and accuracy. As usual, my concentration was disturbed by angry shouting from Goebbels' office. I tried to tune it out, but there was something different about the quality of the shouting that I couldn't quite place. I looked up.

The difference was that there were two people shouting, instead of one shouting and one cringing, or one shouting into the telephone. The other person was Frank. I watched, interested, as they both got louder and redder in the face. Perhaps Frank might win the argument; he'd certainly given Jane a good run for her money the other day, and most people wouldn't take her on. I thought what a pity it was that I was too far away to hear the words. I couldn't get any closer, either, without Goebbels seeing me. Then I had a brilliant idea. Picking up the compilation listing I was working on, I walked confidently over to Tony's desk and leant over it with the listing, carefully keeping my back to the glass partition.

'Tony, could you give me a hand with this?' I asked loudly. 'What's going on in there?' I whispered.

'They're having an argument about buying more DASD. Frank reckons we need another string, and Goebbels doesn't want to blow his budget. Stupid prick,' said Tony quietly, pointing helpfully to the listing.

'How come Goebbels even bothers to argue with him? He's the boss.'

'Goebbels isn't a systems programmer, so he doesn't quite have the confidence in the technical areas to tell Frank to shove off. He'll have to give in in the end, he's just putting up a show. Stupid prick.'

I thought about this.

'Why will he have to give in?'

'Because Frank knows what he's talking about and Goebbels doesn't, his background's in systems analysis and he doesn't know a performance problem from his own dick.' He sniggered. 'Come to think of it, there probably isn't all that much difference.'

Just then Frank came slamming out and stormed off down the corridor, so I had to gather up my listing and go back to my own desk. But the conversation stayed in my mind. A few hours later, when he'd had time to cool down, I went to see Frank.

'Frank?'

'Yeah, what?'

'How did you get to be a systems programmer?'

'Punishment for my sins. Why d'you ask?'

'I want to be one. Is there a course I could do, or something?'

Frank threw back his head and howled with laughter.

***

'What the hell's a systems programmer?' asked Patrick scornfully. 'Listen, Fiona, you've got to help me, how can I get rid of this big zit before Friday?'

'God, Patrick, I'm trying to make a big career decision here, and all you can do is rave on about your spots. Why'd you eat all those chocolate biscuits if you care so much about zits, it's not as if I didn't warn you.'

'Come on, Fi. I can't go on this camp with a huge zit on my chin.'

'Oh well, try taking vitamin B and drinking lots of water.'

'I don't like taking vitamin B, it makes my pee smell funny.'

'Your pee doesn't exactly smell like roses anyway, as we all know since you never bother to flush the loo.'

'Well at least it stops your filthy cat drinking the water. I hate it when he does that, it's disgusting. At night I can hear him lapping and slurping, it makes me want to puke.'

It was true that Moses did have an unfortunate habit of drinking the lavatory water, suspending himself by his back feet on the seat and bracing his front feet on the insides of the bowl. I had no idea how to stop him, so I had concentrated on trying to make sure our mother didn't find out.

'You're just jealous,' I retorted feebly. 'You wish you had an amazing cat like Moses.'

'Oh come on, Fi, please pretty please, give me some of that stuff in the yellow tube, it worked like anything last time. Come on, it's your fault I'm going on this wankers' picnic anyway.'

'If I do, you've got to do my ironing this week.'

'I'll do your bloody ironing, just give me the stuff quick, before it's too late for it to work in time.'

As I went for the Yardley's I felt quite pleased

with myself. Mercilessly instructed by our mother at ten, Patrick irons beautifully.

All this wrangling and bargaining didn't help me solve my career problem, however. I decided to have another go at Frank on Monday.

***

I worked mightily for the rest of the week, determined to make a good impression on both Goebbels and Frank. I got in by nine every morning and only took an hour for lunch, except for Thursday when I had to go shopping. By Friday I was exhausted, but I didn't notice Gobble-guts beaming at me or chucking compliments about. I finally finished testing the latest print program about four o'clock, but Goebbels just grunted and handed me another spec exactly the same as the last one, not even commenting on my new hairstyle, or the fact that I'd finished it in less than a week. I dreamed of a day when I'd be rich and famous, and Goebbels would come crawling to me, begging for a job. 'I'm afraid you'll have to lift your game, Goebbels, if you want to work for me. We don't tolerate second-rate work at MacDougall Associates,' I said to him.

'What!' barked Goebbels. In my enthusiasm for my vision, I must have spoken aloud.

'Oh, nothing, I was just thinking about how I'd approach this program.'

'No doubt you'll approach it the same way you approach everything else I give you to do, by sitting on your backside and doing bloody nothing all week.'

My blood boiled at the injustice of it.

'I finished that last program in four and a half days!'

'It would have taken any decent programmer about two hours, and I bet it's full of errors. Get out of my sight, you make me sick.'

***

'Stupid prick,' said Tony. 'Coming over the pub tonight?'

'Silly bloody arsehole,' said Geoff. 'Going over the road later?'

'Fucking sexist racist bigot bastard,' said Jane. 'Let's go and get pissed.'

So we did.

***

Patrick had already left when I got home. A

note on my pillow said,

'Zit stuff worked wish me luck KTHXBAI.'

***

I dreamed I was an intergalactic space general, conquering worlds populated by huge green draconian creatures, and other worlds populated by small hairy men with beady eyes.

'We will give no quarter,' I told my troops sternly. 'All prisoners are to be shot immediately.'

'A message for you, General MacDougall,' smarmed an obsequious aide de camp, proffering it on a silver tray. I tore open the envelope.

'You have been awarded the Military Cross Extraordinaire with three moons. Proceed at once to Earth for investiture at 0823700 hours gal. std.'

I dropped the message back onto the tray.

'What are these empty honours to me when there are worlds to be conquered? Forward into the heart of the enemy stronghold!'

But what was this? I seemed to hear screams from the lower decks, as though an insurrection were in progress.

'Mutiny!' I shouted, leaping out of bed.

'Officer of the watch, take command!' I raced for the transmat station.

***

I skidded to a halt at the top of the stairs, noting with interest that an insurrection did indeed seem to be in progress. The hall contained Father Morelli, looking extremely Draconian, Patrick, scowling and shuffling his feet, and our mother, swooning. I came the rest of the way down the stairs, wishing I had on my silk pyjamas instead of a pair of Patrick's old flannel ones, and that I didn't have such a crashing hangover.

'Hello, Father Morelli. How nice to see you again. Did you all have a lovely weekend?'

Morelli looked at me with the first sign of genuine interest I'd ever seen. Unfortunately, his next words dispelled for ever any illusions I might have had about how ravishing I looked in Patrick's old pyjamas.

'Miss MacDougall, it may have escaped your notice that it is still Saturday morning,' he remarked frostily, narrowing his beautiful eyes. 'If we might have a word in private, Mrs MacDougall?'

My mother trembled and opened the sitting room door. Morelli trod silently inside, like a cat walking through wet grass. Even his rigid back practically shouted the fact that he hated the sight of our whole family.

I jerked my head at Patrick. Silently we crept upstairs. In my room, Moses jumped off the bed and started sniffing Patrick with great interest, as though he'd been rolling in something funny. Patrick was shivering, as if he'd been out in the rain all night.

'What on earth's the matter? How come you're back already?'

Patrick sank onto my bed, moaning, and buried his face in his hands.

'Come on, tell me. What happened? Are you okay?'

'Jesus, it was terrible. I can't talk about it.'

Suddenly it all fell into place. No wonder Morelli hadn't been interested in me.

'Did he hit on you?'

'Oh, for Christ's sake, Fiona. Is that all you ever think about? Well, you can take it from me that Joe Morelli definitely has no sexual urges, he's far too pure and holy for that. I heard about it all the way back.'

'Patrick! Surely you didn't hit on him? I mean, I know he's gorgeous, but really –'

'Just stop it, okay? Just shut up.'

I couldn't believe it. I'd never seen Patrick this upset, and considering some of the things he'd been caught doing over the years, I'd had rather the impression that he couldn't be this upset by anything. I had to find out what had happened.

'Look, you stay here and calm down, I'll go and make you some hot milk. Get into bed, you look frozen.'

Patrick rolled into bed and buried his face in the pillow.

Silently I crept downstairs, carefully avoiding all the creaky ones.

❧CHAPTER NINETEEN☙

They gaped upon me with their mouths, and said: Fie on thee, fie on thee, we saw it with our eyes.
Psalm 35:21

The door to the sitting room was firmly closed. I didn't dare open it a crack; somehow I knew that Morelli's bat-like ears would detect even the faintest trace of movement. Luckily our house is quite old, and still has keyholes in all the doors. Also luckily, my mother would rather perish in fire and brimstone than let any of these keyholes get clogged up with dust. More than once I've discovered her early in the morning, cleaning inside them with cotton buds and dental floss.

Through the keyhole I had a perfect view of Morelli standing majestically in front of the fireplace. He was livid with rage; vertical lines had appeared at the sides of his mouth, and his whole body was rigid with tension. I could see his nostrils flaring as he breathed, his lips tightly compressed. My mother was speaking, quietly. I wished she weren't quite so ladylike, I couldn't hear a thing. I pressed my ear to the keyhole and held my breath.

The calm, level tones of the Dominican floated through. God, I thought, he must have incredible self-control, to look like that and still sound so calm.

'Mrs MacDougall, all this is beside the point. I'm sure you will appreciate that I simply cannot have this kind of thing happening on our premises. I am, after all, accountable to other parents as well. I could not do otherwise than remove your son immediately. What steps you choose to take are, of course, your own affair; personally, I would recommend counselling.'

I heard my mother again, faintly.

'Well, I think it's only fair to tell you, Mrs MacDougall, that I have yet to see any sign of a genuine vocation in young Patrick.'

A long pause while my mother spoke at length. I looked through again and noticed that Father Morelli seemed to be getting a headache. My mother sometimes has that effect on people.

'Mrs MacDougall, I can assure you that whatever cock and bull story Patrick may have foisted on you and his unfortunate teacher in the past, on this occasion he was caught in the very act, not only of reading this material, but of showing it to the other boys. Now if we are to have any credibility at all as a retreat centre for young boys, this kind of thing absolutely cannot be tolerated. And as for all this about a religious vocation, I would suggest that Patrick might try to raise the standard of his behaviour to something approaching the norm before he starts worrying about entering a state of perfection. Good morning.'

Stunned by the revealed facts, the novel experience of seeing anyone speak harshly to my mother, and the sheer force of his delivery, I failed to notice Morelli moving rapidly towards the door. When he opened it, I fell on his legs.

***

I would like to draw a veil over the subsequent encounter, but it is forever etched on my memory. Morelli remained icily polite while I disentangled myself from the folds of his habit, and even helped me to my feet, but the look of utter contempt and loathing he shot me before stalking out the door will be with me to my dying day. I don't think I've ever met anyone who disliked me quite as much, except

Goebbels, of course. Perhaps they were related? No, on reflection, I was sure Morelli would only deign to have relatives of the utmost purity and beauty. Why he didn't like me was, and is, a mystery. After all, wasn't I pure and beautiful?

I had a lecture from my mother about a) listening at keyholes, b) wearing other people's pyjamas, and c) coming downstairs without a dressing gown when company was present.

Patrick got a lecture from our mother about a) reading stick books, b) going to sleep in other people's beds, and c) getting into any bed fully dressed. She was especially narked that he hadn't taken his shoes off. He also got a lecture from our father about a) wasting everybody's time with a spurious vocation, and b) getting caught.

He didn't speak to me for a week.

***

Of course, I derived immense comfort from my job. The easy camaraderie of true professionals, the satisfaction of a job well done, the sense of making a truly worthwhile contribution to society.

In theory, anyway. As soon as my phone rang things started to go downhill. I didn't realise this immediately, but picked it up happily, thinking how lovely it was having my own phone all to myself again, after so long. Now, when Tony's girlfriends rang up, he either answered the phone himself or, if he wasn't there, we just let it ring, unplugging it if the calls got too frequent.

'Hello, Fiona. It's Fred Morris in accounting here, we're having a bit of a problem with some of the transactions, they're taking forever to finish.'

Oh wow, a real live problem. I felt like Superman. Especially as Fred Morris in Accounts was the Incredible Stinking Man whose biro I'd stolen all those months ago, to do the aptitude test and get this job.

'Well, I'm sure we can help. Which transactions were you having the problem with?'

'It's all the invoicing ones, really. They just seem to sit there forever. It happened on Friday, about four o'clock, but I couldn't get hold of anyone in your department then.'

'So isn't it happening now?'

'No, but we really need to be sure it doesn't happen again. We're supposed to get all the invoices out in time for the last post on Friday, and we hardly got any of them done, so they won't go out now until tonight. It's a real hassle with the weekly accounts.'

'Oh.' I thought frantically. I seemed to remember Frank saying something once about programs using databases, and having performance problems. What was it? Something to do with the way they take turns using the database.

'The only thing different was we were running a Quarterly Report at the time. Could that have anything to do with it?'

I thought it might. The Quarterly Report was a massive program that went through the entire accounts database, doing God knew what to every record. I was positive it was databases I'd heard Frank talking about. Here goes, I thought. I adopted my best tone of technical superiority.

'Oh, of course. That Quarterly Report's a real beast, it goes right through the whole accounts database. Maybe if you got all your invoices out before running it, it might go better.'

Bits of what Frank had said were drifting back to me. Every program that's using a database has a thing called a PSB that it uses to access the database. If one that's set up to let the program read the database is in use, no other program can get in to update that database at all until it's finished. Or if it's writing, nobody can read, or something like that. It had something to do with dirty socks, no, that's right, a dirty update, Frank had called it. Whatever that meant. So, I supposed, all the invoicing transactions, which wrote to the database, must have been held up until the Quarterly Report finished, which would take ages. Sometimes it ran for more than half an hour.

'Yeah, listen Fred, I think you might have a dirty update situation here. Yeah, real bad.' I paused to congratulate myself on sounding like a real expert. 'Yeah, the thing is, once the Quarterly Report gets underway, none of the other transactions can get into the Accounts database, they'd all just hang up until it finished. But, you know, it all has to do with design.' I knew I was on firm ground there, you're always safe if you say something really vague. I experienced a great rush of confidence; here I was at last, talking to a real user and being a computer expert. 'You know, maybe we could change the Quarterly Report program so it lets other transactions in every so often. It'd probably run a bit longer, but that wouldn't really matter, would it?'

'Aah, hell no. We only run it quarterly anyhow.'

'Right.'

'So, d'you reckon you could have it ready for

next time we run it?'

'Oh, well you'd have to talk to Mr Goebbels. I mean, I can't just say we'll do it, it's up to him, you know? Scheduling and that, I don't know what we've got coming up in the next three months. You'd have to talk to him, he's the only one that can authorise things.'

'Oh, okay. And is there any other way we could speed things up in the meantime? I mean, you know, if it's just generally slow?'

'Oh, I'm sure there would be. Ways you could speed it up. You could reorg the database and stuff.' (I tossed this off casually, hoping I'd remembered it right, I'd overheard Frank saying something like it on the phone last week. Whatever it meant, I knew it was something powerful from the respectful way he'd said it.) 'But then too, you'd still have to go through Mr Goebbels for anything like that. Anything that takes man-hours, you know?'

'Yeah. Well, thanks, Fiona, you've been a big help. Catch you later.'

I looked up to find Goebbels looming over my desk. It takes real talent for a tiny little person to loom like that. Goebbels had talent alright. He was breathing in and out, heavily, through his nose, the way Moses does when he's just about to jump on you in a frenzy of biting and kicking. I decided to act naturally, although it never works with Moses.

'Good morning, Mr Goebbels. Did you have a nice weekend?'

He ignored my friendly question.

'Who was that?' he barked.

'Fred Morris, from Accounts. They had a problem on Friday running the Quarterly Report.'

'I don't want you saying anything to people about our applications. You know absolutely nothing about the Accounting application, you have no idea what you're talking about. You are not authorised to make statements about anything like that. You have no right to tell people we can do things when you have no idea whether they're possible or not. How do you think it makes us look?'

'But you and Frank were talking about that program just the other day. You talked about exactly that. Anyway I didn't tell him we'd do it, I said he'd have to talk to you about it.'

'You are not to say anything at all to anybody about our applications, is that clear? You have no right whatever to make such a statement. You know nothing about the application. God, woman, they're already talking about outsourcing to India, they can do that if they want to, you know. The last thing I need is for them to become even more dissatisfied.'

I couldn't really see how they were going to get more dissatisfied by having a query answered. I cast my mind back over my conversation with Fred, and couldn't for the life of me see that I'd committed us to anything. In fact, I'd stressed that I didn't even have the authority to commit us to anything. I wondered how long Goebbels had been standing there, and whether he really knew what I'd said, or had just heard a couple of words and made some wild assumption. I thought this was probably the case; I was sure I remembered looking up fairly late in the conversation and not seeing him.

'Look, all I told him –'

'The point is that you had no right to tell him anything at all. How dare you take it upon yourself to say what this department will and will not do? You are not to say anything to anybody about these matters, you're not competent to make decisions about them.'

'But I didn't –'

'I know what's going to happen next. I'll be getting a phone call from Carl Jacobs wanting to know why we haven't rewritten the Quarterly

Report as we said we would. You have no right to make statements of this kind.'

His speech was starting to take on a Teutonic flavour, so I knew he was really upset.

'Do not ever say anything to anybody about our applications again. Is that clear?'

'Well, okay. You didn't tell me –'

'You should have known. God, woman, how do you think I can run this department with every junior programmer making statements to all and sundry about what we will and won't do?'

I gave up. There was no way I was going to convince him how harmless what I'd said to Fred had really been. I hoped he'd calm down when the phone call from Jacobs never materialised. Not that he'd ever believe me, of course, I knew better than to expect that, but he'd think we'd got away with it, and stop fuming, at least. I reckoned it would take two or three days before he was sure he wasn't going to get a call about it, although with someone as paranoid as Goebbels, who knew, it might take weeks. I wondered tiredly how long it would be before I had enough experience to get another job.

◈CHAPTER TWENTY◈

O Lord God, to whom vengeance belongeth, thou God, to whom vengeance belongeth, shew thyself.
Psalm 94:1

On the way home that night, I fantasised about Goebbels having a heart attack and dropping dead during one of his temper fits. The way his face went purple and his eyes bulged out always looked really unhealthy anyway, I was sure he must at the very least have blood pressure, whatever that was, but I was fairly sure that it led to heart attacks, or a cardiac melanoma or something. I imagined him falling suddenly to the floor in a frenzy of convulsions, all his legs thrashing and foam squirting out between his clenched teeth. I remembered reading a description of someone dying of arsenic poisoning in one of those Sherlock Holmes books, where the victim was in such violent convulsions that his whole body went into a circle backwards, with his head touching his feet. That seemed a fitting end for Goebbels, but I had an idea that you had to sign a poison book to get arsenic. I didn't like the thought of having my name written in a Poison Book, it was creepy. Of course, all medical things are pretty creepy anyway.

Anyway, I thought, what was I doing thinking about poison? You can't just go around poisoning people, you might get caught. Perhaps he could be bitten by a bat, and get that bat disease that everyone was talking about, Henderson Virus or something. I wondered if it was painful. And did you get it by being bitten, or was it more like a cold, that you could get just by breathing the same air or touching a doorknob?

In any case, I felt sure natural causes would get him pretty soon. You just can't spend that much of your life getting angry without it having an effect. Even now, I thought comfortably, hostile antibodies are chewing away at his arteries, lowering his resistance and predisposing him to all kinds of nasty things. In fact I seemed to remember reading something in a magazine about certain types of people being prone to different diseases. I'd ask Patrick when I got home, he always remembered things.

***

I had to postpone my enquiries for several days, because Patrick still wasn't speaking to me, heaven knows why. He went sulking about the place like a sick weasel, and things were pretty chilly with my parents, too. I don't know why I always seem to get blamed for things in our house. I spent the time thinking about a new career. Really, being a computer programmer wasn't turning out to be anything like what I'd expected. Perhaps I could go on the stage. After all, I'd been in the dramatic society at Uni. Then, when my name was in lights all over the world, Goebbels would come cringing and fawning to the stage door for an autograph, and I'd get the bouncers to bash him up. Tim (he still hadn't called me. Why?) had had a case like that when he was doing a summer clerkship, or a bit like it, anyway, well there were bouncers in it who threw someone out of somewhere and then he died, or was injured or something, and then he sued them. I was a bit hazy on the details, but obviously bouncers could be pretty nasty if provoked.

***

'Fiona?'

'What?'

'Can I come in?'

'No, get lost.'

Patrick came in and sat on the end of my bed. Sensitivity isn't one of his failings. I put down my Kindle and looked at him severely.

'What part of "no, get lost" sounded like "yes, come in", shitface?'

Patrick ignored this, as he generally does when it's not what he wants to hear.

'Look, Fi, I've been doing a lot of thinking the last few days.' He looked down shyly and stroked Moses. I couldn't believe my ears. He was finally going to admit he'd brought it all on himself and swear to give up stick books for ever. I smiled fondly. I wouldn't be too hard on him, he'd already suffered enough.

'Yeah, and I've finally got it figured out. Well, the basic idea, we'll have to work on the details a bit.'

I was totally at sea. This didn't sound like any apology I'd ever heard.

'What on earth are you talking about? All you've got to do is stop buying the filthy things.'

'What things?'

'Look, you are talking about stick books, aren't you? And how they got you into all this trouble?'

Patrick's face lit up. 'God, Fiona, I always thought you were dumb. It's taken me days to work it out, and you guessed straight away.'

'It doesn't exactly take Einstein to figure out that all this vocation shit was because you got caught by Miss Peemoller with a stick book.' I thought it was more tactful not to mention Harvey.

Patrick stopped lighting up, and looked irritated.

'God, Fiona. Not that. I'm talking about getting Morelli back.'

I couldn't believe my ears. 'Getting him back! You couldn't wait to get rid of him. What d'you want him for? Anyway, don't you see him every week at school?'

'Not getting him back here, Jesus, Fiona, I mean getting back at him for being such a prick.'

'What, you mean revenge?' The thought was too big for me to grasp entirely, but already I had a terrible sense of uneasiness. Morelli moved in the shadowy world of power, he had nothing to do with us. Look at the trouble he'd caused by just a tiny contact with our family. I wanted nothing to do with him, ever again.

'Are you completely insane? How could you ever get back at someone like him? Anyway, he hasn't done anything wrong, to get back at him for.'

'Are you serious? He made me go to that bloody thing at St Dominic's, for a start. And then he drags me back here and dobs me in to Mum. I never heard the end of it, I'm still not hearing the end of it, she keeps looking at me all sadly all the time, and SIGHING, you know what she's like.'

'But it was your fault, all of it, for having those disgusting stick books in the first place.'

Patrick dismissed this minor detail with an airy wave of his hand.

'I've got it all worked out. First we hide a couple of stick books under his mattress, the really gross ones, then we ring up his boss and dob him in. Anonymously, of course.'

I couldn't help laughing at the thought of Morelli getting caught with a stick book. I knew what that felt like, from my ghastly experience with Goebbels. Then an even funnier thought struck me.

'If he invites you into his bedroom, you'd have more than stick books to accuse him of.'

'Well, of course he's not going to invite me, is he? We'll have to break in.'

'Yeah, right. We can climb over the monastery wall with one of those batman things. If anyone tries to stop us, we'll disable them with a Vulcan nerve pinch and take away their memory by hypnosis.'

Then I realised Patrick wasn't laughing.

***

We squabbled about it for days, on and off. Motivated by his insane desire for revenge against Morelli, Patrick refused to listen to reason, and couldn't understand why I had any problems with his scheme. I was terrified by the thought of Patrick breaking into a monastery, especially one inhabited by Morelli, and even more terrified by the idea of going with him, as he seemed to think I would. For once I was glad to get to the office, where I could forget about the whole thing for a few hours. Not that the office was what you'd call peaceful. The perennial DASD argument between Frank and Goebbels had reached the level of World War Three. Four or five times a day they could be heard screaming and howling at each other. None of us was unaffected by it. All over the fifth floor doors slammed and tempers frayed, and Jane broke a fingernail.

***

'Will you carve, dear?'

'Certainly, my love.'

I squirmed in my chair, half dead with boredom and frustration. We were having another of our interminable weekly dinners with Father Simpson. My parents, since the incident with Father Morelli, had become even more nauseatingly soppy to each other than before, and kept gazing lovingly across the roast, which at their age was disgusting. Patrick, as usual, was sulking because he had to wear a tie and drink milk. Moses, lurking under the table, kept scratching my knee, hoping for a piece of roast lamb. I could feel my stockings being shredded, but couldn't say anything, because Moses was supposed to be upstairs when Father Simpson came to dinner. I wondered idly what it would be like to have my own flat. I wouldn't have to sit through these ghastly dinners pretending to be the Brady Bunch; instead, I would invite only witty, attractive people to my dinner parties. Then I thought about having to clean all the silver myself, and cook everything.

'How is your book coming along, Father?'

Simpson beamed at this untoward display of spurious interest.

'Not badly, thank you, Fiona. Some very interesting questions have arisen on the nature of the human soul in recent months. I have entered into a most enlightening correspondence with...'

He was away for a good quarter of an hour. Fixing a fascinated smile on my face, I turned my attention to how I could persuade Patrick to give up his mad scheme of revenge. Of course I could just refuse to take part in it, but then he'd almost certainly proceed on his own, get caught and then God knew what would happen. Wasn't it the Dominicans who started the Spanish Inquisition? I wasn't sure, but I rather thought it had been. Once inside the monastery, Patrick might never see the light of day again. They might burn him as an heretic. I imagined the flames licking around the foot of the stake, the robed and cowled monks chanting solemnly, their faces shadowed in the moonlight. The Inquisitor General looked like Father Morelli. Then I had an idea.

'Father Simpson, it was the Dominicans who started the Spanish Inquisition, wasn't it?' I kicked Patrick meaningfully under the table.

Father Simpson looked a bit nonplussed at this abrupt change of topic. He adjusted his spectacles thoughtfully.

'Well, not really, Fiona. The Inquisition was

actually set up in 1232 by Pope Gregory the ninth. After the Fourth Lateran Council of 1215, at which...'

This was not what I wanted to hear.

'But the Dominicans ran it, didn't they? I mean, weren't they the ones who burnt people and put them on the rack and everything?'

'Not at the table, dear.'

'Hmm. Both the Dominican and Franciscan orders were associated with the Inquisition, or Holy Office, as it was also known. Of course, they did not actually burn anyone. Executions were carried out by the secular arm, that is, the state. The Spanish Inquisition, of course, refers to that part of the Holy Office operating in Spain, as one might guess from the name.' He paused to simper modestly at his own wit. 'Its function was officially to remove any taint of heretical doctrine, but in fact there were certain political factors...'

Moses was digging his claws into my ankle. Furtively I sneaked a piece of roast lamb under the tablecloth. Simpson was set to go for the night if nobody stopped him; perhaps it would make Patrick think twice about offending a Dominican, but I doubted it; his eyes had already glazed over, and he probably wasn't even listening. I needed to get

Simpson back to the nasty bits.

'But they tortured people, didn't they, before burning them?'

'Fiona! Not at the table!'

And later, 'I can't think what's got into you lately, you used to be such a sweet child. What possessed you to say such a thing in front of Father Simpson, and at the dinner table? And I thought I told you to shut Moses in your room, I've told you and told you how unhygienic it is to have animals under the table. And another thing…'

❧CHAPTER TWENTY-ONE☙

Wherewithal shall a young man cleanse his way: even by ruling himself after thy word.

Psalm 119:9

'But Dad, it was the Dominicans that tortured people, wasn't it?'

'Fiona, that is hardly a suitable topic for the breakfast table. I believe your mother has already mentioned this to you. Why are you so interested in Dominicans all of a sudden, anyway? I should have thought we'd had enough of them lately.'

'Oh, I was just wondering. It's a fascinating period, isn't it?'

'Hmmm.' My father fixed me with a suspicious stare, and retreated behind *The Australian*, with that sort of rustling snap of the paper that says 'subject is closed,' or more precisely, 'I don't want to talk to you any more right now, but I'm still listening in case you say anything you'd rather I didn't hear'.

'Oh, Fiona, don't forget that book you promised to bring me from your office.'

I couldn't believe his gall. In a moment of sisterly confidence I had told Patrick about getting caught by Goebbels holding that filthy magazine with the pig. Now he was convinced that nothing else would do but to have that particular magazine for his evil scheme. Constant pestering over the weekend had not shaken his resolve, and he didn't seem particularly impressed by the Inquisition, either. It was unfortunate that I hadn't been able to stop Father Simpson from revealing that it no longer existed. Otherwise, I felt sure, Patrick would now be in a state of cowed terror, and would be more intent on avoiding Morelli's notice than on his stupid revenge.

***

Work was a positive haven of peace and solace. I settled down to my testing, comfortably secure in the knowledge that everything that could possibly go wrong with my program had already gone wrong with at least one of the fourteen identical programs I'd already written. Presently Frank marched into Goebbels' office clutching a piece of paper, and the shouting resumed. Everything was just as usual.

What wasn't usual was that Frank came out laughing, and didn't even slam the door. Could they have agreed on something? Or, impossible thought, could Frank actually have beaten Goebbels? I looked through Goebbels' glass wall; he looked small, grey and shrunken, and was staring off into space.

***

'You three, come in here, please.'

This was getting stranger and stranger. Goebbels had never said 'please' in my hearing before. Now he wanted all three of us in his office at once. Obviously we were going to get raked over the coals for something. I wondered what it could be. There wasn't much the three of us had in common. It must be the length of our lunch breaks, I decided.

'Sit down.' Goebbels sank into his own chair with a sigh. He really looked unwell, although of course he'd always been ugly, and it's harder to tell when really ugly people are sick. This was another first; normally he didn't ask you to sit down in his office even when he was explaining something for an hour or more; you stood up in Goebbels' office, so that you'd be properly conscious of your grovelling inferiority.

We all sat, in silence. Several minutes passed. Goebbels didn't say anything, and nobody else dared to. I looked sideways at Geoff and Tony, wondering if they were as nervous as I was. There was something really creepy about all of us sitting here in silence like this. It was just like waiting outside the headmistress' study at school, waiting to be given Saturday morning detentions.

When I was about to scream from nerves, Adam, Julie, Steve, Penny and Jane walked in. Goebbels looked up.

'Oh, just grab a couple of chairs from outside, would you?'

We all scrunched in together and looked at Goebbels nervously. Except for Frank, the office now contained the entire staff of our department.

Goebbels cleared his throat and fidgeted with some papers on his desk.

'Some of you already know that Frank Stevens has resigned from this company. He has already left the premises. He will not be replaced. We'll be getting a systems programmer from Katzenjammer Computing to do whatever technical support is required. Right, now I don't want to hear you discussing this matter among yourselves. The subject is closed. That will be all.'

No one was quite brave enough to ask the question.

***

Patrick pounced on me as I got in the door.

'Did you get it?'

I looked at him, baffled.

'Get what?'

'The stick book, the one with the pig. Did you get it?'

'No, I bloody didn't. I told you, I'm not having anything to do with it. And I'm certainly not bringing that filthy stick book home. What if I got knocked over by a bus?'

'What if you did, so what? What's a bus got to do with it, for Chrissake?'

'They'd be looking in my bag for my name and address, that's what. They always do that if you're knocked unconscious. Then they'd find that filthy magazine, I'd probably get hauled straight off to prison.' I remembered with a shudder the time I'd set off the burglar alarm at work and been arrested by the police. They hadn't been a bit nice, even after they'd spoken to Goebbels and dropped the burglary charges, they had still acted as if they thought the whole thing was my fault. They'd taken away my handbag and refused to give me any coffee. And the police station had smelled nasty, like a hospital.

'Oh, come off it, Fi. It's not a criminal offence to have stick books. How could they sell them in the newsagents?'

'Well since you know so much about it, why don't you go and buy one with pigs yourself?'

Patrick looked shocked.

'I'm not having people thinking I'm a pervert.'

***

Sometimes I think I'm the only sane, rational, well-balanced person in the universe. What with Goebbels jackbooting around and carrying on as if Frank had defected to the KGB, and my father looking suspiciously at me through narrowed eyes every time we met, and my mother disinfecting all the light bulbs for the second time that week, and my brother pestering me to procure obscene material, I felt as if I were living in a nightmare. Even Moses persisted in drinking the lavatory water. I was sure that blue stuff couldn't be good for him.

***

Ring. Ring. Ring.

'Hello?'

'Good afternoon, Fiona. It's Miss Peemoller from St Bedivere's. I'd like to speak with your mother, please.'

Oh, God. I remembered the last time I'd spoken to Patrick's form mistress on the phone. It was better not remembered. I decided that this time it wouldn't be a good idea to pretend to be my mother, especially as I'd already been recognised.

'She's in the kitchen, I'll just get her.'

My mother was polishing the underneath of the kitchen table.

'Um, it's Miss Peemoller on the phone for you.'

'Oh, thank you, Fiona. Tell her I'll be there in just a moment.'

I conveyed this message and raced upstairs to listen on the extension.

'Hello, Miss Peemoller.' My mother's vague tones echoed over the wire, sounding oddly far away. 'How lovely to hear from you again. I do hope Patrick's been behaving himself?' Her voice had a wistful note, as of one who hopes for the impossible.

Miss Peemoller evidently didn't wish to commit herself on this point. I gathered she hadn't actually caught him at anything recently.

'Well, Mrs MacDougall, the reason I'm calling is that I had a chat with Father Morelli. He's very concerned about Patrick, and he thinks the three of us should meet and discuss some counselling for him.'

Morelli was the one who needed counselling if he thought it would do Patrick any good. I wondered irritably why he didn't leave us alone, hadn't he done enough harm in our family? All the same, it should be good value to eavesdrop on if they did it here. I hoped my mother's deep commitment to hospitality would lead her to suggest this.

Just then I heard my father coming upstairs, and had to hang up the extension.

***

Sure enough, the following day when I got home from work they were all there, sitting around the coffee table, drinking tea and discussing my brother's spiritual welfare as solemn as cats frying eggs. Morelli got up when I entered the room. The expression on his face didn't indicate whether this was from old-fashioned courtesy or the desire to make a quick getaway in case I got wrapped up in his robes again. I took several minutes pretending to look for the book I'd been reading, but they didn't start talking again until I left the room.

Upstairs, Patrick was eating chocolate biscuits which he'd pinched from the kitchen, and sulking. I chucked the magazine at him; I had caved in and brought it home. Anything for a quiet life. I tactfully avoided mentioning the gathering downstairs.

'What's Morelli and Miss Peemoller doing here?'

'Dunno. I tried to overhear but Mum chased me out.'

Morosely, Patrick offered a chocolate biscuit to Moses.

'Don't give him that, he'll be sick.'

'Good. I hope he does it all over Morelli.'

A gentle tap sounded at the door and our mother came in.

'Darlings, Miss Peemoller and that nice young Father Morelli are staying to dinner. Be sure to wear a tie, Patrick.'

We looked at each other in disgust.

'Oh, and Fiona, do make sure that Moses is away from the dining room, won't you?'

Our mother wafted away, humming gently to herself.

'He must've really got round her. Last time he was here, they were hardly on speaking terms when he left.'

'Last time he was here, Patrick, everybody was hardly on speaking terms. But young! He must be thirty-five if he's a day!'

'You didn't think he was so ancient when you were batting your eyelashes all over him in church.'

'I do not bat my eyelashes. You take that back, Patrick MacDougall.'

'Yes you do, you do it all the time. Honestly Fiona, you're so obvious. You were practically drooling.'

Dance of Chaos

***

I spent the next half hour making myself look as nice as possible, just in case Morelli might be induced to soften his anger a bit. I had the purest possible motives, I thought smugly, as I sprayed on more scent and prized Moses out of the lavatory bowl yet again. I wondered if I could persuade our mother to stop putting blue stuff in the water, and what excuse I could use.

Dinner was light to moderate awful. Patrick had to drink milk, as apparently Father Morelli counted as an honorary vicar, but didn't dare sulk with Morelli across the table from him. I was sitting next to Morelli; Patrick was next to Miss Peemoller. Moses, officially shut in my room, was actually under my chair, batting hopefully at my ankles.

The conversation was really boring, I think it's what's called small talk. When I tried to ask Morelli about the Inquisition, our father fixed me with such a piercing glare that I just shut up. Mostly our father and Morelli discussed the state of the nation, and our mother and Miss Peemoller discussed some art exhibition they'd both been to last weekend. Patrick and I didn't say much, it seemed safer. From time to time I managed to slip some chicken to Moses, who was quietly lacerating my ankles. He had a particularly nasty habit of biting my Achilles tendon.

Everything was fine until my mother served the strudel.

My mother's strudel is wonderful, everyone says so. She's proud of it, with good reason.

And of course it's always served with cream.

It had to be Morelli, naturally. In the middle of some incredibly far-sighted and penetrating (what else?) remark about the political situation in Outer Mongolia or somewhere, he froze. Actually froze, like a statue. A strange expression flitted across his face, his eyes closed for a second.

Then Moses appeared from under the tablecloth. On Morelli's lap. It was amazing, like Attila the Hun meeting Genghis Khan. Then Moses yawned, right in Morelli's face, jumped onto the table, and started to devour his strudel.

Not everyone saw the full impact of that insolent yawn, but I did, and of course so did Morelli. That was the moment when I knew the depths of utter humiliation. I prayed, briefly, that Morelli wouldn't say anything.

Of course, I reckoned without the Dominican Procedure Manual. (In situations of the utmost social embarrassment, the Dominican will make some light remark demonstrating utter savoir-faire. He is not to shriek or climb on furniture.)

'How interesting,' said Morelli. 'I never knew cats had blue tongues.'

CHAPTER TWENTY-TWO

Cursed is he that smiteth his neighbour secretly.
Book of Common Prayer

Even then, I think it would have been alright, just perhaps, if it hadn't been for Miss Peemoller. I could have said he had some rare disease, or was a special breed, or something.

'Oh! I bet he's been drinking the water out of the lavatory! Such a nasty habit, my cat used to do it, but I trained him not to.'

I could have strangled her. Of course her cat wouldn't do anything so crude, it probably had a lace doily under its litter box. I made a desperate effort to recover the situation.

'Why don't we have coffee on the patio?'

Even the Dominican looked grateful. Everybody looked grateful, in fact, except my mother, who spends all day in the house, and was therefore the first person to remember that we didn't actually have a patio.

***

Coffee was served in the back garden, on the lawn furniture, in an atmosphere of what some people call delightful informality and other people call chaos. Actually, I noticed everybody seemed to be getting on much better. Soon Miss Peemoller was telling a funny story about her own school days, and even Morelli looked distinctly mellow, although this could have been a trick of the light. Moses had taken an unaccountable liking to him, and sprawled across his lap, purring loudly and shedding black hairs all over his habit. My mother beamed gently, and passed around little plates of home-made petits fours. My father, liberated by the outdoors, smoked his pipe.

I thought how lovely they all were.

***

'You did WHAT?'

'I put it in his briefcase. When we were having coffee, remember I went inside for a bit?'

'I thought you were going to the lavatory.'

'Well, I was, and then I got this brilliant idea. He left his briefcase in the sitting room, it was full of papers and stuff. I had a bit of a look, they looked like exam papers he was marking. So I just slipped it in the middle of them.'

Patrick looked disgustingly pleased with himself.

'You idiot, he was just starting to like us. You know why he was here tonight, he was having a meeting with Mum and Miss Peemoller about your discipline problem. They were talking about you having counselling and stuff. He's going to hit the roof when he finds a filthy magazine in his exam papers.'

'So what, he won't know it was me.'

'God, Patrick, I can't believe you. What d'you think, he's going to think it was Mum? Or Miss Peemoller, perhaps?'

'He might.' Patrick was starting to look a bit nervous.

'Look, you've got to get it back before he finds it. Make an excuse tomorrow and go and see him. He won't have started doing marking at this time of night, he'll probably leave everything in his briefcase till tomorrow.'

'Shit no, I'm not going anywhere near him. You do it.'

'Me? Me? You want me to go rummaging around in some priest's briefcase looking for stick books? Just forget it, Patrick. No way.'

Which is how I came to be in Joe Morelli's office at St Bedivere's at nine the next morning, having taken a sickie from work.

***

Morelli regarded me impassively across his desk. He had the calm, passionless face of an Inquisitor. Those eyes have seen everything, I thought. I could feel my carefully rehearsed story running out through my toes.

'How may I help you, Miss MacDougall?'

God, he was so formal. I thought about asking him to call me Fiona, but didn't quite dare.

'Um, well, look, it's about Patrick. My brother. You know.'

'Yes, I am indeed acquainted with your brother. Rather better, perhaps, than I might have wished.'

'He's really very nice, you know. We're all

terribly fond of him.'

'I'm sure.'

Morelli waited for me to say something else. I looked frantically round the room. Ah yes, there it was behind his desk. All I had to do was get him out of the room.

'Look, the reason I came to see you, I wanted to ask you not to be too hard on him. It's just a stage he's going through, you know?'

'I do indeed.' Morelli sounded as though his idea of going through a stage wasn't quite the same as mine.

'Miss MacDougall, I appreciate your concern for your brother, but really I feel I might more appropriately discuss this matter with your parents.'

'But they don't understand. Nobody understands,' I wailed. I burst into tears, very convincingly, I thought. Under cover of my handkerchief I risked a quick glance at Morelli. He looked really quite upset.

'Oh, dear, dear,' he murmured. I allowed my mind to fill with the monstrous injustice of it all, and gave way to grief. I sobbed and howled. Crying is one thing I'm really good at. I kept it up for a couple of minutes – careful, I thought, don't overdo it – and then tapered off with an occasional sniff.

Morelli had moved out from behind his desk and was standing with his back to me, looking out the window. I supposed he was tactfully not intruding on my grief.

'I'm sorry, Father Morelli. I worry so much about him, he's been in so much trouble and I just can't bear to think of him getting into any more.'

'Well, that's understandable, and very commendable, but I think you're taking the whole thing too much to heart. It's really not a very major crime, after all. Now, can I get you an aspirin? I'm sure I have some in my briefcase.'

Horror!

'Oh no, no please don't bother. Actually I'm allergic to aspirin, I come out in a rash.'

'I think these are Panadol.' He moved purposefully towards his briefcase.

'No, really, I don't want anything. Perhaps just a glass of water?'

Morelli stopped with his hand poised above his briefcase and gave me a searching look. His eyes gave me the shivers, as though he could read what I was thinking. There was really something a bit sinister about him.

'Very well, a glass of water. I won't be a moment.'

Thank God! As soon as the door closed behind him I leapt across the office and pounced on his briefcase, rummaging frantically through the papers. I was in time, it was still there. I shoved it in my bag, and collapsed back into my chair just as I heard the door opening.

Morelli gave me the water and sat back behind his desk. He was smiling faintly, as if some private thought amused him. I sipped the water to gain time, and wondered how I could conclude the interview gracefully; I hadn't really thought past getting the stick book.

'Are you feeling better now?' The Dominican was all gentle concern, but I couldn't shake the feeling that he was laughing at me.

'Thank you. Look, will you please give Patrick another chance? He's terrified he'll be expelled from school.'

'Miss MacDougall, please, there's really no need to worry about that. I'm sure that with guidance, Patrick will overcome this little problem. I suspect it has far more to do with defying authority than with any genuine interest in this, er, material. I am not without experience in these matters, you know.' He smiled gently, as if he'd made a joke.

'He won't be expelled?'

'No.'

'Not even a bit?'

'Not even a bit. Although it would be difficult, as you put it, to expel someone "a bit". However, you may set your mind at rest. The worst that will happen is that young Patrick will have a few sessions with me, and I'm sure that's not too fearsome, is it?'

He was definitely a sinister character. I was starting to feel just like a chicken being interviewed by a snake. I was glad it was Patrick getting the counselling and not me. Although he was definitely the most attractive man I'd ever seen, but best not to think about that just now, I decided. After all, I was still on a Mission for God.

'No, of course not. Well, thank you so much, Father Morelli, I feel much better now. Thank you for seeing me. I must be going now...'

I got out as fast as I could, and all the time I just couldn't shake that impression that he was laughing at me. But what the hell, I decided as I reached the pavement with a huge sigh of relief. I'd been the one that had fooled him, after all.

***

Patrick's eyes were huge and mournful with anxiety when he got home from school. He looked just like one of those kids with the big heads, in those nasty pictures that my father always calls 'an interesting sociological phenomenon'. He didn't even pester me about whether I'd managed to get the stick book in time or not, just looked at me out of those big eyes, it was pitiful. I felt like kicking him in the head.

'Look, I'm really sorry, Patrick. I tried.'

I saw the blood drain from his face.

'Did he say anything?'

I turned away as if to hide a tear; actually, I could hardly keep from bursting into manic laughter. I let my shoulders shake a bit with it.

'I can't repeat it.' I choked out.

Silence. I turned around, he was just standing there as though he'd been frozen. I felt a bit sorry.

'No, relax, it's okay. I got it, he didn't suspect a

thing. I started crying all over the place and he went to get me a drink of water, and I got it.'

'Fiona, you're wonderful. You're sure he hadn't seen it?'

'Positive. It was mixed up with the papers just like you said. He'd hardly have found it and then put it back there, would he? He hadn't even taken the stuff out, I got there really early, before nine, he was just coming in.'

'You're fantastic. Well, where is it?'

'What d'you mean, where is it?'

'My stick book, where is it?'

'I threw it in the rubbish, as soon as I got out of sight. You didn't think I was going to come all the way home on the tram with it sticking out of my bag, did you?'

'God, Fiona, d'you realise what those things cost? I only get twenty bucks a week, you know. How could you just chuck it in the bin, I hadn't even finished reading that one.'

You just can't get through to some people.

***

'...I swear to God, Fiona, I've just about had it

up to here. Ever since Frank left, he's been the absolute pits. There's nothing to do anyway, he doesn't even need a secretary, for Christ's sake. He just wants to be able to say "My girl will do it for you." Fuck.'

We were having lunch in the Dead Rat. Jane had been holding forth for the entire time we'd been there, letting her food get cold and giving the waitress filthy looks. I tried yet again to lighten the atmosphere a bit.

'Never mind, he might drop dead soon, of a heart attack. My brother says people who rant and rave all the time always get heart attacks or strokes, and the ones that hold it in get cancer.'

'Is he a doctor?'

'No, he's still at school.'

'Oh, right. School kids always know the latest medical discoveries. Must be because they've got their finger on the pulse of the nation. Jesus, Fiona.'

'No, really, he read it in some magazine.'

Jane got a faraway look. 'D'you know what I'd really like?'

'What?'

'I'd like him to have a stroke, and fall on the floor, while I was there, and he'd still be conscious but not be able to move or breathe or anything, and then I'd laugh.'

'There'd have to be nobody else around. It'd be good though, wouldn't it?'

'No, if there were people around I'd just pretend to panic and forget how to do CPR. Then I'd break all his ribs.'

'You couldn't break his ribs in front of people, anyway why his ribs? Why not his kneecaps, or his nose, or something?'

'No, stupid, that's what you do when you give someone cardiac compression, you often break a few of their ribs from the pressure. They told us when I did my St John's that you shouldn't ever tell anybody your name if you've done CPR on them, because even if you saved their life they could sue you for breaking their ribs.'

'Have you done a St John's certificate? God, how yucky. Did you have to practice mouth to mouth and everything?'

'Yeah, they have these rubber dummies that you practice on. Just a head and body, no arms and legs or anything. If you're doing it right you can see the blood going around in these little plastic tubes.'

'Yuk, how gross. But you couldn't do mouth to mouth on Goebbels, oh yuk, it'd be like kissing him. You'd be sick.'

Jane looked broodingly at her knife. 'It'd be worth it. Anyway I'd make sure I didn't do it properly so he wouldn't actually get any air, and I'd break all his ribs and he'd die in agony, and then I'd go and dance on his grave.'

I was silent in awe at so much passion.

'How come you hate him so much?'

'Oh, come on, Fiona, how could you look at that ugly hairy rat bastard, or hear him say two words, and not hate him?'

I had to admit she had a point.

CHAPTER TWENTY-THREE

Such knowledge is too wonderful and excellent for me: I cannot attain unto it.
Psalm 139:5

I felt quite upset after having lunch with Jane. All around me seemed to be hatred and revenge. I didn't like it; happiness is more my thing, really. Patrick still hadn't stopped pestering me about his wild scheme to plant a stick book under Morelli's mattress; even the most passionate and reasoned arguments didn't sway him from his fell purpose. The only reason he hadn't attempted it himself yet was because he was so deeply committed to getting other people to do his dirty work for him. I imagined climbing the wall, breaking into St Dominic's, and getting caught in Morelli's bedroom holding a stick book. Then I imagined the same thing happening to Patrick. Both scenarios were utterly horrible, but it was marginally better if it was Patrick and not me. I supposed that was because if it was Patrick he wouldn't be accused of being there for immoral purposes. But then I thought about my little brother being dragged off to the dungeons and handed over to the secular arm. Somehow I had to talk him out of it before he talked me into it.

I gave some thought to this during the afternoon, because Goebbels was out on some management rort, which meant we could all skive off like the dedicated professionals we were. I knew I had various options.

I could give in and do it. I thought about this for a while. There were several problems with this option. First, of course, there was getting caught. I imagined the tremendous humiliation consequent on getting caught planting a stick book under a priest's mattress. Especially if one were caught by Morelli himself, of whom I was terrified. Then there was the probability of failure. After all, who would ever believe, of Joe Morelli, that he would have a filthy magazine under his mattress? When we rang up to dob him in, which we'd have to do anonymously, would anyone even bother to look under his mattress? In the balance, I rather thought not. And how, if asked, would we say we knew about it?

I could refuse to have anything to do with it,

and let Patrick do it himself. Except that it wouldn't happen to me, all the same arguments obtained. Then, of course, there would be the guilt I'd feel for letting something like that happen to my little brother. All my life I'd been getting him out of trouble; could I really stand by and let him get into the biggest trouble ever, without lifting a finger to stop it? And what if Morelli answered the phone when Patrick rang up? He'd be sure to recognise his voice. I had only a very hazy idea of what went on inside monasteries, but it seemed a fair bet that anyone who happened to be passing might pick up the phone. I'd seen nuns' cells in the movies, and they were always very plain, and never had telephone extensions. Well, that was something I could check out, at least. I heaved the phone book onto my desk. Where to start? Would it be under D for Dominicans, or S for St Dominic's? Probably S.

There was no St Dominic's under S. Well, try D. Dominic, Saint, that would be. God, some people had funny names. I wondered why they didn't change them. Anyway there was nothing under Dominic except a couple of hairdressers. Just on a hunch I tried looking under Morelli, there were quite a few of these, but none of them was in the right place. The Dominicans weren't on Facebook, either, although I noticed with surprise that they seemed to have their own country. Perhaps I could find out their number from their embassy? But the only embassy I found on Facebook for the Dominican Republic was in Egypt. There was a St Dominic's Academy in America, and a grammar school in England, and that seemed to be it. Well, I thought, that really puts paid to the whole scheme, doesn't it? After all, you can't make an anonymous phone call to a place that's ex-directory. And only a complete idiot would mess with people who were so powerful that they had their own country. Was the monastery even Australian soil? Perhaps they would have armed guards.

***

It was with immense satisfaction that I related my findings to Patrick that night. I was prepared for a variety of reactions: shock, disappointment, even denial; I thought he might well insist on verifying it himself, but felt secure in my incontrovertible knowledge of the facts.

I didn't expect him to laugh.

'God, Fiona, you're so dumb. You look up the Catholic church, under C, and then you look up the order and that. Look, I'll show you.' He went to get the phone book, sniggering to himself. I followed him into the hall, keeping an eye out for our mother.

'But Patrick! I found out they've got their own

country, the Dominican Republic! They could do anything, attack us, declare war…'

The little toad was doubled over, laughing.

'Seriously, Patrick. Their own country!' I would slap him if he didn't stop laughing.

'Fiona…oh God, stop it, I'm going to die…'

I whacked him over the head with the phone book. Presently he simmered down to a snigger. He wouldn't tell me what was so funny, every time I asked he'd dissolve into giggles again.

But the laugh was on him because, as I'd thought, there was just the one number.

***

I lay in bed, brooding. I couldn't sleep for worrying about it. I knew that if I didn't do it, sooner or later Patrick would, and utter disaster would ensue. I ran through in my mind all the possible things that could happen, each more terrible than the last. Me in prison. Patrick in prison. The Dominican Republic attacking our country with suicide bombers. Or sending secret ninja assassins to kill us all in our beds. Or causing a Diplomatic Incident, whatever that is. Patrick being expelled from St Bedivere's. My mother finding out that I, or Patrick, had committed burglary and other criminal offences, and been in possession of pornographic material.

Moses was no help either; he lay placidly on my stomach, dribbling on my pyjamas and occasionally biting off a button.

***

I wasn't in the best of form next day, after staying awake worrying half the night. Perhaps if I'd been more than half awake, I would have realised that, when Goebbels started talking about our corporate mission the next morning, it wasn't a joke.

Goebbels had called a meeting, unusually for him, although it wasn't a proper meeting, because instead of all sitting round a table or even just around the office, we had all to stand in a line in front of his desk while he barked at us.

'I have called you in here to inform you of our new corporate mission,' he barked. 'It has been sent to us this morning from America. You are to memorise it at once. Any failure to conform will result in instant dismissal. Are there any questions.'

He glared at us through his facial hair, silently daring us to ask a question. I knew better, but poor Steve never learned. If only he hadn't asked about a copy of the mission, perhaps everything would have been alright.

'I have one copy and I shall read it to you now. The corporate mission is on the company's website and you are to memorise it in your own time. We are united by a common goal. We will treat one another with respect –'

That was when I laughed. I should have held it in, but it was just such a kneejerk, hearing Goebbels, of all people, talking about treating people with respect; for a crazy moment I thought he was cracking a joke.

***

'Look, Patrick, just shut up, will you? I've been subjected to total humiliation at work, and all you can do is go on about your stupid plot against Joe Morelli. It wouldn't work in a million years anyway, just leave me alone, will you?'

'But Fi, look, it's a question of honour.'

'Honour? Honour! Are you from this planet? He catches you with a stick book, a fair cop, red handed, and you're talking about honour? God, Patrick, sometimes I just don't believe you. Look, it's over now anyway, can't you just let it alone?'

'It's bloody not over, I've got to go for these

moronic counselling sessions. It's all your fault, Fiona.'

'...!'

***

The counselling sessions were a trial to us all. Father Morelli, out of the goodness of his saintly heart, had volunteered to do the job of saving Patrick's tacky little soul himself. My mother, being what she was, didn't believe in counselling without cups of tea and lace doilies. This is how Father Morelli came to be spending every Wednesday evening at our house. I was never able to find out what went on in the counselling sessions, which took place in our father's study for an hour before dinner, but dinner was unnerving enough. Patrick, still hell-bent on revenge, used every opportunity to pump Morelli about the layout and routines of his monastery:

Patrick: Hey, Fiona, how would you like to swap rooms this weekend?

Fiona: No, thanks. (My room was nicer than his; it had a window seat, and afternoon sun.)

Patrick: Oh, come on, Fi. I'm doing art this term, I want the morning light for my painting assignment. Anyway, it's nice to wake up with the sun coming in, don't you think, Father?

Morelli: In my order we get up a bit earlier than that, actually.

Fiona: What, earlier than sunrise?

Morelli: Yes, in winter, anyway.

Patrick: What time would that be, exactly? (At the prospect of nailing down a substantial part of the Dominican's routine he had frozen like a hound scenting a rabbit, quivering and pointing with his nose.)

Morelli delicately raised one eyebrow and refrained from answering, turning instead to our father and starting an enlivening political discussion. After dinner, Patrick excused himself with startling speed. I found him in the kitchen, tearing the paper apart.

'What are you looking for?'

'The weather bit. I'm sure it tells you what time the sun comes up.'

'I wrapped the potato peelings in it.'

Patrick then had to be forcibly restrained from racing out and demolishing the rubbish bin in his quest for truth. I only got him calmed down by pointing out that it would also be in tomorrow's paper, and that in any case he could google it. He went on like this all the time, it was frightfully embarrassing.

The quality of home life had taken a drastic turn for the worse, at least in my view. On those evenings when we didn't have Morelli infesting the house, my mother kept up a constant refrain about 'that nice young Father Morelli' until we all wanted to vomit. Nor had she given up on Patrick's vocation, despite the whole thing having been exposed as a scam. She took out a subscription to The Priest and left copies of it lying about the place, and she bought Patrick a whole lot of books about Father Brown, Don Camillo, etc. Patrick, who reads only science fiction and stick books, wasn't impressed.

'Gee, thanks, Mum.'

And later, to me:

'Jesus, what is this shit?'

I couldn't resist winding him up.

'I am sorry that you feel you must blaspheme about our Mother's lovely gift, Patrick. I shall ask Father Morelli to say ten masses for your soul.'

Patrick's reply to this was unrepeatable, but

involved several interesting ideas about Father Morelli and his ancestry and customs.

'That's very creative, Patrick. What a pity you've been called to the priesthood, you could have followed our father into anthropology.'

Then it was my ancestry and customs. In his excitement, he forgot they were the same as his own. After I had gently pointed this out to him, he didn't speak to me for several hours.

ஐCHAPTER TWENTY-FOURଔ

He spake the word, and there came all manner of flies: and lice in all their quarters.
                                    Psalm 105:31

I sighed and turned the page of the dump. I had been working on the problem for two days already, and didn't seem to be any nearer a solution. A perfectly normal print program, after I'd made a few minor adjustments, had suddenly crashed for no apparent reason. I didn't want to ask for help from Tony or Geoff, because I knew they'd only sneer patronisingly and write sections of code for me without explaining anything, and then go and sneak to Goebbels about how incompetent I was.

Hours passed. I could feel my hair growing longer as I stared at incomprehensible pages of stuff that looked like 'f3f44040404040' on the left, and other stuff that looked like '.....k....' on the right. The dump was about eight hundred pages long, and I had absolutely no idea how to read it. If Frank had still been here, I could have got him to show me how to do it, I thought miserably.

'Fiona!'

There was no mistaking that booming, basso profundo screech. I sighed and looked up. Peter was sashaying, there's really no other word for it, at high speed towards my desk. He looked really odd; the black dye had partly grown out, showing light-coloured roots. He was wearing skin-tight, pale green pants tucked into knee-high cowboy boots, the kind with the fur still on, and as well as his usual cubic zirconia studs he'd added a matching necklace, which showed up like anything because the top four buttons of his shirt were undone, revealing a totally hairless chest. The overall effect was quite startling, especially when you remembered that Marsh and Spacknall was one of the oldest and most conservative business houses in Melbourne.

'Honestly, Peter, don't you think you're showing a bit much cleavage for the office?'

He looked at me affrontedly. 'What's the point spending hours waxing it if nobody's going to see it?'

'That necklace... don't you think a tie...'

Peter snorted. 'That prick Jacobs just sacked me. The old fucker. I'd kill him if I wasn't such a coward.'

I was stunned. Peter had never quite fit in to the corporate image, but then he wasn't allowed out to see clients or anything, and he'd been there for ages. I couldn't imagine our old department without him screeching and swishing all over the place.

'Three and a half years I've been here. I worked my guts out and what do I get. It's not fair.'

'Well, you never really did much actual work, as such, did you?'

'Ooh, you bitch! I work harder than anybody in the place.'

'What did he say?'

'He said my appearance wasn't acceptable. The bitchy old queen, after I dieted off three stone and got my eyelashes dyed. I look heaps better than him, the fat bastard.'

'Well, you do look a bit outrageous.'

'God, Fiona, I might have known you'd turn on

me too.'

This was so unfair that I couldn't think of anything else to say. Peter turned on his two inch heels and flounced out, swinging his hips. I was really fond of him, but I had to admit I could see Jacobs' point. I wondered what he'd do now.

'Fiona!'

Goebbels barked my name down the length of the office. Typically, he hadn't even bothered to get up from his chair, he was sitting behind his desk in his office, summoning me like a dog. I thought longingly of telling him to get stuffed.

Goebbels jerked his head. Get in here this instant, that meant. I sighed and went in. It was really no fun at all working here; in a way I almost envied Peter for getting the sack.

'Fiona, I wonder if you realise this is an office, where people are supposed to work, not a bloody tea-party for entertaining your friends?'

'Look, I didn't invite him, he just came in, what can I do about it?'

'I don't give a damn about your sordid arrangements with your friends, I don't want them in here disrupting my department. That creature was screaming loud enough to be heard down on the ground floor. It disturbs people when they're trying to work.'

I went back to my desk. I shot Goebbels with my invisible ray gun. I wished I was an old woman with magic powers so I could put a curse on him. I imagined myself as a village wise woman with a shawl over my head, muttering incantations and stirring a cauldron. All the village people would come to my hut for advice about their problems, and no one would ever dare to offend me. Goebbels, who in my vision was a ratty-looking peasant with greasy hair and a hut right next to the village midden, would break out in great warty sores all over his body and die slowly, in agony, screaming. What a wonderful life. I wouldn't get old like the other peasants because of my knowledge of herbs and potions. Even the village priest, who looked just like Father Morelli, would be very respectful to me, and would consult me about the weather when he wanted to go fishing.

'Get on with your work, don't sit there dreaming. You haven't turned a page in the last twenty minutes.'

God, he couldn't even go past my desk without snarling and growling.

'I was just trying to think of a way to stop people coming in here and disturbing our work.'

'Don't get smart with me, young lady, or you'll be out on your backside.'

***

'Hell no, he doesn't worry me,' said Tony. 'He's always worth a good laugh.'

'Peter who?' said Geoff.

'Christ!' said Jane. 'It'd be the first time that fucker ever gave a rat's arse about anybody's comfort.'

'Get back to your desk. I don't want you hanging around wasting people's time on social chit-chat. Other people want to work,' said Goebbels.

***

On the way home, I realised with a horrible sense of foreboding that it was Wednesday again. I wondered gloomily how many weeks of this we were in for. I wondered whether my mother would invite Morelli to stay for dinner again. I knew she would. My mother's passion for hospitality is exceeded only by her obsession with cleanliness and hygiene.

Patrick greeted me at the door.

'Mum says Moses has to be shut in your room

until Morelli's gone. She said she doesn't want a repetition of last week's Unfortunate Incident.'

'He can't stay in there all night, what if he has to go to the lavatory?'

'Well, you tell her. I'm staying out of it.'

I went into the kitchen. My mother was baking again. A heavenly smell wafted up as she closed the oven.

'Oh, Fiona, darling, I want you to keep Moses in your room tonight.'

'But Mum, he can't stay in there all night. What if he needs to go to the lavatory?'

'Fiona, you know perfectly well he stays in your room all night while you're sleeping. So he can certainly stand being in there for a few hours this evening. I don't want him jumping on the table again in the middle of dinner, it was embarrassing enough last week. I don't know what kind of people Father Morelli must think we are.'

I had a fair idea myself, but it didn't seem like a good idea to enlighten her.

'He thinks we're a really nice Christian family, he told me so.'

It wasn't really that much of an exaggeration. I was sure he realised we were all related to each other.

But even with subtle flattery, there was no shifting my mother from her draconian stance. Moses was banished to my room. I made the bed so he'd be nice and comfortable, and opened the window so he'd have plenty of fresh air and could listen to the noises from outside. He loved to do that; sometimes he'd spend hours on the window sill, pricking up his ears and really paying attention, just like someone listening to the radio. I reckoned he was going to have a lot more fun this evening than I was.

***

I knew my mother was inviting Morelli to stay for dinner, because of having to shut Moses up. For some reason he only ever jumped on the table when we had company; normally he was really quite well behaved. Of course our visitors never believed this.

So I spent quite a long time making myself look specially nice. As I was taking out the hot rollers, Patrick stuck his head in the door.

'God, Fiona, don't you ever give up?'

'I'm doing this for you, you ungrateful little

snot. We don't want him getting the impression we're all ratbags, you always look so scruffy.'

'Well, I don't know. I reckon Morelli'd be more impressed if you wore something grey, with a high neck, and maybe put your hair in a bun.'

'Oh, what? Rack off.'

***

We were all models of decorum. Not being sure there mightn't have been something in Patrick's comments, I put my favourite dress back in the wardrobe and wore a black skirt, with a white blouse buttoned right up. This had the added advantage of not showing Moses' hairs. Of course, after I'd dragged everything out from under my bed looking for the magazine with the article on how to do makeup so that it looks as though you're not wearing any, there was quite a bit of dust on it. There just doesn't seem to be any compromise with clothes; whatever colour you wear, something always shows. Anyway, the light would be fairly dim in the dining room.

Everyone except Patrick was solemnly drinking sherry when I went into the sitting room. Patrick, of course, was sulking. He had remained in his school uniform in an attempt to score brownie points with Morelli, but Morelli didn't look as if he'd noticed.

He was discoursing with my father about some person called Horace. Under cover of pouring myself a glass of sherry, I managed to get my back to him and pull a horrible face at Patrick, which made him get a fit of the giggles. Morelli looked highly affronted. That'll teach you to make snide remarks about my dress, I thought.

'What's that all over your skirt, Fiona?'

Oh, the little rat. I had thought I'd got it all off.

'It couldn't be dust, could it? Gee, you mustn't have vacuumed very thoroughly in your room.'

I could see my mother's ears pricking up. Damn.

'Speaking of housework, Patrick, would you like me to give you a hand to turn your mattress?'

Patrick, having been subtly reminded that I had the goods on him, subsided.

We went into the dining room, where everything had been polished within an inch of its life. It was just like having Father Simpson to dinner. Everything proceeded in terms of the utmost decorum with Moses out of the way. There was no one under the table ripping my stockings, and I started to think that perhaps it hadn't been a bad idea shutting him in my room after all.

Dinner drew towards an amiable close. We were just finishing dessert, and discussing whether it would be nice to have coffee outside again, when there was a terrible racket at the window. The curtains bulged and shook; something seemed to be trying to climb in. Then a little black face appeared under them.

I always think Moses has a particularly attractive face, although I'm aware that not everyone agrees with me. But it wasn't his features that caused all the dismay and consternation.

It was what he had in his mouth.

Scrabbling slightly with his back feet for purchase, Moses executed a beautiful flying leap from the window sill, right across the room onto the table. I always think he looks so elegant when he does those big jumps, as if he were floating in the air. He padded down the length of the table, nimbly avoiding decanters, salt cellars, etc, making affectionate little crooning sounds in his throat, and dropped the rat on Morelli's plate. Then he sat down and looked adoringly at Morelli, purring loudly.

⳯CHAPTER TWENTY-FIVE⳰

The righteous cry, and the Lord heareth them: and delivereth them out of all their troubles.
Psalm 34:17

There was quite a long silence, during which Moses continued to purr loudly. I wondered what Morelli would do. I was sure that even the Dominican Procedure Manual wouldn't cover being presented with a dead rat. My mother couldn't even find the breath to shriek; she was making little gasping sounds, like a landed fish. Patrick was fighting an unholy case of the giggles. Both Morelli and my father appeared to have been carved out of stone.

'Oh, how sweet,' I said. 'He's brought you a present.'

'Oh, Fiona,' said my mother, her whole

demeanour dripping with reproach.

Then I remembered he'd been shut in my room.

'Good heavens, he must have figured out how to open the door!'

Patrick paused in his convulsions to shoot me a glance of withering scorn.

'God, Fiona, you're so dumb. You had your window open.'

'Oh, Fiona.'

How come everybody was suddenly looking at me as though it was my fault? I wasn't the one who'd dropped a dead rat on the table.

'He's got to have fresh air.'

My mother just looked at me. She looked reproachful. My father looked at me. He looked furious. Patrick looked at me, sniggering. Father Morelli considerately refrained from looking in my direction. He was still staring in horrified fascination at the dead rat on his dessert plate.

'I think in this situation you're supposed to put it on the side of your plate,' Patrick said helpfully.

Morelli looked at him with one eyebrow elegantly raised, and started laughing himself.

Moses, offended, jumped off the table, knocking over Morelli's wine glass with his tail as he went. The red wine missed Morelli, but went all over my blouse.

I would really like it if memory drew a kindly veil over the following events, if not the whole evening. I really would. Patrick distinguished himself by rushing around the table and emptying the salt cellar down my front, shouting 'salt for red wine, quick before it sets.' Moses, alarmed by the fast movement and shouting, with his retreat cut off because the door was closed, disgraced himself on the floor. If I hadn't been too soft ever to get around to having him spayed, perhaps it wouldn't have smelt so strong. My mother, overcome either by the fumes of eau de tomcat or the general air of emergency, fainted gracefully in my father's arms. I've always envied my mother's ability to faint gracefully. The one time I ever fainted, overcome by the heat at school assembly, I gave myself a black eye and, on waking, threw up over the games mistress.

By the time things settled down a bit and I had managed to extricate myself from Patrick and brush off most of the salt, Morelli had retreated into a corner clutching his rosary, and Moses was back on the table, investigating the remains of the cheese board.

My father was cross.

'Fiona. Get that rat out of here,' he snapped.

Well, of course. It had to be decently buried, didn't it?

***

I meant it as a compliment. I thought it would help Morelli relax and feel part of the family. Besides, my grandmother always says that, in a crisis, the most important thing is to make sure everybody has something to do.

'Really, Miss MacDougall, I hardly think Christian burial is appropriate for a dead rat.'

He had that old expression back on his face, the one where equal parts of contempt and loathing were overlaid with a thin veneer of saintly patience. I wondered what I'd said to upset him this time. Surely he couldn't be blaming me for Moses' behaviour? Moses had meant well anyway, he liked Morelli a lot.

We had coffee in the sitting room. My father had confiscated the rat and put it in the rubbish bin. The conversation was slightly stilted, and Morelli seemed nervous. When Moses got onto his lap, he jumped and dropped his coffee. White robes aren't really the best thing to wear for dinner at our house.

Morelli left quite early, which was a relief to all of us. Unfortunately, that wasn't the end of the evening. My mother had quite a lot to say about my having left my bedroom window open, which I thought was pretty unfair considering the way she was always going on about adequate ventilation.

***

I finally had to give in and get Tony to help me with the dump. It was no good asking Geoff, I knew he'd refuse. Tony was always good for a bit of assistance, as he could look down the front of my shirt while we were both leaning over the listing.

'Well, okay,' said Tony, masterfully turning back his cuffs. 'Let's have a look at the Listlog first.'

The listlog was the bit that printed right at the end of the job, with all the job control statements and messages from that job.

'Why, we know it cancelled or there wouldn't be a dump.'

Tony looked at me pityingly.

'You always look at the listlog first.' He seemed to feel that closed the subject; obviously he was in the grip of some mindless ritual behaviour. I knew all about mindless ritual behaviour from

Sociology 1; like when people say, 'How are you,' and you always say 'Fine,' no matter how sick/injured/mentally disturbed you really are.

The muscles in Tony's forearms rippled as he turned over the huge listing. He actually had very nice forearms, I noticed. He would have been quite handsome if it hadn't been for his face.

'Well, here we go. Job started, SYS001 assigned... oh.'

'What? Don't laugh, it's not funny. Tony! Don't be a prick, what is it?'

'Hey, Geoff. Get a look at this!'

Geoff ambled over and peered at the listing. He snorted and went back to his desk, sniggering and shaking his head. I looked again at the listlog, but couldn't see anything out of the ordinary, except, of course, the message about the job being cancelled. 'How long did you say you'd been looking at this dump?'

It wasn't fair. They were all against me.

'Three days.'

I hate it when people laugh at me. I really, really hate it.

'Jesus, Fiona. Look at this. Can-celled by op-e-rator. Oh, sorry – you can read, can't you?'

I really hate it worse than anything.

***

It could have been worse, I thought later. At least they didn't rat on me to Goebbels. I sighed with relief as I pushed open our front door. It was Thursday, we wouldn't see Morelli for another six days, and it was quite some time since Patrick had mentioned his wild scheme to plant a stick book under Morelli's mattress; I was starting to cherish a tiny hope that he'd given up the idea, or forgotten about it.

The house was deserted, like the Mary Celeste. In the kitchen, a bowl of cake mixture had been abandoned with a spoon in it, and Patrick's school bag lay open on the table. I put my bag down slowly. I had a very bad feeling about this. My mother has never been known to leave anything lying around in her life, especially something half finished. My skin crawled with foreboding. Could a monster have come up from the cellar and eaten them? But we didn't have a cellar. The back door was open. I went out into the garden, very cautiously.

My mother and Patrick were standing together

under the big pine tree, looking up. I was so relieved to see them both alive and in one piece that it didn't occur to me that anything might be wrong. I went over to join them.

'Hi Mum, Patrick.'

My mother turned on me a look of such reproach that I nearly shrivelled up on the spot.

'What's wrong, Mum?'

Patrick, as usual when something has gone wrong, was sniggering to himself. My mother pointed silently up into the tree.

Moses was crouched on an impossibly thin branch, about twenty feet up. As I watched, horrified, he made a grab for the next branch down, missed, overbalanced, and finally got all four feet in a row on the same branch. He rocked back and forth a few times and just managed to hang on. I could see the whole branch bending under his weight. He was crying, his faint, plaintive wailing drifting down to us.

I looked at my mother. She was looking expectantly back at me. I looked at Patrick. He was also looking expectantly at me. I looked at Moses. He looked trustingly back at me, and went on crying.

Dance of Chaos

I couldn't understand why everyone was looking at me. What was I supposed to do? Climbing a tree was more in Patrick's line.

'Why don't you go up and get him?'

'No way, Fiona, he's your cat, you get him down. I'm not climbing up there and getting a broken neck.'

'Oh, come on, Patrick, you could do it easily. How d'you think I'm supposed to climb a tree in these shoes?'

Patrick shrugged. 'That's your problem, isn't it? Of course, some people might have the brains to get changed first. Then again, others wouldn't.'

'Oh, come on, Patrick. You go up and get him for me.'

'No way, Fiona, forget it. He'll claw me to pieces.'

It didn't seem like a good idea to ask my mother to go up the tree. But I really didn't see what else I could do if Patrick really wouldn't do it, as my father wasn't home. I wasn't even in a position to bargain with Patrick with my mother standing there listening to everything we said. If only she'd go back to the kitchen, perhaps we could come to some arrangement, but she seemed to be rooted to the spot.

'Oh, the poor little thing, listen to him crying.'

I cried a bit myself, but nobody noticed. It was becoming clear that I was actually going to have to climb the tree myself. Why are there never any men around when you need them, I wondered crossly. If this had happened yesterday I bet Father Morelli would have gone up and got him down for me. Where was Tim, and why hadn't he rung me, I wondered, although I couldn't really imagine him climbing a tree either.

'I bet Father Morelli would get him down for me,' I said, hoping to awaken in Patrick a sense of his responsibilities. Like all the other efforts people had made over the years to awaken Patrick to a sense of his responsibilities, it was doomed to failure.

'Yeah, he might. Why don't you ring him up?'

I wished I could postpone the whole situation till my father got home. But Moses was crying. I took off my shoes.

The first branch was within easy reach. I put my hand on it and looked up thoughtfully. Other, quite thick, branches were spaced conveniently above it; it didn't look too difficult. But getting up onto the first branch was going to be a bit of a problem; it was at shoulder height. I thought about how we used to climb trees when I was a kid. It seemed a very long time ago. You had to link both hands over the branch, swing one knee up and over it, and then sort of hitch yourself up. I seemed to remember it being quite easy, but imagining myself doing it now was, somehow, different. Of course, we didn't wear pencil skirts at St Bedivere's.

'Oh, Patrick, come on, please?'

'No.'

I sighed and linked my hands over the branch. I swung my feet off the ground, but the bark hurt my hands and I had to let go.

'Do you think you could just –'

'No.'

I looked around for inspiration. I had been going to ask Patrick to give me a boost up to the first branch, but he was obviously determined to contribute nothing to the enterprise. Then I noticed the garden furniture.

'Look, how about helping me shift the garden table over, I can stand on it and get a start.'

He couldn't really get out of giving me that

much help, not in front of our mother. We carried the garden table, which had been recently scrubbed and still smelt faintly of lavender, over to the tree. I got on the table.

'It's a bit wobbly, could you sort of hold it steady?'

Starting from the table, after a few attempts I was able to get one knee up and heave myself onto the branch. I sat on it and examined the knee, which was grazed. My stockings were already a write-off. I looked dismally up, and tried to count the branches remaining to be ascended.

'Hang on, Moses, I'm coming,' I called up. Moses went on crying.

The next half-dozen or so branches weren't really all that difficult, but then they started to look a bit thin. I wondered nervously if the next one would hold my weight. I remembered that I was a lot heavier than Moses. I looked down; the ground seemed to be a long way off. I looked up. This was a bad idea, as Moses, catching my eye, became excited and started scrabbling around on his tiny branch, dislodging all kinds of crap which fell into my face.

'Get a move on, Fiona, it'll be dark before you get up there at this rate.'

It's wonderful to have sympathetic family members to aid you in your endeavours.

'Darling, are you quite sure it's safe?'

Safe? Who did she think she was kidding? From where I was, it seemed anything but safe. I wondered whose neck I would wring first if I got out of this alive. I scrambled up a couple more branches and stopped.

'Get on with it, Fiona. God, an arthritic old granny could climb a tree faster than that.'

'Hang on, I've got something in my eye.' I hoped it was only a bit of bark, and not an insect. It had occurred to me that there might be spiders in the tree. I finally managed to get the speck out of my eye. My hair was full of pine needles, and bits of crud that Moses had knocked down. I was less than halfway up.

'Oh God, I can't bear to watch. She'll kill herself. Patrick, you look and tell me what's happening.'

'Well, she's sitting on a branch about ten feet up. She looks mighty silly.'

'You shut up, you little rat. I asked you to go up and you were too chicken.'

'I was not!'

'Oh, yes you were. Patrick's a scaredy cat, cowardy cowardy custard, your mother –' I stopped myself hurriedly, remembering that our mother was still there.

Another branch. They were closer together now, and they were all filled in between with little twigs and needles that brushed against my hair and got in my face. Something slipped down my back inside my shirt; I shuddered, and my foot slipped off the branch I was standing on. I clutched frantically at the nearest branch, and managed to stop myself from falling. With the other hand I managed to pull my shirt out of my waistband, and whatever it was fell out. I told myself firmly that it had only been a piece of bark.

I thought about giving up, but Moses was still up there crying, and Patrick was down there laughing. I tried an appeal to his better nature.

'Hey, Patrick?'

'Yeah?'

'If I get killed trying to climb this tree, then will you go up and get him?'

'Oh, yeah, sure, if you get killed.'

Damn. It's so hard to negotiate without blackmail.

The rest of the climb was a nightmare. I snagged my shirt on a twig and ripped a great tear in it. Every time something brushed against my hair, I was convinced it was a huge spider. My clothes became more and more filthy and torn. At one stage I heard a ripping sound from my skirt, and knew with horrible certainty that the back seam had given way.

I finally got within about three feet of Moses, and I just knew that, if I got onto a branch even a millimetre thinner than the one I was on, it would break and send me crashing to earth, which was now so far down that I couldn't even see it through the branches. Moses, presumably heartened by my presence, started wailing like a banshee. I pressed in closer to what I was fairly sure was still the trunk, and prayed.

'Moses? Puss, puss puss, puss, puss, come down to Mummy.'

I heard muffled sniggering from Planet Earth. I couldn't imagine what Patrick thought was so funny. Moses looked at me as if he thought I was insane, and howled even louder.

I went up two more branches; they were

bending like anything now. Finally, I could almost touch him if I stretched my arm right out. I held out my hand to him reassuringly. Moses stood up, arched his back playfully, and danced backwards up the branch. He stopped several feet away, sat down, and looked at me. I looked back at him.

As I climbed around to the other side, a branch finally did break. I shrieked, dangling by my hands, for the moment not even caring if I looked ridiculous. Finally, I managed to feel around and find another branch under my feet. I was soaked with sweat, and my shirt had given way under the arms. I was no nearer to Moses than I had been before.

I pondered the situation for several minutes. I had read somewhere that when you're really stuck, you should reflect quietly, without pressing for a solution. Whoever wrote that had obviously never tried to get a cat out of a tree. After several minutes of quiet reflection, I was standing awkwardly on a very thin branch near the top of a pine tree, with a cat sneering at me from several feet away, a grazed knee, ruined stockings, half the seams on my clothes ripped open, three broken fingernails and God knew what in my hair. I decided it was better to press for a solution.

Moving very, very slowly and carefully, I

manoeuvred myself to a point directly underneath Moses. Then I stopped and remained still for a while, talking softly and calmly to him all the time. I wrapped my legs around the tree and made sure I was as secure as I could be, and then I lunged suddenly and grabbed him by the scruff of the neck.

Moses let out a ghastly scream and lashed out with all four feet, but I did manage to get him over onto my chest, at the expense of some nasty scratches. After he was satisfied that I was bleeding at several points, he settled down and started purring loudly.

Then I realised that there was no way I could get down with one hand.

⍟CHAPTER TWENTY-SIX☙

Behold, how good and joyful a thing it is: brethren, to dwell together in unity! It is like the precious ointment upon the head...
Psalm 133:1–2

I thought at first that I might be able to make a rope out of my pantyhose and lower Moses to safety before climbing down myself, but I couldn't get them off without a) letting go of Moses and b) letting go of the tree, which I was now holding onto with both legs and one hand. I had to admit I was stuck.

The fire brigade men were very nice about it. I couldn't understand why my father was so cross when he got home. After all, how was I supposed to know there was an extension ladder in the shed?

***

The bath water stung in my scratches. After taking one look at my clothes, I had simply dropped them in the rubbish. Moses had eaten a huge dinner and fallen asleep on my bed; he seemed to have forgotten the whole incident already. I didn't think I'd ever been so tired in my life. I dragged myself out of the bath and into my pyjamas, too exhausted even to bend down to pull out the plug. My bed loomed invitingly and I collapsed into it, almost weeping with relief. It was only nine o'clock, but I felt as if a week had passed since I'd got up that morning. I drifted between sleeping and waking, Moses from long habit a comfortable weight at my feet.

'Fiona! Psssst!'

'Go away,' I moaned.

Patrick came in and sat on my bed. I sighed wearily. No doubt he was going to apologise for putting me through such hell by refusing to climb the tree himself. I decided I would forgive him straight away, it would make him go away sooner.

'Listen, Fiona, I've got this really good filthy stick book, for Morelli.'

Oh, God.

'Fine, you can give it to him on Wednesday.'

'No, stupid, for planting under his mattress. When d'you want to do it?'

'Me? Look, forget it. Bugger off, I want to go to sleep.'

'You've got to do it, you said you would.'

'I did not!'

'Anyway, listen, I went back and had another look at the place, they've got ivy growing all the way up the wall, it should be dead simple to climb up.'

'Look, I don't even want to hear about climbing anything, ever again. Just piss off, Patrick, leave me alone.' I was deathly tired, I had scratches, a grazed knee, bruises and I seemed to have pulled all my muscles. If he pestered me any more, I thought I might burst into tears. In fact, I thought I might anyway, it seemed like the most appropriate response to the situation.

'God, Fiona, don't start crying again, you're always crying. Jesus.'

'Look, just leave me alone. I don't care about your stupid vendetta.'

'Oh, come on, Fi, won't it be funny? Just imagine when they find the stick book, how he'll look.'

Oh, God.

'Alright, alright, I'll do it, okay? Just go away now.'

***

I woke up with a headache and a terrible sense of foreboding. The headache was because I'd forgotten to open the window. The sense of foreboding was nebulous, and I couldn't put my finger on what was wrong. I wasn't late for work, I hadn't done anything bad, Moses hadn't done anything bad, as far as I knew Patrick hadn't done anything else that he was likely to get caught for. All through getting dressed, catching the tram to work and an undistinguished day at the office, the feeling of doom stayed with me. It wasn't until I was getting on the tram to come home that it hit me.

I had agreed to climb an ivy-covered wall, penetrate the stronghold of the Dominicans, and plant a pornographic magazine under the mattress of an innocent man. This would result in prison, death, excommunication, or all of the above, not to mention terminal embarrassment.

Well, I'd just have to tell him I'd changed my mind. Charged with Firm Resolution I marched into our house and up to Patrick's room.

All that Firm Resolution didn't do me much good, because Patrick wasn't there. I retreated to my room for some serious worrying.

By the time my mother called me for dinner, I had convinced myself that I had nothing to worry about. The situation was essentially unchanged, Patrick still had his wild scheme and was still convinced that I would help him perpetrate it. True, I had now given him some reason to believe this, but he'd believed it anyway, and at least while he was waiting for me to do it, he wouldn't attempt to do it himself.

Dinner was fairly uncomfortable, as our dining room chairs are unpadded, and some of the bruises I'd acquired going up the pine tree were on my bottom. Also, Patrick, who'd arrived home while I was engaged in Deep Thought, kept catching my eye and winking. I found this really irritating, especially as sooner or later our father, who normally drifts through life in a cloud of Ancient Greek and other arcane stuff, has these occasional flashes of keen-eyed perceptiveness, and tends to start suddenly noticing things just when one would rather he didn't. Sometimes living at home with one's family can be such a drawback.

Neither of us could say anything during the

washing up, as our mother was in and out of the kitchen all the time. Afterwards, I tried to escape to my room, but Patrick caught up with me on the stairs.

'So, when are you going to do it?'

'Soon, okay? First we have to know their routine, there'll be times when they're all in church, then I'll do it. You'll have to find out when all their services are and that.'

'I've been trying to find out off Morelli, but it's hard. Can't you ring up and find out?'

'Oh, for sure. Excuse me, I'm planning to plant a stick book under Father Morelli's mattress and I just wanted to check out your routine so I can do it without getting caught. Forget it, Patrick, if you want me to do it you'll have to find out all the facts first. Look, all you have to do is ask him when you're having your counselling thing.'

'I can't just ask him, he'll think it's funny.'

'Look, just tell him you think you're getting a vocation after all, and you want to know what it's like. Tell him you can't sleep every night thinking about it.'

'He won't believe that.'

'Well, it's just your job to make him believe it.'

'How?'

'Well, you could maybe start off really subtly, have a rosary sticking out of your pocket and ask him a few questions about how he knew he had his vocation. Then, when he tells you, just look really sort of admiring and don't say anything else. Then, if he stays for dinner, you could try to look really far away and just come out with a few remarks about St Francis or something. No, St Dominic, that'd be better.'

'Why can't you do it?'

I had a sudden flash of inspiration.

'Because I'm not going to be here on Wednesday, I'm going out.'

***

'You three. Get in here.'

As if Monday mornings weren't bad enough anyway, Goebbels had to have a meeting. No doubt we were all about to be hauled over the carpet again for some imaginary misdemeanour.

'Right!' Goebbels barked, glaring at us from under his bushy eyebrows. As usual, we had not been invited to sit down, and stood in a line in front of his desk like errant schoolboys. 'From now on we will be running this office on modified flexitime. This folder will be kept in the corner there –' he jabbed an accusing finger at a table just outside his office – 'and you will write in the time you start work each day, the time you go home, and the time you go to lunch and come back. There is to be no carrying over of time from one day to the next, is that clear? You are expected to work a minimum of seven and a half hours per day. Any abuse of the system will result in its being cancelled immediately. Right, that's all.'

'Um, does that mean we can start when we like?'

Goebbels fixed me with a horrid glare.

'No, Fiona, it does not. You may start work between seven-thirty and ten o'clock. There is to be no tardiness, do you understand?'

We all understood. We shuffled out of Goebbels' office like old men on a soup line. How was it that he could even make something good, like being allowed to start work later, sound like a reprimand, I wondered. I thought about the difference it would make to my life being able to start at ten o'clock instead of nine. I could stay in bed till a reasonable time, and miss the rush hour on the tram. Of course, I'd have to stay a lot later, but Goebbels always left promptly at four so as to drive home to Templestowe before the rush hour; he came in at seven-thirty each morning for the same reason, as I'd discovered when I was doing morning shift in the machine room. I thought for a moment about the kind of deep-seated perversion that would make a person deliberately get up before six every morning. So, I concluded, the latter end of the day would pass quite pleasantly without him around. In fact, if I started at ten, I'd only be here at the same time as Goebbels for six hours of the day. I wondered if I could reduce it even further. I could eliminate a further two hours, I realised, by going to lunch at the same time as he got back.

I watched carefully to see when Goebbels went to lunch, and discovered that he went at twelve o'clock on the dot. Right, I thought. I'll go at one and come back at two. Of course, this would mean I'd have to stay till six-thirty every night, but I reckoned it was worth it. I wondered if anybody else would arrive at the same conclusions.

***

The next morning, I ran into Jane in the lift.

'Hi, Jane, you're later then usual.'

'Yeah, well this new flexitime thing, I figure I

can avoid Goebbels as much as possible by starting and finishing late. He gets in at half past seven every morning.'

I smiled to myself. Great minds think alike, as they say.

I settled into my desk, happily aware that if Goebbels wanted to make me suffer, he had only four hours in which to do it. One day, I thought, I'd be the one to make him suffer. When I had Carl Jacobs' job, I thought, I would order him to work nine to five, so he'd have the full force of the rush hour each day. 'This is an office,' I'd tell him superciliously, 'not a bloody amusement park.' Then I'd blow smoke in his face. I didn't smoke, but Goebbels was such a rabid anti-smoker it would be worth it just for that once, even if I got sick.

Jane passed me on her way into Goebbels' office. She looked incredibly smart and put together, as usual. I wondered idly how she managed not to get creases in the back of her shirt.

Goebbels' voice split the Monday morning quiet like a clap of thunder.

'And where the hell do you think you've been all morning?'

I strained but couldn't hear Jane's reply.

Dance of Chaos

'Flexitime! Secretaries don't work on flexitime, you stupid woman. I expect you to be here when I'm here, not when it damned well suits you. This is not a holiday camp we're running here, Madam, let me tell you.'

'Too bloody right it isn't, more like a fucking salt mine, you fascist bastard!'

'What!'

'You heard me, you cunt. You think you're the only person in the world, don't you. Jesus. You short hairy little prick, why don't you jam it up your arse sideways and choke!'

Jane came marching out of Goebbels' office while he was still coughing and spluttering. Geoff, Tony and I sat up straight and watched her out of sight with awe; I wanted to applaud, but didn't quite dare with Goebbels, aka the short hairy little prick, right in my line of sight. I was fascinated. Could it really be possible to talk to Goebbels like that and survive? Had we all been cringing and yes-sir-no-sirring for all these months for no reason?

I waited a few minutes and casually walked out as if I were going to the lavatory. I found Jane muttering darkly and cleaning out her desk drawers, that is if a person who has the contents of her desk drawers all neatly sorted and laid out like surgical tools at all times can ever be said to be cleaning them out.

'Jane, you were wonderful. How on earth did you get up the nerve to talk to him like that?'

'Jesus, Fiona. I lost my temper, what d'you think? Now I'm going to be wonderful and unemployed.'

'Why, are you resigning?'

'God, don't I wish. No, I'm not resigning, but I hardly think I'm going to be around much longer after that little episode, do you?'

'Oh, he couldn't sack you just for that. All you did was call him a few names.'

'Couldn't he? Then why haven't you ever?'

I didn't really have an answer for that. After all, he'd got rid of Scott pretty smartly, without any reason at all that I knew of. And the reason no one had ever called him a short, hairy little prick to his face before, as both Jane and I knew perfectly well, was that we were all far too frightened of him.

✼CHAPTER TWENTY-SEVEN✥

They are corrupt, and become abominable in their doings: there is none that doeth good, no not one.
Psalm 14:2

'He couldn't sack you for that,' I'd said, nevertheless Jane was gone the next day. No one bothered to tell us she'd left, but her desk was empty, and we all knew why. Things were pretty unsettled. Someone had drawn a penis on the whiteboard, with hair sprouting improbably all over it, feet at the bottom and 'S.H.L.P.' written under it. This drove Goebbels into an almost unbelievable paroxysm of rage; he turned deep purple and swelled up like a bullfrog, and for a wonderful moment, I thought he was going to drop dead on the spot with a heart attack. Presently he got his breath, however, and ordered me to clean the whiteboard. A bit later he called me into his office and gave me a huge pile of photocopying to do. Evidently I was going to have to do all the secretarial things until he got a new secretary. Was this what I did all that training for, I asked myself bitterly, but wasn't quite game to say anything.

The photocopier was two floors down and utterly incomprehensible, a great cubical monster of a thing with buttons everywhere. It emitted a menacing growl from time to time. I had never actually worked one before, and spent twenty minutes looking for a slot to put the things into. Then I went to find someone to help me.

In a nasty little area in the corner I found the human equivalent of the photocopying machine; in fact, if she'd had a big green button on her forehead I'd have thought she was a near relative. Squat, square and menacing, she glared up at me from behind a desk half submerged in what looked like a millenium's accumulation of dead bus tickets.

'Um, excuse me, I wonder if you could show me how to use the photocopying machine? I can't find where you put the paper in.'

'God, has it run out again already? I only filled it up this morning.' She glared at me suspiciously. 'You haven't been doing private stuff, have you?'

'I haven't done anything, I can't find the slot to

put it in.'

She snarled at me and waddled off to the machine. When she got there, she removed a little flat box from the side of it. The little box seemed to be full of plain white paper. She slammed it back in.

'What the hell are you on about? There's plenty of paper.'

'But I can't find where you put the things you're copying.'

The woman looked at me with unbelieving disgust, as if she'd found a dead rat in her lunch. I thought it was a bit unfair for anyone who looked like a photocopying machine to look at me like that. Silently, she raised a flat lid on top of the machine.

'You put it under there.'

After giving me another look of utter scorn and loathing, she lurched off back to her lair. I contemplated the open machine. Obviously you had to put the paper in flat. I put it in flat and closed the lid. I pressed the big green button and waited hopefully.

For a second, I thought nothing was going to happen. Then the whole machine started shuddering and groaning. I stepped back nervously. What if the green button was the Self Destruct? Don't be silly, I reassured myself, if it was it'd be red. A blinding light flashed somewhere inside, and suddenly a single sheet of paper shot out one end, into a little tray I hadn't noticed before. I picked it up. It was hot, I hoped it wasn't radioactive. I turned it over. I turned it over again.

It was blank on both sides.

'Um, excuse me. I think the machine's broken, it just gave me one sheet of blank paper.'

***

I really think people are terribly unfair. How was I supposed to know you had to put the stuff in upside down? And one page at a time? It took ages to do it all, and when I got back upstairs Goebbels screamed at me for taking so long. Of course, he probably would have screamed at me anyway.

'God, I hope he gets a new secretary soon,' I remarked later, when he was out to lunch. 'I don't think I can take much more of this.'

Geoff sniggered.

'What's so funny?'

'He's not getting one. H. R. said the size of the department doesn't justify a full time secretary. You're it, Fiona.'

Dance of Chaos

No wonder he was in such a foul mood. But he was in an even worse one the next day, when the drawing of the penis reappeared, even larger, on the whiteboard. This time it had a face, two beady little eyes and a great, fuzzy beard. 'A short, hairy little... person', the caption said.

We all lined up in front of Goebbels' desk, shuffling our feet and carefully not looking at each other. He had waited till three o'clock before calling us in, so he could get both lots of operators.

'You are all aware that there have been filthy drawings appearing on the whiteboard. Now I am aware that some of you think this is funny, it's only what I'd expect from such a slovenly, unprofessional lot of people. God, look at yourselves. You make me sick. Now the whiteboard, as you are perfectly well aware, is to be used only for work purposes, not for sick, juvenile toilet humour. Anybody found putting anything on the whiteboard that is not directly work-related will be instantly dismissed. Is that clear? Now I am prepared to overlook the disgusting, childish graffiti that has appeared over the last two days, but if there is any recurrence of this the culprit will be instantly dismissed. Is that clear?'

***

'I reckon whoever did it ought to get a medal.'

'Oh, you're just juvenile. You are slovenly and unprofessional, look at yourself, you make me sick.'

'Look out, he's coming.'

***

The rest of the day was even more nerve-racking than usual, until four o'clock anyway. Goebbels kept jumping out from behind things and barking. We were all hugely relieved when he went home at his usual time. I was even more relieved to get home, but then with a sinking feeling I remembered that it was Wednesday.

Patrick was in his room. I went in, and found him lounging on his bed with his shoes on, reading Lives of the Saints. I looked for the stick book tucked inside, but no – he was actually reading Lives of the Saints. I found this extremely sinister.

'Hey, Fiona, listen to this. It says he dedicated himself with ardour to the work of his own sanctification. Tosser.'

'Got your rosary?'

'Yeah, I went into the city after school. Got the biggest one I could find.' He brandished an enormous rosary in screaming electric-blue crystal.

'God, Patrick, don't you think you went a bit

overboard? That's not the kind of thing boys usually have. Anyway, d'you know what to do with it?'

'Who cares what you do with it, he's hardly going to challenge me to a praying contest, is he?'

'Who knows what you might provoke him to with that thing? Tell me something else about St Dominic, without looking in the book.' I made a silent bet with myself that he couldn't.

'He invented the Spanish Inquisition.'

'No, he didn't, it was Pope something, after some lateral council or something, don't you remember Father Simpson going on about it at dinner, that time?'

'Did so, it's in here. I'll show you, hang on... shit, I lost my place. Hang on... oh, shit.'

***

I spent the next hour and a half drilling Patrick on the life of St Dominic, foregoing my bath and beauty routine even though Morelli was coming. That's how much I love my brother. But there; some of us just live for others. It went like this:

Me: Tell me one thing St Dominic is famous for.

Patrick: Being a tosser. Ow! Stop it! OW! Paxpaxpax…

Me: What's one thing St Dominic is famous for?

Patrick: Give me a minute… Almost got it…

Me: Come on, do you know the answer or not?

Patrick: Being a saint.

Me: Besides that.

Patrick: Well, I don't know.

Me: I'll give you a clue. He invented something that's used all over the world, even today.

Patrick: Toilet paper?

Me: Don't be stupid, of course not.

Patrick: I know! The double entry bookkeeping system! He invented that.

Me: No, that isn't it.

Patrick: Are you sure? Here, give me that book.

Me: Ow! Get off!

Patrick: Dammit, Fiona, now you've torn it.

Me: It was your fault. You shouldn't have tried

to grab it.

Patrick: Bitch! Nothing's ever your bloody fault, is it?

Me: No, it usually isn't, because I think what I'm doing. Like now, I am helping you keep up your sordid little pretence of wanting to be a priest. And I don't have to do that, I'd rather be doing other stuff, actually. Some people would appreciate having a sister that helps them.

Patrick: !!!!

Me: Now come on, do you know what he invented or not?

Patrick: (sullenly) No.

Me: He invented the rosary! Now do you see why it's important to know this stuff? You can work that in when you're waving it about.

Patrick: I'm not going to be waving it about, Fiona, just let it sort of casually hang out of my pocket. You know, in a subtle way.

Me: Whatever. Tell me one thing he did when he was a student.

Patrick: Um... drank a lot of beer?

Me: Besides that. Something that not all

students do.

Patrick: Cheated on his exams?

Me: No.

Patrick: Buggered a goat?

Me: Look, if you're not going to take this seriously…

***

'Wow. Wow.'

'Moses! Stop it. Leave Father Morelli alone.'

'Mrrrrrao. Wow.'

'Moses! Come here.'

He didn't, of course. Instead, he sat up and batted gently at Morelli's rosary, which hung off his belt.

'Moses! Leave that alone.'

'Don't worry, Miss MacDougall, he's not bothering me. Would he like a piece of chicken, do you think?'

I held my breath. Feeding Moses at the table was anathema to my mother, and I couldn't imagine what had got into Morelli to make him so mellow. I wondered if I could use it to create a Thin End of the Wedge. It was just possible that my mother's reverence for The Cloth would overcome her mania for hygiene.

'Wow! Wow!'

'I'm sure he would, Father.'

Morelli handed Moses a piece of chicken. Moses bolted it down and jumped onto Morelli's lap. Morelli carried on discussing Attic Synthesizers, or something, with my father while Moses turned around in a number of circles and settled down, purring loudly. I couldn't figure out what had made him take such an undeserved liking to Morelli, but it certainly seemed to be having a salutary effect on him. Several times during the course of the meal I noticed him furtively stroking Moses under the table. Perhaps Patrick's rosary had put him in a good mood.

Nothing awful happened during dinner, which must have been a great surprise to everybody after the previous two weeks. Moses stayed on Morelli's lap, purring, and occasionally taking a swipe at his fork when he wanted another bit of chicken. When we moved into the sitting room for coffee, he followed at Morelli's heels, and jumped back onto his lap as soon as he sat down. Patrick was respectful and deferential. My mother was charming, and seemed not to have noticed Morelli feeding Moses at the dinner table. My father was his usual vague self. Morelli actually seemed quite jovial. At last he must have decided we're nice people after all, I thought.

It was only when he was leaving, and I went to let him out, that I wondered.

'Oh, by the way, Miss MacDougall, if Patrick is going to wave that rosary around, it might be an idea if he learned how to use it.'

❧CHAPTER TWENTY-EIGHT☙

*False witnesses did rise up: they laid to
my charge things that I knew not.*
Psalm 35:11

Patrick wasn't at all pleased when I told him what Morelli had said about his rosary. He made a number of unsuitable remarks about Morelli's probable ancestry and habits, which I thought was a bit unfair, considering he'd been the one to say that it didn't matter if he didn't know how to use it. I wanted to know what he'd done with it to give himself away, but he had become sulky, and wouldn't tell me. He wouldn't tell me anything else either, which was just fine with me. I was heartily sick of the whole 'going to be a priest' thing.

***

The penis had appeared on the whiteboard

again next morning. This time it had a bubble coming out of the top saying 'Get back to vork, Kaffirs!'. Goebbels was in his office with the door shut, very red in the face and screaming into the telephone. He was obviously shouting at the top of his voice, but I couldn't make out the words. I went over and had a closer look at the whiteboard. The penis had glasses and a beard; it was really a very clever likeness.

'Good likeness, isn't it?'

'Did you do it, Geoff?'

'Huh! Wouldn't tell you if I did. Whoever did it'd better keep bloody quiet, he's in there now screaming to H. R. Reckons he'll sack the whole department if it doesn't stop.'

'God, I wish I knew. It wasn't you, was it, Tony?'

Tony wasn't able to do anything except giggle inanely.

'Must be one of the operators, then. If it isn't one of us.'

'Must be.' Geoff looked suspiciously smug. I just knew he was the one; apart from anything else he, like Goebbels, was another early starter, so he'd have the opportunity. On the other hand, it might have been done overnight. Then it could be any one of us: the night shift operators, the morning shift operators, the cleaning lady… no, the cleaning lady wouldn't know about the 'short hairy little prick' remark, not having been there when Jane said it. And, given the hours Goebbels kept, she'd probably never even seen him, so she could hardly draw this wickedly accurate caricature of him.

There was no peace at all that day. After he finished his screaming match with the H. R. department, Goebbels rushed out of his office like a bear in heat, and ordered me to clean the whiteboard. Then he spent the rest of the day patrolling around the floor, stopping at each desk to growl, and bark 'Get on with your work.'

He kept rushing back to peer at the whiteboard, in case it had suddenly acquired a fresh drawing. We were all worn out by the time he left at four o'clock, scattering dire warnings.

'Hey, guys. Look what I found.' Geoff held up a stick book, open at the centrefold. She was certainly pretty, but I thought the picture was a bit rude.

'I reckon we should stick it up on the inside of his cupboard door, he'll find it when he goes to hang up his coat.'

'Yeah, great. He won't be so quick to accuse us, once everybody knows he's a dirty pervert.'

We stuck up the centrefold with sticky tape and closed the cupboard. Then we opened it. The effect was striking, he couldn't miss it.

Tony wasn't satisfied.

'I reckon that one's too wimpy. What happened to that other magazine, the one with the pig? Fiona had it last.'

I would rather not have remembered.

'I threw it in the rubbish, you creep.'

'Bet you didn't. I bet you really took it home.'

'I did not!'

'I bet you read it every night.'

Geoff cracked up. What juvenile minds one comes in contact with in the working world, I thought loftily to myself as I stalked back to my desk. I was above this childish horseplay, made of finer stuff than these crass peasants. I imagined myself as a philosopher, in a tower. No, a sorcerer. Casting spells and reading ancient tomes of magic, I passed my days and nights far above the rabble who toiled in the fields below my enchanted castle.

Dance of Chaos

Occasionally a bat would fly in through one of the high, gothic windows, bearing a message from one of my fellow sorcerers in far-off lands. Suddenly a shadow fell across my crystal ball. I looked up, but, sadly, it was not a bat.

'Hello, Fiona,' said Carl Jacobs.

'Oh, hello, Mr Jacobs, I didn't see you there.'

'Lost in thought, I see.'

'Yes, pretty well.'

'Hmmm. That's a nice chair you've got.'

'Yes, isn't it? It's really comfortable.'

'I'm sure it is. Mr Goebbels not in?'

'Oh, no, he's gone home. He always goes home at four o'clock.'

'Does he, indeed? Well, perhaps you'd ask him to come and see me tomorrow morning.'

Jacobs loomed off in his majestic way, and I forgot all about him.

***

When I got home, Patrick jumped on me and dragged me up to his room.

'Fiona, I need you to help me. I have to know how to use the rosary, by next Wednesday.'

'So google it, what am I, an automatic teaching service? Ask Morelli, you've got him for Divinity, haven't you? Or get someone else to ask him, would be better.'

Patrick said something extremely rude, which I shall not repeat, about Father Morelli.

'Well, ask Mum then.'

'I'm not going near Mum till dinner, she told me to clean my room again. I'm supposed to be up here doing it.'

'Well, why don't you, then?'

'I already did, I shoved everything under the bed and sprayed Mr Sheen everywhere, she'll smell that and think it's clean.'

This made sense. I made a mental note to do the same in my own room.

'So are you going to help me or not?'

I sighed and sat down at his computer. I'd find the instructions for him and then perhaps I could have some peace and quiet until dinner. I fancied a nice long soak in the bath, with my new lilac bath salts.

I opened up Google and typed in 'How to use a rosary.' It immediately responded with 1,250,000 results. I love Google; I'm sure one day it will replace the entire school system. I picked one that looked good, and got a rude shock. It seemed demonically complicated. Apparently it's not enough to know the Hail Mary and the Our Father; you have to know eighty squillion other special prayers. Better print it out, I thought. Dad wasn't home yet. I sent it off to print on the printer in Dad's study, which we all had to share. That would take a couple of minutes, so while I was waiting I looked at Patrick's browser history.

'Um, Patrick, you might want to delete your history.'

'Why?'

'Well, I'm just taking a punt here, but Mum might not be thrilled to know you've been going to a site called "Boobpedia". Or "youporn.com". I mean, just a wild guess, but it kind of detracts from the whole pure, saintly, I want to be a priest thing.'

***

'Um. Excuse me?'

'Well, what is it?' Gracious as ever, the little

ray of sunshine, otherwise known as the Short Hairy Little Prick, sat behind his desk and glared angrily at me out of his little red eyes.

'Well, Mr Jacobs was in here yesterday, after you went home? He said would you go and see him this morning.'

'You stupid woman! Why didn't you tell me before?'

'I just got in. You said we could start at ten...'

'Oh, what's the use. Get out of my sight, you make me sick.' Goebbels shot me a look of pure hatred out of his piggy little eyes and stamped off muttering to himself. I could tell he was wondering if I was a new sort of kaffir. I was a bit surprised, you'd have thought he'd be in a good mood this morning, as there was nothing on the whiteboard.

***

He was back before long, steaming worse than ever.

'Fiona. Get into my office now!' he barked. In fact, he probably would have thundered if he hadn't screamed himself hoarse the day before, on the phone to H. R.

I followed him into the office.

'It is not enough that you haven't done a stroke of work since the day you started here. It is not enough that you've stolen the managing director's special chair out of the boardroom. It is not enough that you have given the managing director the impression that I'm off playing golf half the bloody day. You couldn't even be bothered to give me his message. You are the most idle, destructive employee this company has ever had the misfortune to be saddled with. You have done nothing but cause trouble since you've been here. Have you got anything to say for yourself?'

I had, actually, but he got going again before I had a chance to draw breath.

'You are totally incompetent, it takes you two hours even to do a bit of simple photocopying. I've had enough of you, this department does not tolerate slackers. Or dishonesty!'

'Dishonesty?' I was genuinely amazed; although I was pretty well used to Goebbels and his outbursts by now, his accusations had always had some connection, however tenuous, with reality. But I'd never so much as taken home a pen from the office. They didn't have nice ones.

'Don't play innocent with me, Missy.' God, he was offensive. I wished I could take a deep breath, split my shirt and turn green, like the Incredible

Hulk. I'd pick him up by his feet, swing him around my head a few times, and bash his brains out on the wall. Or perhaps I'd let him beg for mercy for a few minutes first, and then tear him slowly limb from limb.

While I was contemplating this pleasant fantasy, I had, unfortunately, missed the actual accusation. I'd better find out what it is this time, I thought, just in case it's something really bad.

'Um, I'm sorry, I didn't quite catch...'

For a moment I thought he was going to swell up and burst. Then he seemed to get a grip on himself.

'I am referring to your falsification of the timesheets.'

'What?'

'Don't say what to me. You know perfectly well what I'm talking about. You take two hour lunch breaks and put down an hour. You go to lunch at twelve o'clock and come back at two, and write down that you went at one. Do you think I'm stupid?'

Yes.

'No, of course not. But –'

'I don't care what you think. I don't care if you think I'm stupid, I don't give a damn what you think. This cheating on your times had better stop, or else you'll wind up in more trouble than you know what to do with.'

'But I didn't –'

'I don't want to hear it. Now get out of my sight.'

'Look, I've never –'

'I said I don't want to hear it, now get back to work, are you deaf?'

***

I spent the rest of the day fuming. Nobody had ever accused me of anything like that. I wished I'd thought of it first and done it, since I had evidently been found guilty of it anyway, without even being allowed to deny it. I couldn't even go and talk to Jane about it, Goebbels had already sacked her. I wondered why he hadn't sacked me, since he obviously hated me so much. Perhaps he was about to. Perhaps, even now, my pink slip was being got ready in the depths of H. R. I thought, with a shiver, of being sacked for dishonesty. How would I ever be able to get another job, it would be almost like having a criminal record. I imagined still living with my parents, unemployed, when I was forty.

It didn't bear thinking about, so I didn't.

☙CHAPTER TWENTY-NINE❧

I will take no wicked thing in hand; I hate the sins of unfaithfulness: there shall no such cleave unto me.
Psalm 101:4

I meant not to think about Goebbels and his paranoid delusions, but it kept popping into my mind. By the time I got home that night, I had worked myself into a state of nervous irritation. I wanted to kick him in the head until he was dead, as that old song of Peter's went. Failing that, I thought it would be rather nice to kick somebody else.

Patrick met me at the door and followed me upstairs. I greeted him with sisterly affection.

'Bugger off, Patrick.'

'No, I won't. You promised, Fi, come on, when're you going to do it? If you leave it much longer Morelli'll die of old age first.'

'Look, for the last time, I'm not doing it.'

'You promised.'

'No, I didn't, that wasn't a promise, it was just, just, a sort of statement of intention. And my intention's changed, okay? It's a silly idea and we could get into untold trouble, and I'm not having anything to do with it.'

'You said you would. You did, Fiona.'

I tried another tack. 'Look, how would it look, getting caught breaking and entering in a monastery? I'm going out with a law student, for God's sake. A *graduate* law student.'

'Really? I thought he dumped you again. Back on, are you?'

'We will be, as soon as he calls me.' Why hadn't he, I wondered. I was sure it hadn't taken him this long to call me, all the other times he'd given me the flick.

Patrick snorted. 'Yeah, right. Face it, Fiona, the guy's a complete waste of space, and you're better off without him.'

Was I? I wasn't sure. But then common sense

reasserted itself. If I gave up on Tim, I'd have to go through it all again with someone else. All that first date bullshit, all of it. It was all just too much trouble, and I didn't even know anyone else suitable, and Tim, when he was around, could be a lot of fun. What the hell business was it of Patrick's, anyway?

'Mind your own business, Patrick.' I brought out the heavy artillery. 'You're too young to understand.'

'I'm not too young to add up four months, that's how long since you heard from him, isn't it?'

'Look, just leave Tim out of this. It's none of your business, anyway.'

'I'm just saying, Fiona, the guy dumps you and then you don't hear from him for four months, doesn't that suggest that it might be over? He's probably got someone else by now.'

'You don't know anything about it.'

'I know that Tim's a tosser.'

'Whatever. Listen, you wouldn't believe what that bloody Goebbels did today. He accused me of cheating on my timesheets.'

Patrick, of course, received this news in a

caring and supportive way.

'Did you do it?'

'Of course I didn't do it! I never even thought about it! He just assumed that because he goes to lunch at twelve o'clock everybody else does too, and I actually go from one to two, so he reckons I've been taking two hours for lunch and only putting down one.'

Patrick shrugged. 'Well, if you're going to get blamed for it anyway, you might as well do it.'

'Thanks very much, Patrick, that's a really great idea. He'll be spying on me more than ever now, so why not give him some really good ammunition. I'm on two written warnings, you know.'

'Whatever. Anyway, doing this job on Morelli'll take your mind off it.'

'Patrick. I. Am. Not. Doing. It.'

'But you promised, you did, you said you'd do it, you did you did you did.'

'I did not. I only said I'd think about it. Well, I've thought about it, and I'm not doing it.' This was a bit unfair, as I had, in fact, said I'd do it. I'd been in bed after an incredibly gruelling couple of hours rescuing Moses from the big tree, and I would probably have agreed to murder the Dalai Lama if it had meant he'd leave me alone. I made a mental note that, the next time I was in that kind of situation, it would be best to pretend to be asleep; that way I couldn't say anything that could come against me later. The word is father to the deed, or something like that, anyway. I was sure I remembered my grandmother saying something like it.

'You did so promise. You know you did, Fiona. And I *acted in reliance on that promise.*'

Damn, now he was quoting Tim, the little hypocrite. Acting in reliance is one of those law things, apparently if you say something and someone else relies on what you said and does something because of it that turns out badly for them, they can sue you. Tim was always rabbiting on about things like that, which was one reason I didn't really mind all that much having a break from him.

Patrick was still pestering me. He went on and on and on, it was like a dripping tap. I felt as if my head was going to burst. By the time our mother called us for dinner, I had had all I could take. Something slid sideways in my head.

'Alright, alright, I'll do it! I'll do it tonight,

after dinner. Give me the stick book.'

***

I changed into a black sweater and jeans. It was what I'd seen people wear on television for burgling art galleries and banks and things, so I assumed it was the correct attire for the job. My grandmother always says that if you've got the right clothes you're halfway there. I tucked my hair up under a black beret. All that black made me look pale, so I added more blusher and another coat of mascara. Patrick came in with the stick book, and burst out laughing.

'You need a tinderbox and a fifty foot coil of rope.'

'What for? What the hell's a tinderbox, anyway?'

'It's what they used in the dark ages, sort of a mediæval Bic lighter.'

'I don't smoke. What would I need a lighter for?'

'Never mind. Aren't you going to wait till it's dark?'

'It will be by the time I get there. Tell Mum I went over to Gloria's place, if she asks.'

'Okay. Fiona?'

'What?'

'Good luck.'

***

It wasn't actually quite dark yet when I got to St Dominic's. I had looked it up in the Melway's, so I knew where it was, but I'd forgotten how much the evenings had lengthened. I reconnoitred from across the street; it was on a corner, and there was only a low stone wall around the outside, so the grounds were quite easy of access, but the building itself was huge, and very closed-looking. There was some ivy growing on it, but it didn't really look all that strong. I couldn't really see all that much of the building past the trees and bushes all around the outside, but it was obviously quite large. On the other hand, I seemed to remember reading somewhere that monasteries are usually built hollow inside, like a doughnut, so perhaps it wasn't really all that big. There must be corridors going all around, I thought, with rows and rows of monks' cells on each side. And cloisters, I remembered, lots of cloisters, whatever they were.

It was then that I got the creeping feeling of doom.

I realised that, once inside, I would have no idea of how to find Morelli's room.

***

Whatever loose piece of machinery had slipped in my head before, I reflected as I thought the whole thing out over a cappuccino in a nearby café, had definitely gone back to its rightful place. The more I thought about it, the less confident I was about a) being able to get inside the building, b) finding Morelli's room, and c) getting away undetected. I also remembered that I'd forgotten to find out from Patrick when they'd all be at Vespers, or whatever. And to make matters worse, the church was next door. I had thought they'd have their own chapel inside the monastery, but clearly they'd be going between the two buildings at some point, putting them all outside the building, possibly at the very moment I was getting in or getting out. I had a very, very bad feeling about the whole thing. I wondered how Doctor Who would handle it. But then the Tardis would materialise inside the building, so he wouldn't have that problem to start with. And he could use it for a quick getaway, too. Of course, the Doctor had the advantage of being a man, I reflected gloomily. Why was he always a man, I wondered. If you were constantly regenerating into different bodies, it seemed to me that the law of averages would mean that sometimes it would have to be a female body. But there was no denying that being a man was an advantage for him. If surprised red-handed in Morelli's room, at least he wouldn't be suspected of being there for immoral purposes. It didn't matter how innocent you were of a thing, I thought, remembering Goebbels' outburst earlier that day. If people thought you'd done it, it was really the same as having done it. I wondered if I'd hit on the governing principle of the universe.

Then I thought a bit more about my current problem, and realised that it really wasn't a problem at all.

***

I staggered upstairs, feeling thoroughly bruised in mind and spirit. Patrick shot out of his room as I reached the top. He'd doubtless been awaiting my return with bated breath, and wondering whether to send in the cavalry.

'Did you do it?'

'Sure. It was easy.' I assumed an air of nonchalant bravado. 'No trouble at all.'

Having disposed of the filthy magazine in a rubbish bin on the way home, I felt I'd dealt effectively with the whole problem, and the matter was closed. Patrick, however, was jonesing for the gory details, and followed me into my room, settling on the window seat with the air of one not to be swayed from his fell purpose.

'Come on, tell me everything.'

Unfortunately, I hadn't bothered to think of everything.

'I climbed over the wall. I got in through a ground floor window. Then I found his room, shoved the stick book under his mattress and went out the same way I went in. End of story. If you weren't such a wimp, you'd have done it yourself.'

Patrick was almost speechless with awe. His eyes were as big as saucers.

'Weren't you scared?'

'Course not. I'm not a wimp like you.'

This was pretty unfair, but having got Patrick on the down side for once, I wasn't going to waste it.

'How did you find his room?'

Oh, hell. I thought frantically.

'Their names are on the doors, they've all got little labels. I just walked along the corridor until I found the right room, it was easy as. God, it was lucky he wasn't in bed sick, now I come to think of it.'

I didn't have to pretend to shiver; just thinking about what it would have been like actually going in there was enough. My dramatic efforts were wasted, though; Patrick was too busy gloating.

'When are we going to ring up the abbot, then?'

'I already did that, from a phone box on the way home.'

'Why a phone box? Did you forget your mobile?'

'I thought it was more untraceable to use a phone box, in case they've got Calling Number Display. I put my hanky over the mouthpiece in case Morelli answered the phone, so he wouldn't recognise my voice.'

'Good thinking. What did you say?'

'I just told them to look under Joe Morelli's mattress. The guy sounded really shocked.'

'God, Fi, you're so brave. I didn't think you had it in you.'

I had to admit I was quite impressed myself.

❧CHAPTER THIRTY ☙

Thou hast turned my heaviness into joy: thou hast put off my sackcloth, and girded me with gladness.
Psalm 30:12

Going in to work on Monday, I felt relaxed for the first time in what seemed to be months. Having secured my home base at last, I now felt ready for anything; even the prospect of seeing Goebbels when I walked into the office didn't seem too nerve-racking. I hadn't realised how much Patrick's wild scheme of revenge had been weighing on me until I'd resolved it. Of course, my father was still a little cool, since he'd got the bill from the Fire Brigade, but he'd get over it soon enough; he was much too vague to be able to hold a grudge for long.

Goebbels wasn't in his office when I arrived.

There was a huge penis drawn on the whiteboard, with Goebbels' face on it and a bubble coming out of its mouth that said 'I sack secretaries'. It had little thin arms, and was holding a book labelled '*How to Win Friends and Influence People*'. Someone was really going to get it, I thought smugly, knowing it couldn't be me. Then I remembered that Goebbels didn't care if things were really one's fault or not, and felt a bit less smug.

Tony looked up from his listing.

'Good likeness, isn't it?'

'God, Tony, he's going to go right over the top when he sees that. Shouldn't we clean it off?'

'Naah. He called in sick, probably going for a job interview.'

Geoff sniggered. 'Who'd hire him?'

'This company did.'

'Yeah, well they're fuckwits, aren't they?'

'Language, please, gentlemen. Let us conduct ourselves with decorum.'

'Fuck off.'

***

Dance of Chaos

I actually got quite a lot done that day. Without Goebbels glaring out through his glass wall all the time you could really relax and concentrate, and I found my testing going really well. By four o'clock I had my whole program tested and debugged, and was ready to print off the final listing. We kept the last compiled listing of every program in a hanging file. I printed it off, and then, because Goebbels never let anybody work on more than one thing at a time, I had nothing to do. I decided I might as well wander down to the computer room and pick up the listing, then I could get it filed and go home early. Surely even Goebbels wouldn't expect me to hang around the office for another two hours when I had absolutely nothing to do? Anyway, he wouldn't know.

Steve and Adam were on duty that afternoon. As Goebbels wasn't there, they were taking it easy, with their feet up on the console table. I had to knock for ages before they heard me. Eventually Steve shuffled over to the door.

'Hi, Steve. Can I get my listing?'

'Oh, bugger off, Fiona, we just cleared the printer half an hour ago.'

'Oh, what? You've got nothing else to do, come on. I want to get it in the folder and go home.'

'No, rack off.'

'Gimme a break, will you? God, you're so slack. Look, I'll get it off myself.' I pushed past him into the computer room.

Steve rushed over and flung himself dramatically in front of the printer.

'You're not touching it. Union rules.'

'Oh, what?'

They were both falling about laughing. Seeing my chance, I quickly reached past Steve and hit the Stop button on the printer. We had a bit of a tussle, but Steve was laughing so much that I eventually managed to hit Form Feed a couple of times as well, sending the last couple of pages round to the back. We skidded around opposite sides of the printer, colliding with a crash on the other side.

Steve was faster than me, no doubt because of wearing runners. He had the listing out and was away before I could stop him. I chased him around the disk drives a couple of times, but it was hopeless. Four inch heels just aren't the thing to chase people in, and by that time I was laughing pretty hard myself. He took refuge behind the console with Adam.

'Surrender or die,' I shouted. 'We have you

surrounded.'

'I wave my privates at your aunties, you silly little English kernigget.'

They started throwing biros at me. I ducked behind a disk drive. Some of the biros landed within reach, and I grabbed one. I advanced towards the console, brandishing it threateningly.

'Lay down your arms. You cannot hope to stand against the Mighty Javelin of Korindos.'

'We will never surrender. Villain, do your worst.'

'Alright then, prepare to die, thou varlet.' I threw the Mighty Javelin of Korindos at him. It flew majestically through the air. For once I had managed to aim something in the right direction. I wished all the kids at St Bedivere's, who'd always picked me last for basketball teams, could see it.

At the last possible instant, Steve ducked, and the biro sailed harmlessly over his head, clattering against the CPU. He laughed derisively.

'Ha, ha, missed again.'

'Rooooooooooooooooooooooooooo.' A dreadful moaning sound filled the computer room. Then silence. Real silence, not the background hum that you get used to hearing. We all stopped laughing. I looked around. All the lights had gone out on the CPU and peripherals.

'Shit, a power failure.'

'No, look, the overhead lights are still on.'

'Well, what's happened, then? Could it have blown a fuse?'

Adam turned around and looked at the CPU. Then he turned back and looked at me. The silence was deafening.

'Jesus, Fiona, you hit the Emergency Stop.'

***

'...and furthermore, gobble gobble gobble idle destructive gobble gobble useless gobble gobble wanton destruction gobble gobble gobble...'

And half an hour later he still hadn't run out of breath.

'... gobble gobble gobble off the premises immediately.'

***

I walked down the familiar steps for the last time. Perhaps crying might have worked, I thought, but I just hadn't been able to muster the enthusiasm for it. I didn't feel like going home yet, so I wandered down St Kilda Road, thinking vaguely about cappuccino. The weather had turned really warm, and a little breeze ruffled my hair. I thought about never having to listen to Goebbels again, and felt slightly more cheerful. Computers hadn't turned out to be that much fun after all, I reflected, not really like on Blake's Seven at all.

As I passed the big Police building, a recruiting poster caught my eye.

THE END

Fiona's story continues in Gift of Continence.

ಒPROLOGUEಅ

I never really wanted to get married. Tim had been pestering me for years, on and off, I generally tried to avoid the subject.

But then, one day, I saw this incredibly perfect dress. Of course I had to try it on.

The dress was magic. I still think so. It had some supernatural quality that defied analysis, as Tim would have said. He often said things like that, which I suppose should have been a warning. Anyway, when I looked in the glass I almost didn't recognise myself. Except for my red hair, I could have been Scarlett O'Hara.

I didn't just get married on the strength of that, though. After all, I'm not stupid. I checked it out most carefully.

It was pure silk, and all hand-finished. How could I go wrong?

ཨCHAPTER ONEལྷ

'First the Banns of all that are to be married together must be published in the Church three several Sundays, during the time of Morning Service, or of Evening Service (if there be no Morning Service), immediately after the second Lesson...'

'Fiona! Get out of there this instant, do you hear me? It's after ten, the hairdresser's here.'

'Go away, I'm busy.'

'Fiona!' The doorknob rattled violently. For all I knew, my mother had a passkey. I wished I'd thought of putting a chair under the knob. Although why that would stop anyone coming in, I've never been able to figure out. Ah well, life is full of mysteries. I turned on the hot tap to drown out my mother and a cloud of steam filled the bathroom. Moses, crouched on the basin, watched me balefully through the swirling mist, rather like the Hound of the Baskervilles.

It was a great comfort to me to have Moses with me on my wedding day. My mother had wanted to put him in a kennel, but I had really had to put my foot down about that. I was already going to be separated from him for the whole honeymoon. Men are so funny about things like that. I lay back in the hot water and imagined that I was the captain of a vast schooner, carrying a precious cargo of peacocks and ivory to the Spanish Main, whatever that is.

'Fiona! Open this damn door or I'll break it down.'

Thank God, Gloria had arrived. Now it was safe to come out. I had been locked in the bathroom for the last two and a half hours because I couldn't face my mother unadulterated. Having dodged out on her parental responsibilities for twenty-two years, she had been hounding me for the past week, trying to give me a talk about the birds and the bees. I could hear her scuffling with Gloria in the hall.

'But I have to talk to her.'

'Don't worry, Mrs M, Fiona knows all about

sex. She got it off the lavatory wall, same as the rest of us.'

Evidently my mother retreated in some confusion, because when I came out there was only Gloria, looking evil and dangerous in a black mask. She took it off when she saw me, revealing a stupendous black eye.

'I didn't want your old bag of a mother to see this. Got it at karate last night. Bloody moron, I told him I was being your bridesmaid today, you'd think people could show a little consideration.'

'D'you want to see the cake? It's amazing, six layers.'

'Christ. Did she make it herself?'

'Of course. She's been at it nonstop for weeks, in between trying to give me The Talk.'

'Still trying, I noticed.'

We sneaked furtively down the stairs to the sitting room. My mother had insisted on having the reception at home, just the way she'd insisted on everything else. I sometimes wondered if everyone realised who was getting married here.

The cake rose majestically from a sea of white tulle with little pink rosebuds scattered through it.

Six layers of white frosting, lace, and God knew what else. I had to admit it looked lovely. Gloria tiptoed over to the cake and bent to examine it.

'Holy Jesus, there's a hole in it!'

'What d'you mean, a hole? There couldn't be. What sort of hole?'

But when I looked, it was all too obvious what sort of a hole it was. You could even see the tongue marks around the edge if you looked closely.

'Oh God, Moses. It's the marzipan icing, he loves it. Someone must've left the door open.'

'Well Jesus, Fi, we've got to do something. Cover it up or something. Did she have any icing left over?'

'God, I don't know. I've been staying out of her way so she wouldn't start telling me about sex.'

'Go and have a look in the kitchen. I'll stand here in front of it, just sort of casually.'

I left Gloria standing casually in front of the cake and dashed for the kitchen, clutching my towel. My little brother, Patrick, was there, eating something out of a large mixing bowl. I skidded to a halt.

'Patrick, thank God! Moses ate a hole in the cake, is there any of that marzipan icing left we can cover it with?'

Patrick looked innocent, which I knew meant trouble.

'Well, not actually left, not as such, no.'

I grabbed the bowl. Sure enough there were a few tiny scraps of marzipan icing clinging to the edges.

'You greedy little shit!' I howled. 'Now what am I going to do?'

Attracted by the noise, my father wandered into the kitchen.

'Ah, Fiona. I think your mother was looking for you. Is something wrong?'

It's not easy to break the habit of fifteen years.

'Oh no. Everything's fine. I just wanted to spend some time with Patrick, things won't be the same after...'

My father went predictably misty.

'Well do put something on, you'll catch cold wandering about like that. Although in some areas of Central Australia...'

He wandered off, mumbling to himself. I quickly filled Patrick in on the situation.

'Oh, don't worry. They always freeze the bottom layer for your anniversary. So no-one'll be looking at it down there.' He sniggered; presumably the words 'down there' had sparked off some association in his incessant preoccupation with sex. I looked at him doubtfully. Wedding protocol wasn't something I'd really expected Patrick to know much about.

'Are you sure?'

'Yeah, the bottom layer, or else it's the top one, Mum was on about it the other day.'

'Oh, great. What if it's the top layer, you dork? Quick, we've got to hide it before Mum sees it.'

'What about Tippex?'

'Have you got any?'

'No.'

I looked about for something to hit him with. Speed was definitely of the essence.

'What about flour and water? That's white. Quick, give me that bowl.'

We mixed some flour and water and dashed

back to the sitting room with it. Gloria was there, standing casually in front of the cake and listening to our father, who seemed to be describing the burial customs of Samoa. She didn't miss a beat.

'Good heavens, Mr M, Mrs M'll have a fit if she catches you in here with your pipe. I'd better open a window. And I think Fiona was looking for you, she's upstairs.'

Patrick and I dodged behind the hat stand as our father wandered past. It wasn't difficult to avoid notice; he's never really quite there.

We filled in the hole with the paste we'd made.

'That's no good, I can see the finger marks.'

'We'll have to sort of scrape it over. Get a piece of cardboard or something.'

'What about this?'

Using the bottom edge of the china shepherdess, Gloria masterfully scraped over the patch. We all stepped back to admire her work.

'Jesus, it's not the same shade of white.'

'Don't be silly, white's white. You can't have shades in it.'

'No, look. You can see it.'

It wasn't the same shade of white.

Gloria rose to the occasion, as I knew she would.

'Well, we'll just have to cover it up with something. Look, we'll pull a bit of this material up in front of it.'

'Why don't we just turn the whole thing around so it's at the back?'

'God, you're a dork, Patrick. It's on a semicircular thing, look. No, this is the best way. Look, all we've got to do is pull it up a bit, see?'

She let go and the tulle fell back down.

'We'll have to stick it with something. A pin or something.'

We looked around the immaculate room. Of course there were no pins. Superfluous objects are not allowed to hang around in my mother's rooms.

'Fiona, go and get a pin. We'll stand in front of it.'

'No way, I'm not going back upstairs without you. Mum's up there.'

I wiped the china shepherdess on my towel, to give myself time to think. I didn't think of anything.

'Shit, I've got one!' Gloria was unbuttoning her shirt.

'Look the other way, Patrick.' He was getting a glazed look to his eyes which was positively obscene. Gloria pulled a safety pin out of her bra strap.

'You'll have to lend me a bra, okay?'

'Mine won't fit you.'

'Oh, never mind, I don't really need one. What's the point of all that martial arts and stuff, if your tits don't stay up?' She jabbed the safety pin into the cake.

'That's no good, you can see it.' I didn't want to be negative, but it stuck out a mile. Patrick didn't say anything, he was angling around trying to look into Gloria's shirt.

Gloria looped a bit of the tulle around the exposed part of the safety pin. It sort of worked.

'Well, that's going to have to do.'

* * *

My mother was practically foaming at the mouth by the time we got upstairs. She followed me and Gloria into my room; the hairdresser was curled up in my armchair reading a magazine.

'Here they are, Kerry. At last. And mind you keep Moses out of the room if he comes back inside, Fiona. Kerry's allergic.' She shot me a filthy look. Moses was on top of the wardrobe, luckily she hadn't noticed him. I wondered what she was so upset about, after all the wedding wasn't until four o'clock.

Gloria threw herself onto my bed and lit one of her black cigarettes. She hadn't done her shirt back up. The bra was red satin. I hastily got into position in front of my dressing table to distract my mother, she didn't like Gloria anyway. I'm not sure why. I looked at Kerry in the glass. I wasn't sure I wanted my hair done by someone with green spikes, but it was too late to get another hairdresser. I closed my eyes and imagined that I was the captain of an interstellar spaceship, on a mission to save the galaxy.

* * *

I felt really weird when I woke up. I couldn't remember who I was, or anything about my life. I grasped futilely at shreds of my dream, which might have had something to do with the Navy. No good, I couldn't remember that either. Panicking, I opened my eyes and saw two strange-looking women and a huge black cat; I seemed to recognise the cat, but had no idea about either of the women.

Fortunately this state only lasted a few seconds, actually until I moved and one of the strange women moved with me, and I realised I was looking in a mirror. Then everything came flooding back, and I really started to panic.

I looked like Elizabeth the First. My hair rose vertically up from my head into what appeared to be a solid mass about eight inches high. My fringe had totally disappeared, and the whole thing was the wrong colour, sort of a pale washed-out ginger. I had gone to sleep with nice, thick red hair, and woken up a freak. I turned and looked at the hairdresser in total disbelief. She didn't look so good herself, her nose and eyes were bright red, which clashed unpleasantly with her green spiked hair. I'd cry too, I thought bitterly, with remorse, if I'd done this to a fellow human being. If she even was human.

The hairdresser sneezed all over me. It was the last straw, and I'm afraid I rather lost it. After the hairdresser had departed, weeping pitifully between sneezes, I ripped into Gloria for not watching what she'd been up to. By this time my mother, attracted by the noise, was outside tapping at the door in a ladylike manner.

'Go away,' I shouted, in a frenzy of grief and terror.

Gloria, who had been reading some trashy paperback while I was being mutilated, was quick enough to save her own neck. Quick as a flash she did up all her shirt buttons and resumed her mask just as my mother opened the door.

'Darling, whatever is the matter?'

'Look at my hair, just look at it!' I shouted.

'It looks lovely. Darling, I came up to tell you Tim's on the phone.' She bustled off to ruin someone else's life.

'I can't talk to him,' I wailed. 'Oh God, this is the worst day of my life.'

'For Christ's sake, Fiona, settle down. You're getting married in four hours.'

'No way! I am not getting married looking like this.'

'Well, it's too late to get out of it now.'

'I don't care. I am not leaving this house. Tim wouldn't want me looking like this anyway. What did she do to my fringe, for God's sake? She must have plucked it, the bitch.'

'Look, go and talk to Tim. We'll fix your hair, don't worry.'

'Fix it! How can you fix it, it's the wrong colour! Oh God, I wish I was dead.' I got into bed and pulled the covers up over my head. I wasn't exaggerating, I really felt suicidal. My hair had always been my best feature.

I heard Gloria going away. Good, I thought. If everyone would just leave me alone perhaps I could go to sleep and wake up and it would all have been a bad dream. Moses thudded onto the bed and raked at the doona. I pulled him under it and buried my nose in his lovely rich smell. Nothing smells quite like a tomcat.

Presently Gloria came back and ripped off the covers. I wondered how I had come to have a best friend so devoid of sensitivity.

'Come on, get up, you can't lie there all day feeling sorry for yourself. Tim's ringing back in half an hour, I told him you were in the loo throwing up.'

Perhaps it wasn't so bad after all. Gloria certainly didn't seem to think it was the end of the world. I got up cautiously and sat on the edge of the bed.

'Okay. Now we'll just take it all out and start again.' Gloria sat down beside me and poked at my hair experimentally. A worried frown appeared on her face and she poked around a bit more.

'Jesus, Fiona, it's got no ends.'

* * *

Ten minutes of poking later, we were both seriously worried. Gloria's temper was showing signs of fraying.

'Jesus Christ on a bicycle. It can't be a perpetual fucking Mobius strip. What the hell has she done?'

'It must be the hairspray.'

'That or the fucking snot she kept spraying all over you. Fuck, I thought we were all going to drown.'

I felt sick, both at the thought of the Hairdresser from Hell sneezing all over me while I was asleep and also what my mother would say if she overheard Gloria's language.

* * *

We were in the bathroom washing out the industrial strength spray when a shriek of outrage ripped through the house. I had been dreading the moment when Patrick discovered he was to wear the kilt. I had realised some weeks ago that, as he had failed to show any interest whatever in my wedding plans, this detail had escaped him. It didn't really seem kind to warn him, so I hadn't. Truth, the enemy of kindness, as my grandmother always says. It had been my mother's idea for Dad and Patrick to be in Highland dress, but who argues with my mother?

We found Patrick standing in the middle of his room, arms folded, looking bootfaced. Our mother was facing him, they were squared off like two tomcats disputing a garbage can.

'I don't care. I'm not looking like a poofter in front of everyone.'

'Patrick Aloysius MacDougall, how dare you use that language. Your father isn't ashamed to wear the kilt, and you shouldn't be either. Now I don't want to hear another word...'

And so on, and so forth. I had to admit Patrick had a point. Our father might not have been ashamed to appear in Highland dress, but then he didn't have weedy little skinny legs like Patrick. Really an ankle length job would have been better.

As there was clearly nothing to be done, Gloria and I started to ease gently backwards out of the room. With my mother in full cry, I was uncomfortably aware of my hair dripping on the carpet, and Gloria's mask.

Just as we were about to accomplish a silent escape, with verve, elan etc, another cry of outrage rang through the house. This one sounded more like a wounded bull. It was my father, who presently erupted from my parents' room clutching his kilt and roaring incoherently.

'Jesus, what's his problem?' screeched Gloria.

A general confusion ensued, with my mother trying simultaneously to look reproving at Gloria's language and to be a ministering angel to my father. Gloria and I retreated a little way to be out of the centre of it.

'Holy God,' muttered Gloria. 'It's a wonder she doesn't trip over her own back legs.'

The trouble emerged. Moses, at some stage since it was laid out on the bed, had slept on my father's kilt (when had he found the time?). The kilt was now covered in black fur.

Cat fur, as my readers will no doubt be aware, is extremely difficult to remove from any woollen material. Added to this injury was the insult that, my father seemed to feel, had been sustained by Clan MacDougall. I couldn't really see the problem myself, Moses leaves fur on all my stuff and I don't feel insulted. Still, my father is, as I may have mentioned, a bit eccentric. I think something happens to people's brains when they turn forty. As for the actual fur itself, you could hardly see it. The

MacDougall tartan is one of those ghastly boring old ones with just black and red, in a sort of nasty blocky design. I was glad I didn't have to wear it, it would murder my hair.

'God, my hair!' In the excitement I'd forgotten about it.

'And what the devil, may I ask, are you doing, dripping all over the carpet with the hairdresser already gone?'

Oh, shit.

'She fell in the bath, Mr M. Don't you worry, we'll have it good as new in two shakes. Come on, Fiona.'

I was left wondering why nobody but me had noticed the mask.

Also by Tabitha Ormiston-Smith

NOVELS

Gift of Continence: With the perfect wedding dress, what can go wrong? A great deal, as Fiona McDougall rapidly discovers. From the wedding from hell onwards, Fiona successively discovers that her new husband is stingy, bad-tempered and an adulterer.

Where The Heart Is: Widowed, broke and unemployed, Fiona moves to the country to save money. But she is not prepared for the realities of country life…or for whom she will meet.

King's Ransom: What really went on back in 1193? Was Richard Lionheart really the hero we think? Was John really that bad? And who was Robin Hood, no really, who was he?

The Secret Summer of Peter Fotheringay: Left at boarding school over the Christmas holidays, Peter expects to have a boring time. But when he goes exploring in the school's disused attic, he finds something that will change his world forever.

COLLECTION

Once Upon A Dragon: Collected short fiction. A non-themed, cross-genre collection of short fiction, including fantasy, science fiction and horror as well as general fiction.

NOVELLAS

Melanie's Diary: Melanie's life is out of control. Her status-hungry parents have forced her grandmother into a home, and she's under siege from the school bully. But things are going to get a lot worse before they get better...

Dancing Feet: Ashley is devastated when her widowed father returns from his business trip with a new wife and her two daughters in tow. Pushed to one side by the interlopers, can she make a new life for herself?

Operation Tomcat (Operation Tomcat Book 1): Left almost penniless after divorcing her cheating husband, Tammy moves to the country to reinvent her life. But life in a country town isn't as simple as it looks...

Operation Camilla (Operation Tomcat Book 2): A sleazy solicitor hacks into a dating website in order to boost his failing family law practice. But he doesn't count on Tom...

Operation Badger (Operation Tomcat Book 3): Detective Senior Constable Ben Jackson is handsome, kind, diligent, dedicated and a total mensch. He's also as thick as two planks.

His girlfriend, Tammy, is clever as anything, but sillier than a wet hen.

And then there is Tom. Tom is a cat.

NON-FICTION

Grammar Without Tears: Historical and fictional characters explain common grammatical errors in a funny-as-hell book that will forever change the way you see grammar.

Fifty Shades of Grammar: Everyone, it's said, has one book inside him, but getting it out can be problematical. Perhaps you can't English very well, or you work long hours and just don't have time, or you started writing and then got stuck? Fear not, for help is at hand.

Packed with friendly, no-nonsense advice, Fifty Shades of Grammar will answer all those questions you were too afraid to ask. From sentence structure to punctuation, from setting up your workspace to support your efforts to overcoming the dreaded 'writer's block', from traps and pitfalls to avoid to editing, the problems faced by the novice writer are clearly addressed – and with LOLCATS!

With this book at your side, the only variables will be your talent and your commitment.

www.ingramcontent.com/pod-product-compliance
Ingram Content Group UK Ltd.
Pitfield, Milton Keynes, MK11 3LW, UK
UKHW041409180426
11947UKWH00007B/26